Thank you for helping me
raise addiction awareness.

*Moral Dissipation is dedicated to my one-year-old daughter Oriana in hopes that this book will help end the opiate epidemic in Vermont and far beyond, so less people in her generation will have to struggle with addiction. It is also dedicated to my loving mother who voluntarily spent so much time helping me edit and providing feedback and encouragement. I love you both more than words can describe.*

**www.mascotbooks.com**

*Moral Dissipation*

**For more information, please contact:**
Mascot Books
560 Herndon Parkway #120
Herndon, VA 20170
info@mascotbooks.com

Library of Congress Control Number: 2015920600

CPSIA Code: PBANG0116A
ISBN-13: 978-1-63177-238-2

Printed in the United States

# MORAL DISSIPATION

**WHEN YOU'RE AN ADDICT THERE IS NO RIGHT, THERE IS NO WRONG...**
**THE ONLY THING THAT MATTERS IS THE HIGH**

## by S.M. JARVIS

# CONTENTS

# CHAPTER ONE:
## Innocence

If you think a ticket is something you get for speeding, a bun is a bunny rabbit, and a sub is a teacher, you don't know how lucky you are. Those words meant those things for me too, at one time in my life, before the accident. Now, a ticket is a bag of heroin, a bun is ten bags, and a sub is Suboxone, an opiate blocker. My name is Ryan Landry, and these things have defined my life for the past ten years. I used to fear jail, but sitting here, in this cell, thinking about my past, I've come to realize I'm lucky just to be alive. Over the past decade, my hometown of Arelington, Vermont has developed a widespread opiate problem, and I want to share my part in it with you.

———•———

The future was bright and so was the sun in my eyes, as I carved in and out of narrowly spaced trees, flinging snow in every direction at lightning speed. Luckily, I had just returned from snowboard camp out west, where I'd learned to wear a helmet from watching pro-riders get into gnarly accidents. Previously, I'd boycotted helmets because I didn't think they were cool.

I usually rode with a few friends, Will in particular, but none of my buddies had agreed to join me on the slopes that day. Too shy to ask anyone I wasn't really good friends with, I'd trekked up to the mountain solo. The woods were my thing. The park was great too, but I'd come close to breaking some bones on jumps and rails, and wanted to avoid that. All I needed to be happy was my board, music, and the mountain. I had no memory of my father (he died from cancer when I was just an infant), but my mother had told me he was the happiest anytime he was on a snowboard. Riding made me feel connected to him in a way nothing else could.

Taking it easy for my first run, my mind drifted back to my mother's wedding. Even though I hadn't known my father, I felt like I had from my mother's vivid descriptions of how nice and laid back he was. After years of going through countless photos of him on snowboarding trips, at the beach in Cape Cod with my mother, and holding me as a baby, I thought I knew him pretty well. I had the feeling he was smiling down on me, telling me it was okay that my mother had found someone. Seeing her beaming up at her new husband that day, I vowed to accept him, because I wanted my mother to be happy. Don, who was now my stepfather, wasn't a bad guy at all. He let my mom keep my father's last name with no complaints (which I really appreciated), and he gave me my half-brother, who was my best friend—but he did try to act like he was my dad; I didn't like that.

"Wow, this is such an epic powder day! I can't believe no one wanted to join me!" I thought, as I sped down the back country terrain. It had been a few years since it had snowed enough for these trails to be open, and I wasn't familiar with them, but that didn't stop me. There was a sign on the trail entrance that said 'Woods close at 3:00 p.m. Don't ride alone,' but conditions were so nice that I couldn't resist temptation.

Taking my eyes off the trail for only a second, I fumbled with the volume on my phone. One of my favorite Eminem songs had come on and I wanted to turn it up to get my adrenaline pumping. The trail split, and I went right without thinking. That was the wrong choice.

My stomach flipped as I felt myself freefalling at an alarming speed. What had happened? Had I fallen off a cliff? Was I going to die?

*Snap!* My body landed on a tree branch, cracking it in half, and I continued to fall into the blackness, finally coming to the ground with a loud thud.

I'm unsure to this day how long I was unconscious; when I awoke, my body was enveloped with piercing pain. It was coming from everywhere. I needed to escape, but I couldn't move or see; I was buried in snow. Struggling I dug a small tunnel to the top of the snow pile I had landed in; it wasn't much, but at least I could breathe easier and see something other than snow. Judging by the tiny sliver of sun barely peeping through the trees, it was pretty safe to assume I'd been out for a while. The mountain was most likely closed.

There was no hope of being found if my phone was dead. Eminem was no longer blasting in my ears; my nerves prickled, as I recalled having it in my hand before the accident. There was no way I would find it without being able to move. If the phone wasn't dead because the battery ran out, I guessed it would be water damaged. I was doomed. My only hope was my mother. We'd made dinner plans, and I was never late. I said a silent prayer she would track the GPS on my phone when I was late and send some help, and then I slipped into a coma.

———•———

"Your concussion would have been much worse if you weren't wearing a helmet; you're lucky to be alive," the specialist told me during my release after a blurred hospital stay.

"When can I snowboard again?" I asked, glancing down at my scarred leg and wincing. I had taken a pretty crazy fall, broken my left femur on the tree, and gotten a really bad concussion, along with some other minor injuries. My prayers had been answered. My mother had worried when I failed to show up to dinner. She'd called and texted me multiple times, and then gotten on our family account to use an app to find my phone and realized it was still on the mountain after dark. Growing up, I had hated how my mother was such a worrier. After the accident I resolved never to complain again when she would fret about the smallest problems and go out of her way to make sure things were as they should be.

"You're out for this season, for sure, and I would recommend taking it extra careful if you choose to go next year. It depends on your rehabilitation—how quickly you're able to walk again, and how fast your broken bone heals. Here is some information on health and rehab centers for patients who need to learn to walk again after injuries like yours," she said, handing me a pamphlet.

When I got home, my brother Tim was right by my side.

"Dude, it sucks so bad you can't walk, but we can still play video games," he offered. I wasn't much into video games. I preferred being outside, playing sports and exploring nature, but I was thankful for the offer. We played a few games of Madden, and then he ran off to hang out with Brandon, his best friend from next door.

Thankful that he had spent a little time with me, I hid my jealousy that I wasn't well enough to join him. Tim, Brandon, and I did everything together. We'd play basketball, go for bike rides, fish at the lake access near our house, do our homework, and sometimes play video games. Basically the only thing I did without them was snowboard. Brandon's older sister, Ashley, was an avid snowboarder, and I really wanted to ask her to ride. There had been a few times when I considered walking next door to see if she wanted to join me on a trip to the mountain, but I had been too nervous. My friend Will was my snowboarding partner; when he couldn't go, there were one or two more people I might tag along with, but I usually rode with him or by myself. Even though I had been against using alcohol and drugs, he had gotten me to smoke a little weed with him occasionally when we were on the mountain. It relaxed me, put me in the zone, and wasn't addictive in the least bit.

The days dragged by, and I resented having to spend so much time in my room, working on the assignments Tim had picked up for me at school. I had never enjoyed going to class, but it sure beat this.

Still in denial of the severity of my accident, I told my mom I didn't need physical therapy.

"Ryan, if you ever want a chance at snowboarding again, you're going to need professional help getting that leg back in working order," she insisted, wheeling me to the car. After a short drive, we arrived at a small brown building with a green 'Arelington Physical Therapy' sign. Reluctantly, I wheeled myself up to the door and told my mom to wait in the car. That was where I met my first girlfriend, Layla.

"Hey, skinny boy, you have any more hydrocodone, Dilaudid, or whatever they gave you for that leg?" a girl whispered to me while I was waiting to be called in for my PT session. Nervously I glanced around to make sure she was indeed talking to me. No one else was in sight, so I responded.

"I think I have two left. I've been taking them as directed and I'm still in pain, but I don't want to ask for more. I heard they're supposed to be addictive."

"Ha, addictive, you're cute," she snorted.

I was confused. Did she just call me cute? She scribbled something down on a piece of paper and handed it to me.

"I'm almost done PT for my ankle, rolled it when I was fucked up. That's my number; give me a call when you're done your appointment and we'll hang. You're so innocent, it's cute," she said, rising and hobbling to the door as the physical therapist's assistant called her name.

It wasn't much longer until my own name was called.

I had flipped the paper over and over in my hand as I waited, contemplating calling the girl. She wasn't very attractive and was considerably older than me, but I had never gotten a girl's number before, and the forecast for the remainder of my winter was pretty glum—so I figured, why not?

I waited until I felt a little more comfortable with my crutches, so I wouldn't embarrass myself. Finally, I worked up the courage to dial the number she had etched onto the torn piece of paper. Her shocked tone told me she hadn't really been expecting me to call. I was so nervous I nearly hung up, but my nerves settled down a bit when she said she was glad I called and invited me to hang out.

Partying with Layla was thrilling, mostly because I was usually wasted out of my mind. I was hesitant at first, but she promised that if I tried anything I didn't like, she would bring me home right away. She introduced me to Adderall, cocaine, and alcohol, and provided me with money and drugs whenever I wanted. My physical pain soon faded, and I began walking without my crutches. As I spent more and more time with Layla, I stopped dwelling on my ruined snowboarding season, and we became an official item.

I dated her for about three months—just long enough to begin down the tortuous, self-destructive path that would eventually lead me to this very jail cell.

One afternoon, Layla and I went over to one of her friend's houses to drink after I got out of school. It was the fateful evening that I was introduced to an 80 mg OxyContin pill, or 80's, as we called them.

"Hey, Ryan," my new friend Tina slurred, "you have to try this oxy, my boyfriend's mom got them for her back problems."

I was more than eager to try a new mind-altering substance. Having just started to drink and do coke in full force, I loved the way drugs and alcohol enabled me to be social and outgoing. When I was drunk or high, I was confident enough to make new friends and didn't care what anyone thought of me. I forgot all about my injury and my stepfather constantly trying to act like he was my dad, and just enjoyed life. A new way to get high seemed great; there was a mysterious side of myself just waiting to be revealed. Gone were the days when I only took medication as directed and steered clear of all drugs except smoking weed on the mountain. I had heard 'don't do drugs' all through my life, in school and from my mother, but what was a little pill going to do? Of course, I wouldn't try anything stupid, like crack and heroin—or so I thought.

Tina instructed me to only take a tiny bit of the pill. "We can crush this up and it will get all of us high," she said, breaking out her ID and crushing the pill after she had removed the outer coating.

I stared at the fine powder on the table and watched as my friends took lines one by one, snorting it up their noses and nodding out. Tina gave me my line, and I couldn't help but feeling like I would need more. It hadn't been long since I'd started to use cocaine, and already I took much bigger lines than that. I considered asking for more, but I was getting it free, so I didn't complain. At the time, I was not aware that the street value of 80's in Vermont was eighty dollars. At such a high price, one would assume no one would be able to afford to get addicted to these—but I did.

The fine powder from the pill went up my nose so smoothly; I almost didn't even notice it. The drip wasn't bad either; snorting things is usually combined with a bitter taste in the back of the throat that grosses many people out. I had been a bit put-off at first, but quickly came to love it, because it was always accompanied by the rush of whatever drug I was doing. The sensation of the drip triggered my body to morph from reality into a dream-like state, and the bitter taste became welcoming, because my brain associated it with the great feeling that followed.

As the days went by, I spent more and more time with Layla at Tina's house. Her boyfriend had a drug connect, a scrubby-looking middle aged man from New York City named Black. He had money to spare from a car accident settlement, and would supply us with drugs for a decent price. I struck up a deal with him to buy in quantity, to save even more, and started selling cocaine and oxys to kids at my school. This led to me finally talking to girls my age who were much better looking than Layla. I no longer needed her to supply me with drugs and alcohol. The money I was making enabled me to fund my habit and buy nice new clothes, computers, CDs, rims for my car, and anything else I wanted.

I broke up with Layla. She was heartbroken, and insisted we remain friends. That worked out for me, because I still got money and drugs from her, but no longer had to admit she was my girlfriend. Each day we did more and more drugs, but we didn't notice a difference day-to-day; we were too dazed.

"Bet you can't snort that whole smiley face!" Tina said to me, as she finished breaking out a huge line of cocaine in the shape of a smiley face on the coffee table. I accepted the challenge, and then made a shape for her to snort. Then my phone buzzed, and I was off to sell one of my classmates a ball.

I found out, years later, that my mother had suspected I was dealing some kind of drug, and asked her good friend, Brandon and Ashley's mom from next door, to have Ashley try to find out what I was up to and put a stop to it.

Looking back, I find it funny that Ashley and I never hung out growing up, because our mothers and brothers were friends and we both loved to snowboard. I wanted to talk to her, but she was always out doing things with her countless friends and we didn't hang out with the same people in school. Ashley was very anti-drug, because her father and older brother had passed away from overdoses. She told her mother she wasn't going to text me because I was a dirtbag. I often wonder what would have happened if she had texted me and we had started dating then. At that point, I wasn't too far gone; I was just getting started, and she may have been successful in saving me. She didn't, and nothing I can do now will change that.

Life went on like this for the remaining months of high school and into the summer. Eventually, Black moved back to the city, but took my number with him.

## CHAPTER TWO:
# Fear

I know I should stay out of my son's bedroom. He is almost eighteen, a young adult, and he deserves his privacy, but I am so worried about him. I found a chest filled with money, lots and lots of money, in his bedroom. He won't tell me where it's from, and he's becoming more and more distant.

Ryan is the best at giving hugs. He knows just what to do or say to brighten my day, and can make me laugh even when I want to cry, but something has changed. The spark in his eyes is gone; he's glued to his cell phone, and always runs off to go meet up with friends. I am happy that he is social, but I think something more is going on. I believe that Ryan is selling drugs out of my house.

"Take off that hat and look me in the eye. You better not lie to me, boy!" My husband's angry words from last night are still fresh in my mind. No matter what either of us do or say, we just can't get through to Ryan like we used to. He was just a newborn when his father died, but he is still reluctant to follow Don's rules. We both care about him deeply, and I hope he knows that.

My friend from next door recently told me her daughter,

Ashley, thinks Ryan is selling cocaine, but doesn't want to get involved because he is a dirtbag. That breaks my heart. My son is a sweet and intelligent boy with good intentions, not a 'dirtbag.'

I've tried time and time again to talk to him, but he brushes me off. Maybe, if I catch him with drugs, I can call the cops and have them put a stop to it—but I don't want to get my own son in trouble. I am lost. I hope there is something I can do, before it's too late. As a mother, there is nothing you want to do more than to protect your children, but when they won't let you in, it makes it hard.

Should we take away his car? Ryan is a dedicated boy, taking the car won't stop him from doing whatever he's doing. If he really wants to do it, he will find a way.

"He's going to college soon, hopefully he will smarten up; he's really talented, I'm sure he will get a great job when he graduates and stop these shenanigans," my friend re-assured me over lunch one day. I don't want to discuss these problems with my friends, or taint my son's reputation, but I'm worried and don't know where else to seek advice.

"Maybe he's not doing drugs and is just selling them, and that's why he has so much money?" Another friend offered a glimmer of hope, but my gut is telling me she's wrong. My gut instincts have never failed me. Whether that is a good or bad thing, I'm not sure. Since I have no experience with this type of situation, all I can do is worry, and that doesn't help.

# CHAPTER THREE:
# College

After high school graduation, I started taking classes at Arelington College while still living at my mom and Don's house. I was fortunate enough that they paid my tuition; campus was close to home, so paying extra for an apartment didn't make sense. The photo and web design portfolio I had started in high school expanded as I excelled in my courses freshman year. One of the girls I had been selling cocaine to in high school, Miranda, became my girlfriend. She was a step up from Layla, looks-wise, and much closer in age. Life was great.

While I was in college, I worked at Stars, the local grocery store. I sold 80's out of there for almost four years without ever getting caught. My customers would come in, buy something small, pay me for the merchandise and the oxys, and I would put the drugs in the Stars bag with their pack of gum or gallon of milk. On top of working almost full-time and taking a complete course load, I was also driving roughly seven hours each way to New York City once a week, to meet up with Black and re-up on drugs. Through him, I could get a script of sixty 80's for only a hundred dollars. The street value of drugs was much lower in

New York City and he cut me a deal, so I turned quite a profit bringing them back up to Vermont.

If I sold all of the 80's, I could have made over $4,000 on just one trip to NYC. If I had stopped doing drugs and saved the cash, I could have been set for life. That was not what happened, though. I was in a drug haze, constantly high on 80's, which had quickly become my number one choice drug. I stopped selling cocaine, because it wasn't as profitable and I preferred 80's. The first time I tried an oxy 80, back in Tina's living room, the tiny line split between friends was more than enough. Now I had built up a tolerance to the drug, and I was forever chasing that original high. I could snort multiple 80's at a time, which would make most people literally vomit. Miranda had switched from cocaine to 80's as well, and since she was my girlfriend, she no longer paid for them. I bought her clothes and jewelry, and we spent hours together just getting high and zoning out.

At that point, I still did some things that I had loved growing up, like hiking and biking. Will asked me to go snowboarding a few times; I declined, not wanting to hold him up, since I was sure I wouldn't be ready for the park or woods. When my trips to the mountain had ceased, I felt less connected to my late father, but I wasn't concerned. I was in the haze of the high, day in and day out. Soon after being introduced to opiates, I stopped smoking weed, because it made me paranoid and I didn't like the combination.

One day, Miranda and I went for a hike and rewarded ourselves with a couple of pills at the top. We were never without drugs, but I wasn't consciously aware of it at the time. I was starting to get a deviated septum from snorting so many things, but it didn't even bother me, because I was always high. It was hard to believe that, not long ago, I cringed at the thought of snorting anything and never thought I'd do drugs except for smoking an occasional bowl of weed. Now they were the center of my universe.

Drives with Miranda to NYC to re-up were a blast for me. Occasionally my friends Violet and Will would tag along. Will was one of the few friends I'd had before drugs, and he'd gotten caught up in the opiate whirlwind right along with me. I can't remember how I met Violet, most likely from dealing.

"Hey, Miranda, pass the book! Stop hogging it!" Will called from the backseat to Miranda, who was riding shotgun as I drove. Miranda finished snorting her line off of my Subaru driver's manual, and passed it to Will and Violet in the back.

We spent the entire trip high, which made it seem short and enjoyable. I drove every time. I loved driving. My silver Subaru meant everything to me. I washed it daily and polished the new black rims. No one else was allowed to drive it. The book was passed back up to the front, and Miranda took the wheel while I snorted my lines. I felt the calming rush of the painkiller envelop my body, and held my foot steady on the gas pedal at 110 miles per hour. The hazy world slipped by me, and any care became obsolete.

Once we had parked on the outskirts of the city, we took the subway to see Black. Taking a brief detour in Times Square to get some food, we saw some NYPD officers and took pictures with them.

"This picture is epic. Look at us all, chillin' with the NYPD. The cops are posing with me like we're boys," I laughed, passing the camera around to my friends as we got back on the subway toward the sketchier part of the city. If only the officers had known what we were up to, they would have been taking mugshots instead of selfies.

Leaving my friends at a rundown burger joint I made the last leg of the trip on foot to Black's apartment solo. Miranda would often join when I was selling drugs, but when I went to buy 80's in the city, I went alone; Black wanted to deal with only me. I should have been afraid to enter the dingy fourth floor apartment, where Black hung out with a crew of strung-out middle aged men with gold teeth, gang tattoos, and baggy jeans with guns tucked in them, but I was on so many drugs that even fear wasn't real to me. I had a gun myself, but I always left it back in the car. Black didn't allow visitors who were not part of his NYC crew to show up with guns. I was fairly certain he wasn't going to rob me anyway; I was worthless to him. The gun I had was to protect myself against people who were going to rob me back in Vermont, which actually happened later. At the time, I just thought I was cool because I had a gun.

The subway ride back was one I will never forget. There was an old Asian woman with short grey hair, double fisting beer out of two crumbled paper bags in the train car. We could see her as it pulled up to the station, and we purposely chose to sit nearby for entertainment. I usually don't like to sing in front of anyone, but I found myself belting out lyrics to song after song with Miranda, Will, Violet, and the drunken old woman.

I couldn't think of any other way I wanted to spend my Sunday morning at 4:00 a.m.

The joyful tunes came to an end. We were all coming down from our highs, and were a bit drowsy upon arriving back at the car. I gave each of my friends a pill to snort and took two for myself. After snorting them in the car, I put it in drive and heard clunk, clunk as I tried to drive away.

"Fuck. I think my tire is flat," I said, more to myself than anything. "I think I have a spare in the trunk, does anyone know how to change a tire?" My uncle, who I was close with as a child, worked at an auto body shop down the road from my mom's house. I should have known how to change a tire, but I had never bothered to learn, and neither had any of my friends. After over an hour of attempting to read the torn up manual, the four of us finally managed to get the donut tire on the car. It was getting light already, and I was just barely going to make it back for my 1:00 p.m. design class if we made no stops.

My friends all passed out in the car, and I snorted the Adderall I'd brought along to help me focus and stay awake. Adderall was a great drug for road trips, because it kept me alert and prevented me from nodding out. Finally arriving at campus I dumped my friends on the side of the road to find their own way home from Arelington College, and ran from the parking lot into class.

"Ryan, you're late again," my teacher embarrassed me, calling me out in front of the entire class as I tried to slip through the door.

He was lucky I made it, running on no sleep. He had no

idea what I had to get through to even show up for his class, but I loved all of the web design and photography classes I was taking. I wanted to learn, and I didn't want my mother and stepfather asking questions, like I knew they would if they heard I hadn't been showing up for class. I quickly became proficient in HTML, JavaScript, CSS, Adobe InDesign, Photoshop, Illustrator, and more. My teachers praised my work and gave me excellent grades, even though I would frequently fall asleep in class or show up late.

When class was finally over, I snorted another pill in my car and headed home. I can only imagine how horrible I must have looked, judging by the lines of worry on my mother's face when I tried to sneak in and make it to my room without conversation. Running on forty-eight hours without sleep and plenty of drugs, I could feel my eyelids drooping severely.

"Ryan, sweetie, come here. Where have you been?" she inquired, as I looked at the floor and tried to push past her on the way to my room.

"Class and Miranda's. I spent the night," I said, avoiding eye contact and continuing down the hallway. She followed me, entering my room, where I sprawled out across the bed. My limbs felt heavy, as though gravity was pushing them down harder than usual, but my head was in the clouds. All I wanted was my mother to leave me alone so I could drift into a relaxing, drug-induced slumber. She kept talking. I vaguely remember hearing something about her concern for me, how she hoped I wasn't selling drugs, and how she didn't want me to end up dead or in jail, blah, blah, blah. I wonder how long she sat by my bed that day, and what she said. I couldn't have stayed awake if I had wanted to. She was still sitting beside me when I lost consciousness. It's not that I didn't care about how she felt. I did. Well, the old Ryan cared, the person I still believed I was.

My college career was a haze. Most of my days were very similar—school work, drugs, working at Stars, and traveling to NYC. My mother's worry grew, and she tried a number of different things to get through to me. Her efforts ranged from offering to help me and spend more time with me, to threatening to kick me out of the house and pull me out of college. Nothing worked. The more she cared, the less I noticed. You don't notice much when you're constantly on painkillers. They numb your pain and emotions while clouding logic, until, slowly, your perception of the world changes. It happens so gradually that you aren't even aware.

Miranda broke up with me. Or I broke up with her. I'm not really sure which. We just seemed to drift apart. I spent more and more time traveling to NYC, working and doing drugs. She'd chosen an out-of-state college to attend when she graduated high school, and I would've been heartbroken if I hadn't been so busy getting high. I had back-up girls to hang out with anyway, so I wasn't worried.

One evening, soon after our break-up, I was drinking with a friend in the Arelington College parking lot. She was pretty wasted, and tried to unzip my pants with a bottle of vodka in her hand. It spilled and got all over, soaking through my jeans and running onto the floor. I would have been furious if I had been a little more sober, but my attention was soon directed to the blue lights behind me.

"How much have you had to drink tonight?" the cop asked me as soon as I rolled down my window.

"I haven't been drinking; my friend just spilled some vodka on my jeans, but we weren't driving anyway, just sitting in the parking lot," I responded.

"Step out of the vehicle," he instructed me. I obliged, knowing that if the car was searched and he found the drug scripts I'd stashed in multiple spots or the baggie of cocaine I had in my backpack, I would be in a lot more trouble than I currently was.

"Would you be willing to do a few field sobriety tests?" he questioned.

I nodded in agreement, preferring sobriety tests over a Breathalyzer that I was sure to fail.

"Please take nine steps, heel-to-toe, across this line," he said, motioning to one of the white designated parking spot lines. "When you finish, please turn around on one foot and return in the same manner."

My head started spinning, but I was able to complete the task, careful not to wobble off of the white line, start before he instructed, or use my arms to balance.

"Very good; now, can I have you stand on one foot and count one thousand one, one thousand two, one thousand three, and so on, out loud, until I tell you to stop?" he inquired.

"I've never been very good at standing on one foot, but sure, I'll give it a try." Concentrating on my standing leg, yet trying to look relaxed and remembering to count by the thousands proved to be a very difficult task; however, I only wobbled once, and made it the entire time without falling.

"This is the last test; can I just have you follow my flashlight with your eyes?" he asked, shining the light at my pinned-out pupils.

"Okay," I said, trailing his light back and forth with my gaze.

"Your eyes are jerking a bit, so I'm going to have to ask you to take a Breathalyzer."

"Fuck. Fuck. Fuck," I thought to myself. There was nothing I could do to hide my BAC, which I estimated was over the legal limit. I considered denying the test, but I knew if I did I would be immediately arrested, and because I'd been taking shots, my BAC would continue to rise.

"Do I really have to take a Breathalyzer? I wasn't driving, and I did the walking tests just fine. I really don't see what the point is." I tried to convince the officer not to make me blow.

"You were in the car, with the keys in the ignition, so I want to make sure you're not impaired. It should only take a minute." He dismissed my concerns and returned to his cruiser to retrieve the breathalyzing device.

"Take a big breath and then blow into this until you hear a beep," I was instructed.

My mind raced. "Maybe if I just blow out the air that is in my mouth and not exhale from deep within my chest, I can trick the machine," I thought to myself.

That failed. I wasn't able to blow for long enough, and the officer had to instruct me to try a second time. After what seemed like an eternity, I heard a small beep, caught my breath, and looked up, anxious to hear my fate.

"You blew .16. That is twice the legal limit for someone who is twenty-one or older, and you're underage." My heart dropped. I wondered how my drunk friend was going to get home, and what was going to happen to me.

"You are now under arrest," the officer stated calmly, pulling my hands behind my back and inserting my wrists into cold metal cuffs.

The following hour or so was a blur. I can remember swaying back and forth in a zoned out state, sitting on the hard plastic rear-seat of the cop cruiser during the short ride to the police station, and wondering to myself why my hands were behind my back. I sat up with a jolt, suddenly remembering my predicament, as if I was just realizing for the first time what was going on.

Flashes of this experience are still crystal clear for me, while others remain blurred. One memory that still stands out was when the officer taking my fingerprints confused my pointer finger and my ring finger.

"You must be drunk, not me," I thought to myself, as he lifted up my ring finger and called it an index finger.

My mugshots from that night must have been slightly comical; I can remember I was wearing a shirt that said, "Sex, Drugs, And Dubstep," and I must have looked gone out of my mind. After reading me my rights, I answered a series of questions and the officer wrote me a ticket.

"DUI Number One?" I read the ticket out loud in a stunned slur. "But I wasn't driving!" I protested. My brain had registered that I was receiving a DUI, and that I was most likely going to lose my license.

"You're lucky we're not sending you to jail for the night. We will see you in court," the officer replied. After he took my license and keys, I was free to go.

"Little does he know, I gave him my expired license and I keep a spare key under my car," I thought to myself, stumbling off into the night. The police station was not far from Arelington College, and I was still inebriated when I arrived at my car, but that didn't stop me from snorting another oxy and driving home.

My head throbbed, my limbs ached, and I was greeted harshly by an intense hangover the following morning. My physical pain, combined with emotional guilt and the fear of losing my license, was too much to bear. My mother was going to be so disappointed about the DUI. I floundered around in bed, trying to reach my nightstand to retrieve my secret stash of 80's. I was running low and was supposed to re-up the next day. I knew I should've saved them to sell, but I needed something to take my pain away, or at least partially numb the pounding in my skull.

Finally I retrieved the tiny pouch holding the cure to my treacherous hangover. "Thank God for these," I thought to myself, crushing one up as quickly as I could with shaky hands while resisting the urge to vomit. After snorting two of them, I wasn't experiencing any type of euphoria, but my vicious hangover symptoms were almost instantly subdued.

———— •◆• ————

A few months later, I sat in court for the fourth time. Apparently, when you're charged with a DUI, one hearing is not enough—

you have to keep going back. These court appearances were a blur for me. I should have remained sober, but I was so ashamed that I was there in the first place, I'd taken some pills to calm my nerves before each session. Looking down at my fresh white button-up shirt, I could see my mother next to me out of the corner of my eye. She had helped me hire a lawyer, and took time off of work to accompany me to court each hearing. I knew this was painful for her, and I was so overcome with guilt, I couldn't even look her in the eye; luckily, I had the pills to ease the pain.

I was issued a fine of $1,000 for my DUI and a separate $500 fine for underage drinking. My license was taken away for six months, and I couldn't get it back until I completed a CRASH course. I was also required to get SR22 insurance for high risk drivers for three years. This was all on top of the lawyer fees. In total, I spent around $10,000 on the DUI. The money I had made from dealing lessened the blow financially, but my parents took away my car, which made my oxy operation a lot more difficult.

Then there was CRASH. Wanting to get it over with as quickly as possible, I opted for the weekend overnight course, instead of the afternoon courses a few times a week for multiple weeks, even though the weekend course was slightly more expensive.

"Wow, I guess a lot of people get DUIs," I told my mother when I was put on a waiting list for the weekend course. I felt slightly better; if so many people get DUIs, they can't be that bad. I could tell my mother was beside herself with worry.

"What about the background checks when you go to apply for jobs? What about all the money you have just wasted? How are you going to get to class, since I can't drive you to school every day?" Her list of questions and concerns went on and on. I was not nearly as concerned as I should have been, or as I would have been if I wasn't on so many drugs.

The dreaded day came for me to attend the overnight weekend CRASH program. I'd heard rumors about the program directors going through your belongings to search for drugs, alcohol, or any other contraband that was strictly prohibited from entering the facility, so I knew I had to be strategic with my packing.

I had used up most of my recent stash, and it was nearing re-up time again. I needed to figure out how to get a little extra cash to throw Brianna, so she'd let me use her car again for my weekly trip to NYC. Brianna was one of my custys (I called all of my drug customers 'custys'). I'd been using her car for New York trips ever since my parents took mine away. We were sleeping together at the time, but since she wasn't officially my girlfriend, I told her I would give her some money each time I took her car. I didn't yet bring her with me.

Using her car, I drove myself to CRASH. I didn't care that I had no license, and wasn't worried about them checking to see how I had arrived. My only concern had been making money over the weekend, and I had taken many pills to get myself through the boredom.

I pulled up at the secluded colony of log cabins buried deep in the woods and parked Brianna's car. Shoving as many pills as I could into the soles of my shoes and grabbing my overnight bag, I headed towards the entrance. If I had been going here for a romantic getaway with a girlfriend, I would have been thrilled. The log cabins looked very cozy; I wished I had a female companion, no rules, and a lot of drugs.

In sharp contrast to my wishes, I was greeted by two over-sized men who took my bags and immediately started going through them as I signed in. They even had me take my shoes off and dump them upside down. Luckily, my precious cargo did not fall out. I was admitted into the facility and, much to my dismay, they took my cell phone, promising to return it at quiet hours, which started at 9:00 p.m.

"It's only 7:00 a.m.! This is going to be awful! Thank God I brought some drugs," I thought to myself as I met my roommate Mark who was only older than me by a few years. He had just returned from fighting in Afghanistan, suffered from severe PTSD, and was already on DUI Number Two.

"This shit sucks, bro. It's my second time here. I could really use some opiates right about now. They took my stash at the door; those bastards almost didn't let me in. I wanted to just say fuck 'em, but I need to get my license back, ya know?"

As I listened to him talk, I knew we were going to get along. Maybe this place wasn't so bad after all. Now I realize that if I had met Mark prior to my snowboarding accident, we wouldn't have been friends. I would have been disgusted by his lack of ambition, and how he was dumb enough to get two DUIs. I knew for sure I wouldn't be coming back here again.

"I got some stuff, if you have the cash," I said to him. His eyes lit up; he passed over the bills, and we shared a few lines before getting called off to our 7:30 a.m. activity.

Along with about twenty other people of all different ages

and backgrounds with a DUI in common, Mark and I watched a series of movies showing young people with bright futures dying in drunken driving accidents. There were segments that depicted intoxicated drivers surviving fatal accidents and getting years of jail time for killing their friends. I saw tears welling up in the eyes of some of my peers as they watched while I zoned out, imagining I was somewhere else.

"I am an amazing driver; even drunk, I wouldn't crash badly enough to kill someone," I thought to myself.

After the films, we had to go around in a circle and tell our stories. How had we ended up here? Everyone else's was way worse than mine.

"This is so stupid, I don't belong here," I told myself, listening to the twenty-one-year-old girl next to me tell how she killed her best friend in an accident involving alcohol when she was seventeen, and had just been released from prison. What I should have been thinking was how lucky I was that I didn't kill myself or anyone else with my drunk driving, but my head was in the clouds. I was only focused on my current situation, and everything else seemed foreign and surreal. I had been an emotional and empathetic person, but the drugs wouldn't let me sympathize with the poor souls around me.

"Are you kidding me?" I mumbled out loud when we were introduced to our next activity. I wondered when we were going to get a break; my drugs were starting to wear off, and I wasn't feeling great.

"I want each of you to take a piece of paper and some crayons. Draw your future as you want it to be. Then stand up, one-by-one, and share with the group how your DUI has made it harder for you to achieve your goals," our instructor explained as she passed out paper and crayons.

"I am not fucked up enough to do this," I thought to myself. At the time, my future seemed pretty clear. I was going to stack some money, finish school, get out of the drug game, get a high-paying web design job that would also let me put my photography skills to use, buy a house and design that bitch (I was a big fan of interior design and decorating), get married, have two kids, and live happily ever after. I thought I was on track for that plan. My DUI seemed like a very small bump in the road to success.

It felt like a century had passed before quiet hours finally came. When I got my phone back, I had hundreds of texts from regulars needing their fixes. I had a stash out in Brianna's car, and gave them directions to the CRASH building. I should have been worried that I might get caught, kicked out of program, and arrested, but I wasn't. After sneaking out to the parking lot to sell, I retired to my room with Mark.

"Man, this CRASH shit has really taken a lot out of me, I feel like crap," I said to Mark as I broke out my secret shoe stash of 80's. They always seemed to help me when I was fighting off any type of illness, either physical or emotional.

"I just feel like shit because I'm jonesing for a line," Mark said, passing me eighty dollars and holding his hand out for a pill. I tossed him one.

"This guy must be a real junkie, he just had one this morning," I thought to myself, not even realizing how long it had been since I had gone a day without drugs. I never really realized, because I always had them. I didn't need to take them; they were basically free for me, and helped me get through whatever awful situation I had managed to get myself into, so I figured, why not?

The next day dragged on just as the first had. The only positive thing was I made some new connects and custys at CRASH. One guy I met could get me cheap scripts of Adderall, and another one had a benzo hook-up. Black wasn't always able to come through with scripts of 80's each week, and if I couldn't use Brianna's car to travel to New York, I was afraid my funds would run out. I had to have back-ups.

My mother had taken $10,000 from my bedroom, promising to return it when I let her know where I got it from and stopped sneaking around. I had spent $10,000 on CRASH, and was easily doing around $2,000 of drugs a week myself. My cash pile had begun to dwindle.

# CHAPTER FOUR:
# Realization

"Finally, a break from the chaos," I thought, hopping in the backseat of my mom's car next to Tim. My stepfather was at the wheel, with my mother by his side. We were headed off to our yearly family vacation on Cape Cod. Ritually, we stayed in a little cabin a block away from the beach that my mom and Don rented out; it was our summer tradition. Judging by my baby pictures, my mom started it with my dad, but I didn't mind that she carried it on with Don, as long as he didn't try to boss me around. Tim and I really looked forward to Cape Cod. Even if we were arguing before the trip, all feuds were put on pause when we hopped in the car toward the Cape.

I'd warned my custys I would be out of town for a week and many of them had stocked up on supply, which left me with a generous amount of spending money. Switching my phone to silent mode, I vowed not to look at it the entire time. I just wanted to enjoy myself. With everything that had been happening lately, my life was racing by in a drug-induced flash. I wanted to slow down and relax by the ocean.

We arrived at our cabin, and after we had unpacked, Tim

and I ran down to the beach to throw the football. Once we worked up a sweat, we raced into the crisp ocean water to cool off. Soon we were joined by Don and my mother, who set up beach chairs and towels. After a delicious lunch of homemade sandwiches from the cooler my mother had graciously toted down, we played a few family games of bocce ball. Life was good. I had missed days like this, before the drugs and the hustle. I planned to get out of the drug game before I finished college, and focus on things that mattered, like family and finding a future wife—not just some drug girl who could care less who I was, as long as she got hooked up with free drugs. Maybe it could be Brianna, but she was pretty deep into 80's. I wondered if she was ever planning to quit. Looking back now, I can see how immature of me it was to need the crutch of a woman. I should have realized I was also deep into drugs, and focused on bettering myself before searching for someone to save me.

In the evening, Tim and I went shopping down by the beach. I bought some funny T-shirts and some new hats to color coordinate with outfits in my expansive wardrobe. I had much more money than Tim, so I bought him a few things as well. I'd taken a good amount of opiates to get me through the five-hour car-ride, and they were slowly starting to wear off. It was time for dinner, but I felt sick. I opted to stay back at the cabin and get some sleep while Tim, Mom, and Don mounted their rental bikes and took off down the Cape Cod Rail Trail to get some fried clams and lobster. Disappointed that I felt so crummy, I cursed myself for not bringing any drugs. They always seemed to revive me whenever I felt like I was coming down with something. I really hadn't wanted to do any drugs while I was on vacation with my family, but if it had kept me from being sick, I would have.

"Too bad I didn't know I was going to be sick," I thought to myself as I lay on the couch in the cabin, watching TV. I took a larger than normal dose of Tylenol, which didn't even touch my symptoms. They continued to get worse, but somehow I managed to drift off to sleep. At the time, I didn't realize that taking Tylenol was completely pointless. My body had developed such a high tolerance to painkillers that taking an entire bottle of Tylenol wouldn't have done a thing, except for attack my liver, depleting it of an enzyme necessary for life and slowly and painfully killing me. It was a good thing I didn't take the whole bottle, but when I awoke, I wished I had.

My eyes cracked open and I was overwhelmed by nausea; my entire body ached, and my hands were shaking. I let out a dull moan and tried to roll over on the couch. I had no idea what time it was, but I guessed somewhere close to 4:00 a.m. The sun was not yet peeking through the cabin window, but the darkness that encompassed our tiny dwelling during the night hours had lifted. The searing pain that had throbbed in my head the night before was back, a hundred times stronger.

"What is this, some kind of flu?" I wondered to myself. It was bad, worse than anything I had ever experienced in my life. The time Novocain didn't work when I was having a tooth pulled, or when I broke my femur on the mountain were previously the worst pains I had ever felt. This feeling made those pains seem like nothing. I would have gladly gone back to any prior painful experience in my eighteen years of life to get away from the one I was currently battling. The only thing I could think of was making it go away. I wished I could fall back asleep, but it was impossible. I was trapped in this excruciatingly painful hell.

"Mom," I tried to yell, but I could barely speak because I was in so much pain. I didn't even bother taking any more Tylenol, even though the bottle was nearly full beside the couch. I needed something stronger. Why did I have to be sick when I was on vacation? If I had been home, I could have just gotten some drugs and been better in no time.

All of a sudden, it hit me. I wasn't sick. These were withdrawal symptoms. It couldn't be. Was I really addicted to drugs? I had done a lot of cocaine when I first met Layla, but I could always stop for a few weeks and then start up again. Sure, I had the constant nagging feeling that I wanted more, but I could push that away. Maybe the reason it had been easier to push my coke cravings away was that they were replaced with OxyContin. I remembered the feeling that Mark had described to me when he was craving and constantly on my case for opiates at CRASH. These feelings were similar, only much worse.

I dug in my pockets and pulled out my phone—seventy-five missed calls and eighty new texts. Wow. I had only been gone one day! If I hadn't been feeling as shitty as I was, I would have wondered what the hell was wrong with people. I would have thought, "I can't go on vacation for just a week, you really need your drugs that badly?" But I didn't think that. I thought, "Uh... ow...no wonder I have so many texts; my custys all feel like this too, and they want it to stop." The pre-drug Ryan would have felt overwhelmingly guilty for enabling so many people to ruin their lives, but my brain was mush. I couldn't think about anything, it was too physically painful. I wanted to off myself. My head pounded, my legs ached in places I never knew existed, I had cold chills even though it was summer, and the god-awful nausea felt like it would never cease.

I was glad my mother didn't stir when I tried to call her name. The pain was so bad that I couldn't talk and didn't want to be around anyone. I just wanted it to go away.

It seemed like years had passed by the time my family members rose and started filtering into the living room.

"Ryan, you slept on the couch all night?" my mother said, surprised.

"Uuuuuhhhh," I grunted back, not opening my eyes and clutching my stomach. I could hear her walk over to me, and felt her place her warm hand on my back. I didn't want to be touched. I wanted to die.

"What's wrong, dear, you don't look well," she said. Her voice was filled with concern, but it was not troubling to me; I didn't have any emotions or feelings except for pain. It overcame my entire being. I would have given away all the money I had for just one pill. I knew one wouldn't even get me high, but it might help kick this unbearable feeling, and that was the only thing on my mind.

After trying to get me to respond for entirely too long, my mother finally gave up, and headed down to the beach with the rest of the family.

"You get your rest, Ryan. If you feel better later, we are

going to the flea market this afternoon, then we might take a trip into P-town, and we're getting dinner at your favorite seafood place," she said as they left.

"You could have told me you had a million dollars waiting for me at my favorite seafood place, and I still wouldn't get off this couch," I thought to myself. The only thing I was budging for was an oxy, and getting one here seemed close to impossible.

My phone flashed again with more incoming texts from people wanting drugs. With shaking hands, I clutched my phone and sent out a mass text to almost everyone in my contacts. It read, "Can anyone bring 80's to Cape Cod right now...I will pay you a lot." I hit send and waited. Every response I got was along the lines of "Naw, man, I'm dry, I need some too," or "Cape Cod, that's like more than four hours away, sorry bro, no can do." I was lost. I needed to think of something. Phone in hand, I navigated over to the mobile search browser; maybe Google had some cures for withdrawal symptoms.

I didn't like what I found. OxyContin was an opiate, and was highly addictive. It was derived from opium, and basically the equivalent of synthetic heroin. I guess I had known this all along in the back of my mind, but seeing it written out in plain text and feeling worse than I did after my snowboarding accident, I could no longer deny the horrific truth—I was addicted.

"But Tina's boyfriend's mom had gotten a prescription for her back; they can't be that bad, can they?" I tried to reason with myself, but the nausea in my gut told me they were much worse than I had originally thought.

"I got hydrocodone to numb the pain when I had my

wisdom teeth removed, and doctors prescribed me pain medication after my snowboarding accident." I tried to rationalize my newly discovered addiction over and over again, but the strength of an 80 milligram OxyContin was far superior to hydrocodone, and both of those were only prescribed to be taken orally.

"Prescription medication is highly addictive and should be used with extreme caution," I remembered hearing on radio commercials, from my mother, Don, and teachers, but I hadn't listened. I had been told weed was bad too, but Will and I used to blaze and shred with no problems before I started doing opiates. When I stopped smoking marijuana because it made me paranoid, I'd quit cold turkey and it was easy—but this was different.

I flicked my nose and sniffled a bit; the pain from over a year of daily snorting was very acute. I had never noticed it before because I was constantly high. Suddenly aware that I had been high every day for around two years, I was shocked the possibility of addiction hadn't occurred to me earlier. When I was younger and sober, a year seemed like a long time. Sitting on the tan leather couch in the cozy Cape Cod cabin, I pondered how the past year had gone by so quickly. One day blended into the next, and I had not even noticed time slipping away.

"What the hell is wrong with me?" I thought to myself. I just needed to find something to make this pain go away, and then I would slowly wean myself off of painkillers and return to being the carefree individual I was before this whole mess.

On shaky legs, I mustered the strength to get off the couch and head out into the daylight. Squinting, as the sun tore into my eyes, magnifying the pain in my head, I stepped back inside to fetch my sunglasses. I should have gone to join my family on the beach, but I wasn't going anywhere until I found something to stop this horrible pain. Walking a few blocks in the direction of the fishing pier I noticed a shady-looking drugstore down a side street. I entered, catching a whiff of the potent scent of marijuana. There was a thin man who looked to be in his mid-thirties behind the counter. He had bags under his eyes, and despite a skeleton-like frame, his face was puffy. There were red blotches all over his face that looked like oversized scabs. I knew I should turn around, go back to the cabin, and deal with this agonizing self-inflicted pain without medication, but the pain overcame my self-control. I had to at least try to get relief.

"This guy looks sketchy, maybe he will know where to get some painkillers," I thought to myself. Approaching a complete stranger to ask for drugs was not something I had ever pictured myself doing. I knew my mother would be deeply disappointed if she ever found out; a wave of guilt momentarily washed over me, but was quickly driven away by the severe flu-like symptoms that encompassed my body.

I walked briskly past the pain relief section, not even bothering to browse. Nothing there would help me.

"I'm in a lot of pain. Nothing you have here will do. Do you know where I can get something a little stronger?" I asked the man behind the counter, expecting to get turned away. He held up a finger as if to tell me to wait, and opened a small door behind him, leading into the shack-like house that was connected to the store. Hope and anticipation of relieving these excruciating symptoms made them fade momentarily.

In less than a minute, the man returned and slid a tiny clear baggy containing fine brown powder across the counter towards me.

"Twenty-five dollars," he said. My heart lurched and dropped down into my stomach. I almost turned and left, fairly certain the small bag contained heroin, but instead, I took twenty-five dollars out of my wallet and gave it to the man. It went against everything I had thought I stood for, but my overwhelming desire to try absolutely anything to make the pain go away outweighed my moral compass. I put my hand over the baggy, closed it tightly, and nearly ran out of the shop.

I didn't know too much about heroin (other than that I had promised myself I would never touch it), but I knew it was a painkiller just like my beloved pills, and could be snorted or even smoked.

"Score," I thought to myself; I most definitely was not going to shoot anything up. One of the main differences between pills and heroin is that you never know how potent the heroin is. Oxys were always the same. Eighty milligrams was 80 milligrams, and that never changed. In my detoxing state, I briefly wondered if this was highly potent heroin that could potentially cause me to overdose.

"Oh well, I'd rather die than be in this much pain for the rest of the week," I thought to myself. I needed to take it as soon as possible. I couldn't wait until I got back to the cabin. Taking it there wouldn't have been a good idea anyway, in case one of my family members came back from the beach to check on me. I walked a few houses down from the shop where I had scored the drugs, and slipped in-between two buildings. Crouching down, I attempted to snort the heroin. There wasn't a good place for me to break out a line, and the warm ocean breeze wasn't helpful either. Not wanting to lose any of the contents of my precious package, I sealed up the baggy and headed back to the store.

"Do you have a bathroom I could use?" I said to the man behind the counter. He pointed to the back left corner of the store, to a sign that said 'Employees Only.'

"Don't be long," he said, as I hurried into the dingy hallway and found the restroom. The floor was mostly dirt, and the sink looked as if it hadn't been cleaned in years. I didn't care. My hands shook as I emptied a portion of the baggy onto the sink into a line. I'm sure there was dirt mixed in, but the heroin was a similar color, so I couldn't tell and I didn't care.

The potent powder entered my nostrils and, almost immediately, I was enveloped in pure euphoria. My dreadful detox symptoms lifted, and a blissful high took their place. I was in heaven. The best part was that I hadn't even used the whole bag, and I was high. This stuff was cheap! Bustling out of the store, I could barely hide my happiness. I raced back to the cabin, carefully hid the treasured bag of drugs, and headed to join my family at the beach. It was a gorgeous day, something I had failed to notice before, when all I could think about was the pain. I should have felt guilt when I saw the enormous smile on my mother's face as I joined my family in a game of bocce ball, but I was in paradise; nothing could touch this feeling.

For the remaining days we were in Cape Cod, I frequented the heroin shop, making excuses to sneak away for a few minutes.

Tim always wanted to come with me. I was not sure if he was suspicious of my behavior, or genuinely wanted to spend time with his older brother, but I had to tell him no. On the last day, I was sad to go, but anxious to get back home. I missed selling drugs. I was drawn to the hustle. Running around dealing was thrilling for me; it filled the hole in my soul that the snowboard accident left. Not only did it fulfill my thrill-seeking desires, but if I was always on the move, I wouldn't have time to think about my drug problem. I knew deep down I needed to get help, but with help from the heroin, I convinced myself I was fine. I could fix this on my own.

## Chapter Five:
# Denial

Heroin had saved me from my agony in Cape Cod, but I still hadn't admitted to myself that I had done it. I was not one to break promises. I could not remember ever breaking a single one before. Now I had broken a promise to the person who mattered most in my life—myself. Addicts don't like to admit anything. The use of drugs shoots them into a superficial elation that allows them to escape reality. I was living in that illusion. With drugs, my world was perfect. There was nothing to admit, nothing to worry about, nothing to fear.

The panic only set in when I started to come down from a high and my supply was low. I was no longer interested in making money; I just wanted to stay well. My vow to wean myself off of opiates upon my return was long since forgotten. Each time my high began to wear off, the uneasiness set in with astonishing speed. I couldn't even enjoy being high like I used to. Each time I used, I was inevitably plotting ways to obtain my next fix.

Brianna had become my steady girlfriend, and the two of us spent all of our time finding drugs, selling drugs, and getting high. I managed to get my license and my car back, but I needed to ask my mother to help me pay for my increased insurance rate. She obliged, saying she would use the money she took from my room to cover the extra cost, but she wanted me to promise her I would stop sneaking around. I quickly promised and got back behind the wheel. Of course, that was another promise I would break. Lies, deceit, and broken promises were becoming a trend for me. I would have been immensely disappointed in myself, but personal shame was an emotion that had vanished with the drug use.

My four-year college career passed in a hazy flash. Instead of enjoying myself like normal eighteen to twenty-one year olds do in college, with sports, beer pong, and parties, my life was focused on drugs. Attending class less and less, I barely scraped by with passing grades. Even in my clouded state of mind, I was a very talented designer. My teachers wanted to see me succeed, and constantly tried to motivate me to come to class and get photo or web design internships. I only did the bare minimum of what was required to graduate; I didn't have time for design work along with my job at Stars, dealing drugs, and feeding my habit. My mother encouraged me to quit working at Stars, since I had college paid for and a place to live. She had no idea how badly I needed a constant cash flow.

Early one morning, Brianna and I were on the interstate, headed back from picking up a script in NYC. We had done a lot of opiates and I was nodding in and out of consciousness.

"Too bad I'm out of Adderall, I could really use a pick-me-up," I thought to myself, as I gazed at Brianna fast asleep in my passenger seat. Finally, I saw the sign for my town: 'Arelington 2 miles,' it read.

"Almost home, I can do this," I thought to myself. My eyelids drooped and finally shut. Suddenly, I snapped back into consciousness with a rush of adrenaline, as my Subaru tore across the rumble strip and barreled toward the tree line. In sheer panic, I slammed on the breaks, but it was too late.

# CHAPTER SIX:
## Virginia

Beep. Beep. Beep. The sterile stench of the hospital filled my nostrils. White coats filtered in and out, and the steady beeping of one of the machines I was hooked up to drilled into my skull like piercing daggers. Flashbacks of my snowboarding accident and previous hospital stay darted through my semi-conscious mind. Pain took over my body, and I screamed out in agony. Feeling a warm hand on mine, I clenched my eyes shut tighter, not wanting to face my mother. Finally, I cracked open an eye. Sure enough, tears were streaming down her face, and I was pretty banged up in a hospital bed.

"What happened? Did we crash? Is Brianna okay?" I asked, not sure if I wanted to know the answers to these questions. My mother informed me that Brianna had not broken any bones, because her body was so relaxed on impact, but because of the way she had been sleeping in the front seat when the airbag deployed, she had a punctured lung and was in a coma. She kept talking and crying, but all I could think about was the pain. A nurse entered the room; I must have asked my mom to get her and tell her that I was still in pain, because she hurried in and went directly to check my IV.

"You're hooked up to an IV containing quite heavy painkillers, I'm surprised your level of pain is still so high," she said to me when I let her know my pain was an eleven on a scale of one to ten. She bustled out of the room returning in what seemed like a million years with a few more nurses and a doctor, but the large white clock on the eggshell colored wall told me it had only been three minutes.

"Hello, Ryan, I'm Doctor Jones," said a tall, stern-looking man in scrubs and a white hospital suit coat. He was holding a clipboard with some paperwork. I could see RX imprinted on one of the papers. It was the symbol used to trademark medical prescriptions, and triggered an intense craving to get high. They said I was already on painkillers, but they were only slightly numbing my withdrawal symptoms and not even touching the pain from the accident.

I stared at the doctor and said nothing, mentally willing him to not ask questions and to up my dosage of pain meds. How could I trick him into giving me more medication? I had to think of something, but nothing was coming to mind. I was too out of it.

"I don't know what you guys are doing wrong, but I'm still in a lot of pain, so obviously someone here isn't doing their job." I glared past him at the nurse, trying to guilt her into upping my dose. She stared back at me, shaking her head.

"You are a very lucky young man. If you had been just a foot over to the left, you most likely would not have survived. Instead, you escaped with a broken wrist and only a few scrapes and bruises. With all of the fluids and Dilaudid we have going through this IV, I can't imagine you're still in pain. It could just be the shock of what happened causing you to think you are really in more pain than you are," the doctor continued.

I knew what Dilaudid was. Dilaudid was great. It was a prescription painkiller that gave a phenomenal high, but it was not as strong as oxy 80's, and I needed a hell of a lot more than what they were giving me to ease this pain. I didn't know what to do. I couldn't leave until they discharged me.

The police had taken my cell phone and belongings as evidence. There was a lock on my phone, and I was always careful to erase my text messages and put my dealers and custys under fake names. I was pretty sure they wouldn't find anything incriminating if they were to look, but there was no way I could call anyone to come bring me some drugs.

"I'm so glad I stashed the script we just picked up in the roof of my car," I thought to myself. I didn't want to be caught with a script after getting in an accident, especially if Brianna died. They said she was stable, and I was thanking the Lord she hadn't been killed and praying for her save recovery. I knew if she died and the script was discovered, I would do some jail time for sure.

"I'm not built for jail; I'm too small and cute. I would be somebody's bitch in a second, and I would kill myself before that happened," I thought. Little did I know that jail, although far from pleasant, might have actually been the best place for me at the time.

I needed to leave. If I could find my car and get that script, I would be all set.

"Ryan!" I snapped out of my dazed thoughts. The doctor had been saying my name for God knows how long.

"What?" I slurred when he finally got my attention.

"We will need to keep you here for a day or so, to make sure you don't have any internal bleeding and nothing comes up that we may have overlooked by mistake. Usually people in your condition aren't in this much pain, so we want to keep a close eye on you." I could see my mother listening to him with lines of worry etched across her face. That was absolutely not going to work. If they didn't up my dosage of Dilaudid through that IV, there was no way I was going to stay here another minute. He turned to walk out of the room, saying he would be back to check on me in a few hours. I had to do something.

Thinking fast, I blurted out, "I'm fine! I'm not in any pain at all! It must have just been in my head, like you said. Can I leave now?" I hadn't taken time to think this plan through, and was completely unprepared for his response.

He turned around smiling, and said, "Oh, good, if you are feeling fine, we will remove the IV and monitor your pain levels for a few hours; if you are still feeling fine, we will discharge you."

I froze with panic. There was absolutely no way I could stay here completely off of painkillers. The pain was already so great; I couldn't even think about how Brianna was or worry about the damage to my car or my mother's pained facial expressions. The only thing that mattered was getting high. I considered jumping up and running as soon as he disconnected my IV, but my legs were cramped and I was in so much pain I didn't think I would make it very far. There was also the matter of the awful hospital gown I was in. After removing me from the car, they had cut off all my clothes and I had nothing to wear on my feet. With no phone, there was no way I could easily get some drugs. If I tried to escape, my mother and the hospital staff would come running after me.

"Ryan, what is it, sweetheart?" It was impossible to hide my worry from my mother. She saw right through me. She knew something was very wrong, but she just didn't know what it was.

I couldn't speak. "How did I get myself into this situation?" I thought, as a feeling of rage shook through my body. I could feel my heart tingling with burning anxiety and my fists clenched in frustration. It wasn't fair. I had become so accustomed to turning to drugs to ease my physical and emotional pain that I was not equipped to deal with such a distressing situation. I wanted to jump out of my own skin, punch my mother and the doctors in the face, and flee. But there I was, stuck to an IV in an uncomfortable hospital bed. There was no way out.

"Don't!" I yelled, as the doctor approached to remove the IV from my arm. "I can't stay here for a few hours with no pain medication," I whimpered.

"Ryan, what's going on?" the doctor asked. He must have noticed my drug-seeking behavior and was trying to get me to come clean.

"I thought you just said you were okay," my mother interjected.

I knew I needed help. I really wanted my old life back. Maybe if I told them what was going on, they could help me get off opiates slowly and less painfully. An addiction was the last thing I wanted to admit to my mother and out loud to myself, but the alternative was to stay in the hospital for hours in deadly amounts of pain, while pretending I had no pain so they would release me. That seemed impossible.

"You can't remove that IV… because I am already suffering from severe withdrawal symptoms from opiate addiction, on top of the wounds from my accident. If you take away the tiny amount of painkillers you're currently putting into my body and make me stay here, I feel like I will die. Please. Don't do it," I begged.

What happened after that was a blur. I remember my mother crying, the doctor talking about treatment options and opiate blockers, and my twenty-one-year-old self sitting with my eyes shut, wishing I was anywhere but in that hospital room.

Then I was introduced to Suboxone—subs, stops, or strips, as I would later refer to them. Stops were the street name for Suboxone in a pill form, because the orange pill was formed in the shape of a stop sign. Strips were the term we used for Suboxone strips, which looked like a flat orange rectangle and came inside of a blue and white rectangular package. They were like a drug version of Listerine breath mint strips. Suboxone is a form of buprenorphine, or bupe, as we called it on the streets. Buprenorphine is used to treat opiate addiction.

The doctor explained that Suboxone was an opiate blocker, so if I took some, I couldn't get high on heroin or painkillers even if I wanted to.

"Awesome, that could help with the mental part of my addiction, but what about my physical pain?" I thought.

As if the doctor had heard me, he continued. "Suboxone and buprenorphine have affects similar to opiates, and can help improve physical withdrawal symptoms. The catch is that Suboxone is also highly addictive, and it can be even harder to wean yourself from this drug than from heroin and other opiates. It is only to be taken orally. Don't snort it or inject it if you want to cure your opiate addiction without developing a buprenorphine addiction. I trust your mother will supervise your use," he said to my mother and me, embarrassing me.

"Drugs to cure your pain, more drugs to cure your addiction—this world is fucked. If hospitals didn't prescribe pills to begin with, I wouldn't even be in this predicament, but at least they're not making me quit cold turkey," I thought to myself.

The doctor wrote me a prescription for Suboxone, which my mother took control of, saying she would only let me have the prescribed amount and she would have to watch me take it. I was infuriated.

"What am I, a child?" I screamed at her. It was not her fault. The doctor had recommended her supervision, and she was just concerned about me, but I didn't see it that way. The way I saw it, I was a twenty-one-year-old being treated like I was twelve and it was rude and unfair. The whole world seems like it is out to get you when you are detoxing from drugs.

The Suboxone did help a lot. It was a relief from my intense symptoms, and I knew I couldn't get high, so it alleviated my cravings for the most part. Then there was the depression. I didn't want to interact with anyone. Things I used to love, like design, snowboarding, other sports, and exploring the outdoors, seemed bland and uninteresting. My mood swings were crazy and unpredictable. I never slept.

Insomnia was just a part of what the doctor called post-acute withdrawal syndrome, but it was a bitch. I would lay awake at night, my legs constantly twitching from restless leg syndrome, yet another side effect I would have to live with for who knows how long. I would try to think of anything to calm me down, but nothing helped. Even with the subs, every second ticked by slowly as I tried to count sheep or do anything else that might naturally induce slumber. My brain was still exploding from anxiety and my heart was sullen. Each day I was off pain-killers seemed like a miracle. Twenty-four hours may not seem like a long time to most people, but to an addict craving drugs, it seemed like a century. Stairs were the worst; every time I had to go up a staircase, my leg muscles screamed out in pain. My back hurt too, most likely from an injury I'd gotten when I was on opiates that I didn't even realize because my body was numbed by pain. Now I felt everything.

I had a lot to be thankful for. I was alive, I had a family that loved me, a degree from a reputable college, my uncle's auto body shop fixed my car for a very good price using the last of the money my mother had taken from my bedroom years ago, Brianna had come out of her coma, and I was not in jail. I didn't feel thankful. I didn't feel happy. I felt anxious, lost, depressed, and restless.

My mother insisted that I go to rehab. She wanted me to be monitored by professionals and get proper treatment. There was no way in hell that was going to fly. I wasn't going to be locked in a facility with drug addicts, like I was some kind of crazy person. Hell no.

The only other alternative was that I join Tim and Brandon when they moved to Virginia for school in a few months, to get away from the negative influences in my life. My baby brother was leaving the state for school. I was proud of him. He was finally doing something that wasn't following me, but now I was being forced to follow him. I didn't want to leave Vermont. My custys were here, and my dealers were close by. How would I ever survive in Virginia? I didn't have any connects or custys there. My mind raced; I had to think of a way to convince my mother to let me stay in Vermont and live with her. I didn't want to live at home, but there was no way I could afford an apartment, and my parents refused to help me pay for one unless I moved to Virginia.

Rent was cheaper in the little town just outside Virginia Beach where my brother and Brandon had found an apartment than it was in Vermont. My mother promised to cover it for me for the first three months, to give me some time to get on my feet and get hired as a web designer or photographer. The job market in the south was not great, but having a bachelor's degree from Vermont gave me a leg up. Maybe I could actually get my life on track. Still taking my prescribed Suboxone with my mother's supervision, I was staying off opiates for the most part. I would wait until the Suboxone wore off, get high on some heroin or oxy, and then use the Suboxone to cure my withdrawal symptoms. It was a vicious cycle. Brianna had also scored a Suboxone prescription after coming out of her coma, and preferred it to opiates. I didn't understand. Suboxone was nice, but nothing compared to oxy.

"I am not going to Virginia unless Brianna comes with me," I protested when my mother tried to convince me I needed to move. It was a good idea to get away from my drug connects, and with Brianna by my side, I wouldn't have to suffer through my depression, drug cravings, and anxiety alone. It was possible that if I left Arelington, where the opiate problem was getting increasingly worse, I could have started over and gotten on the right path. It sounded great in theory, but that was not what happened.

My mom and Don agreed to let Brianna be the fourth roommate in the three-bedroom apartment Tim and Brandon were planning on moving into. They were having trouble finding a third roommate in Virginia, and having four people split rent made it even cheaper, which was appealing.

Our apartment was settled in a gated community in a small town outside of Virginia Beach. Although the town was slightly run-down, our little area was quite nice. It included a pool, hot tub, tennis court, basketball court, workout facility, and numerous other amenities. It was the perfect getaway to focus on myself and try to beat this horrible addiction. Brianna was going to quit with me. Not being in this completely alone was the only thing that kept me going.

I couldn't have picked a better time to get out of the drug game. The FDA had banned 80's. They were no longer being made. I felt like a part of me was destroyed. It was bittersweet. I still had some 80's stashed away, along with an array of various other painkillers—Percocet, Vicodin, Dilaudid, and a few benzos (short for benzodiazepines), like Valium and Xanax. The benzos put a small dent in the violent anxiety that came with detox, and lasted long after. They were part of the arsenal of drugs I used to stay away from opiates. I stashed the substantial assortment of drugs in the bottom of my suitcase, and stuffed it in the back of my Subaru with all of my other belongings.

My plan was to give up opiates, because even though they made me feel so wonderful, they were destroying my life. After trying them, I had forgotten my initial fear of addiction; taking drugs had seemed like no big deal. I'd felt like I was in control. I'm sure most people feel the same way. "It could never happen to me," I always thought about early death, addiction, STDs, and other horrible things that I heard about in the news and in school. Many things that seem like they could never happen do, and I was finding that out the hard way. I still hadn't fully admitted to myself that I was an addict. I knew I was addicted, but I would tell myself I was just an innocent person that got caught up in some bad stuff, and I was going to easily get out of it.

As long as I wasn't doing heroin, I didn't feel like a junkie. Pills didn't seem that bad, because doctors prescribed them. The little voice in my head that told me otherwise was silenced by the drugs. The lines between good and bad and right and wrong were blurred when I was using. As I drove the eleven hours to our little town outside Virginia Beach with Brianna riding shotgun, I couldn't help but think about the collection of drugs at the bottom of my suitcase. What if I needed to go back to opiates? Would they be enough to keep me going until I found a steady connect? Even though there was an adequate amount of drugs in my trunk to get me thrown in jail for years and to make the average person faded for weeks, I could burn through it in a day if I let myself. After my experience in Cape Cod, I felt fairly confident that I could just ask around and score some drugs, but I really didn't want to. I needed to get my life on track. I used to think that only scumbags used heroin, but I quickly learned that anyone, regardless of age, race, social class, and upbringing, could fall victim to drug addiction.

Brianna was passed out in the passenger's seat. "How can she fall asleep so easily?" I wondered. "Is she using again, or do the subs really have that much of an effect of her?" Brianna and I had been together for quite a while, and she was pretty hardcore addicted, but her addiction wasn't nearly as strong as mine. "Am I responsible for her addiction?" I pushed the thought out of my mind and continued to drive, wishing I had some Adderall, 80's, or even a beer in the front seat. I wanted to pull over and get the drugs out of my trunk, but Brandon and Tim were following me. They disapproved of my addiction. My hands thumped against the steering wheel, and my legs jiggled as I drove. I had to constantly be moving, but I wasn't sure why. I couldn't control it. My brain was as restless as my body; the only time I was completely satisfied was when I was on drugs. I never stopped to think if anyone else ever noticed my compulsive movement, or if it had started so slowly that no one picked up on it, like the subtle changes in my appearance.

Even with my addiction, I still had dreams, goals, and aspirations. I wanted to become a web designer, and also do photography on the side. With my degree, I was right on track. The only thing holding me back was my addiction. It knew no limits.

Finally, we arrived in Virginia and began to unpack. Tim and Brandon wanted to organize everything and make the apartment feel like home. Brianna and I dragged our belongings into our room and then cracked open some beer. Normally it would have bothered me that my things weren't put away and I would have gone straight to organizing, but that wasn't even a thought now. The only thing in my mind was getting rid of the cravings. Beer seemed like a good idea. It wasn't.

In the days that followed, my roommates and I set up our apartment and played a hell of a lot of beer pong. I was only using subs and benzos, and was feeling okay for the most part, but still hadn't applied to any jobs. Since I had been off the opiates, I was almost always drunk and on benzos. When you combine the two, it causes a lot of memory loss. There were days that went by without me knowing. One day, I woke up in my bed thinking it was Tuesday, when really it was Saturday.

What had I done? The dents and scratches in my car told me I had driven, and a new number in my phone told me I had made a drug connect. Brandon and Tim told me I had stolen a lot of food and DVDs from a few local stores.

"Dude, I can't believe you don't remember grabbing those DVDs and walking out of the store while you flipped the camera off! Then we got into your car and you pulled out onto a busy street going the wrong way! I thought I was going to die! You jumped the median and scratched the shit out of your car. You really don't remember?" Brandon went on and on about how crazy my driving was and how he was pumped to have a bunch of free movies, but he had feared for his life. I remembered nothing. As far as I knew, I was winning in beer pong with Brianna against Tim and Brandon on Tuesday night. Then I woke up, sprawled out in my bed with Brianna beside me and a raging hangover. I remembered not even a second of anything that had happened in between.

I must have done opiates somehow. I had a new number in my phone, presumably my new drug connect. The contact name said 'Terrorist.' The person I had gotten drugs from must have looked like a terrorist. I was unsure if Brianna had been with me when I met Terrorist, or if she knew I was using again. She looked sickly. I didn't want to wake her.

Drugs numb you. They take you over and eat away at your soul. Everything that you once stood for crumbles to nothing when you're under the influence. Drugs mean everything. They don't care that you had a bright future, they don't care that your family loves you. They don't care if you have children, which, luckily, I didn't.

I needed to fix myself, but I couldn't even think about getting my life on track in this condition. I'd run out of subs, and ransacked the room as quietly as I could in search of any type of opiates. I found nothing. My cash supply was dwindling. I needed to act fast.

I uncovered more and more details from my four day black out by calling Terrorist. He lived in a sketchy neighborhood a few blocks away and sold a shit-ton of drugs. I had gotten crack and heroin from him and we had done some together.

"You a crazy little white boy! I can't believe you don't remember meetin' me. You came up to me in the shoppin' center parkin' lot, drivin' that flashy little car of yours, and asked if I could help you out," he told me, summarizing a series of events that I almost didn't believe had happened. I was in shock that four entire days of my life were missing in my head, but my body had kept going, making horrible decisions without consulting my brain.

I asked if he would front me some dope. He was shocked at my lack of fear and rejected me immediately, but offered a proposition.

"You wanna get some dope? Take that little car of yours to the back entrance of the department store near Causeway Block and wait. When my boy Ace sees you, he will jump into your ride with a stolen TV. Bring it to me in Causeway Block, and I'll give ya some dope." Terrorist's proposal was risky, but I had no other options. I promised myself that, after this, I would get a job.

"Word. I'll do it," I agreed. I wondered how much dope we were talking about, but at this point it didn't matter. As long as it cured the wave of hell I had brought upon myself, nothing else mattered.

Hanging up the phone, I grabbed my keys and wobbled out of the apartment in the same clothes I had woken up in. Who knows how long I had been in that outfit? I'm pretty sure it was at least a week. I could feel Tim and Brandon staring at the back of my head as I fumbled for my shoes. Their disapproving stares burned through me like daggers. I ignored it. The physical pain from withdrawal was a million times worse than the embarrassment I felt from their worry and displeasure.

"Be careful, bro," Brandon said as I left. I could sense my own brother just shaking his head. He had nothing to say to me. I should have been concerned that our relationship was worse than ever. Tim and Brandon were my best friends; they were family. They didn't know where I was going or what I was doing, but they could tell it was bad and didn't want to be any part of it.

My hands were shaking as I pulled around the back of the department store near Causeway Block, just minutes from my apartment. Terrorist ran Causeway Block. Anyone who came down that street had to get the clear from him. His neighborhood was so bad that cops didn't even drive down there. If something happened there, the pigs just turned a blind eye. Once we got the TV from the shopping center parking lot to the beginning of the block, we were safe—until we left the street again. I had not even lived in Virginia for three months, and already I was going to be banned from my local shopping center, in the best case scenario.

I should have put something over the license plate of my car, so it couldn't be identified if I parked in a spot where the cameras could see me. I didn't know the shopping center well enough to be sure I wasn't going to get caught on video surveillance, but even that didn't bother me.

My hands shook on the steering wheel more from withdrawal pain than from nerves. I sent Terrorist a text to let him know I was in position. Just minutes later, a large African American man carrying a huge flat screen TV, trailed by mall security, came barreling at my vehicle.

"This must be Ace," I thought to myself, as I popped my trunk and unlocked all four of my Impreza doors. Ace slammed the TV in the trunk and darted into my backseat.

"Move it, whiteboy!" he yelled, and I peeled out of the parking lot just as security arrived at my car.

They had my plates for sure. My heart was thudding in my chest, and Ace was laughing in the backseat.

"That's what you call a clean getaway," he chuckled, as my Subaru careened into Causeway Block.

"Clean getaway, he must be smoking crack," I thought. I meant he must be crazy, but it occurred to me after that he was most likely literally smoking crack, and on all sorts of other drugs. I said nothing.

My car screeched to a stop in front of Terrorist's spot. He was waiting for us outside, baggy of dope in hand, as promised.

My heart sank. It was only a ticket. One single bag. I was hoping for a bun. I should have known there was no way Terrorist would give me anything more than a ticket, but it was all I needed to feel well enough to apply for a job.

It was time to suit up. I got home all doped out and feeling much better. Brandon and Tim barely looked at me when I walked in the door. Only Brandon spoke.

"Glad you made it home okay, buddy."

Tim had taken to ignoring me to show his resentment for my behavior.

Brianna had woken up and was furious with me. As soon as I had entered my room to shower and dress, she flung herself out of bed, nearly knocking me over.

"You asshole!" she screamed, pathetically punching me and scratching my face.

"What have I done," I wondered, holding her arms back so she would stop hitting me.

"I thought we were quitting opiates," she screeched. "So much for that! You got me drunk, left me alone, went out and got high! I found your stash and did some of it while you were gone because I was so pissed, and now I'm withdrawing and I can tell you aren't, because you look high as shit!"

As she hounded me at the top of her lungs, all I could think was, "You bitch. You did my revival stash, that's why I woke up in such bad shape and couldn't find any drugs!" Even when I was fucked up out of my mind, I tried to keep a revival stash of drugs to help ease the withdrawal symptoms that would inevitably hit me hard when I woke up. I didn't remember the past few days of my life, so I had believed that I was just so messed up that I had forgotten, until now. I had left an emergency stash, and Brianna had done it. I was beyond pissed. It was all her fault that I had to be a getaway driver for a robbery and that I was surely not allowed back at the local shopping center.

We screamed back and forth for almost an hour, and then I finally pushed past a weak and withdrawing Brianna and jumped into the shower.

I emerged from the bathroom forty-five minutes later looking pretty dapper. To the untrained eye, I was a productive member of society.

"Time to get a job," I thought to myself, snagging my resume off my desk planning to head to a few local design firms. I had a list of every place within an hour radius of our apartment that would potentially hire me. My mother had sent it from Vermont, along with a gift basket of homemade food. She was the best.

I started off at Landsing Designs, a company just minutes from my house that designed websites for all different types of businesses, large and small. I didn't have an interview and hadn't even applied, but when I walked in, the receptionist said the hiring manager was free if I would like to speak with him.

Luckily, I had brought my photography portfolio along with my resume, and my web design portfolio was easily accessible online. The receptionist led me to a brightly colored room with modern features and superb interior design, where I was greeted by a small man with glasses. He introduced himself and I gave him a firm handshake. After an hour of fluent conversation and reviewing my portfolio, I left feeling great.

I called my mom for the first time in a long while.

"Ryan! Honey, how are you doing? It's so good to hear from you!" I could tell she was glowing as she spoke into the phone. My mother's love for me radiated all the way from Vermont, and filled my insides with a warm comforting glow.

"You had an interview! That's amazing! How did it go?" she asked. I could tell she was beyond thrilled.

"I nailed it," I said. "I should know by this time tomorrow if I get the job."

Her excitement was contagious. I hung up the phone and headed home to celebrate. As I neared my apartment, my joy suddenly turned into panic. I had done the entire ticket Terrorist had given me. What if Landsing Designs called to say I got the job and they wanted me to come in? I couldn't start work if I was sickly.

"Maybe Brianna still has some of the subs she was pre-scribed," I thought to myself. She would hopefully lend me a few, just to make sure I could make it to work if I was hired. Then I remembered how badly she was withdrawing, and figured she most likely didn't have any left.

I arrived home to find Brianna passed out drunk on our second story deck in a pile of vomit.

"That's you, bro," Brandon said to me, pointing at Brianna. "She was freakin' out about not having any drugs, took a ton of shots to ease her pain, then passed out and puked in her sleep." I could tell my brother and Brandon were starting to regret agree-ing to have Brianna and me as roommates. This was not at all how I had wanted to celebrate my successful interview.

After cleaning Brianna's puke, I left her on the porch floor, threw back a few straight shots of vodka, and took to my bed. The shots and the heroin helped me fall peacefully asleep, only to be woken at the crack of dawn by the ringing of my cell phone.

"Dammnit, why didn't I put that on vibrate?" I thought to myself, about to silence my phone and take some more shots, since I was completely out of drugs again. Then I noticed the number on the phone was from Landsing Designs, and I strug-gled to answer.

"Ryan Landry?" The chipper voice of the small man I spoke with the day before rushed through the phone and almost knocked me out with pain. Any loud noises were unwelcomed when I was suffering from withdrawal.

"This is," I managed to muster the strength to reply.

He went on and on, describing the job and the duties, and

said, "I would love to hire you as one of our designers, starting at twenty dollars an hour, pending your background check and successful completion of a urinalysis."

My heart felt like a boomerang, as it went from hopeful elation at the mention of twenty dollars an hour to dire dismay when I heard the term urinalysis. I agreed to come in to have my urine screened the following morning, and quickly got off the phone.

"With the exception of the DUI, my background should be pretty clean; now, how the hell am I going to pass a piss test?" I thought to myself. I was withdrawing pretty badly. I needed to find something, or I wasn't going to make it. I rolled over on something hard. Reaching my hand under my limp body, I uncovered a script bottle with a few orange octagonal pills.

Subs! Where had these come from? Brianna must have been holding out on me—I was going to kill her! Or maybe she'd hidden these on herself when she was blacked out, and really didn't know about them. I helped myself to a few pills. I knew I couldn't take a whole one or I would never be able to get it out of my system. I broke off a tiny piece and snorted it. I was still in pain, barely able to function, but it was better than nothing. I stashed the other pills I had stolen from my girlfriend's script bottle under the mattress, and headed out to the store.

I had to get a drug cleanse kit. It was the only way I had any hope of passing the screening the following day. With no money, I had no choice but to steal it. Shoving it in my pocket proved a difficult task, I was so clumsy and obvious, but no one even suspected me. I left the drugstore parking lot with the cleanse kit in my oversized shorts pocket. I had considered asking Tim or Brandon to piss for me, but I knew they wouldn't. Besides, they frequently smoked weed, and that was sure to show up on the test, as it stays in your system for much longer than opiates. I silently thanked myself for no longer smoking weed.

Opiates take between twenty-four and forty-eight hours to get out of your system, depending on metabolism and a variety of other factors. Luckily, I had a beast of a metabolism. Even before I was a drug user, I was the skinniest kid in school and ate the most. It was nearly impossible to build muscle, and I was often picked on for being such a twig. Now my fast metabolism was finally working in my favor.

After pounding the disgusting drug cleanse drink, I spent the entire day drinking water and going to the bathroom while suffering withdrawal symptoms that were coming on in full force. It was hell. This was the only way I was going to survive. My parents weren't covering my rent this upcoming month, and I had no money for food, gas, or drugs.

I was mid-piss and Brianna came raging into the bathroom, infuriated beyond control. She knocked right into me and I fell into the tub, splattering urine all over the bathroom floor and walls.

"Where are they?" she demanded.

"What are you talking about?" I asked, at first genuinely confused, then remembering taking some of her subs earlier in the day. I had intended to tell her, hoping she would be okay with it since my job interview had gone well and potentially working for this design company was such a great opportunity for me.

Seeing her now, I knew I had been hugely mistaken. I decided to play dumb.

"I don't know what you're taking about, Brianna, quit being such a psycho. You just made me pee all over the bathroom, and I had to clean up your puke yesterday. You probably took more subs than you thought when you were drunk."

"I woke up in the middle of the night on the floor covered in dry puke, so you didn't do a very good job cleaning me. I searched for the subs and finally found them. After taking some, I was able to fall asleep, so I know they must have been on the bed, and they're not anymore. You're lying, I know it!" she screeched.

"I don't know where they are. Leave me alone. I'm detoxing for a job, and I don't want to hear your shit," I retorted.

I didn't even feel guilty about lying to my girlfriend. She was turning into a bitch.

The next day, I returned to Landsing Designs for the dreaded piss test, still feeling severely under the weather. The same receptionist I had seen when I went in for my interview greeted me warmly and gave me a small cup to pee in. She was pretty hot, and I awkwardly blushed as she handed me the container.

"Don't worry, everyone has to do it; just leave the container in there when you're finished," she said, sensing my unease. I smiled and said nothing. Sober, I couldn't handle the embarrassment. Not being able to take any opiates for the second full day in a row was draining. My physical pain was thrashing at my withering body from every angle. I did my best to hide it, while longing to get high, or at least crawl back into bed and waste away.

"Your background check came up all clear; as long as the drug test checks out, you should be working with us next Monday," the receptionist told me when I was finished. She said I would receive a call in a day or two with the results, and I was all set to leave.

The Virginia sun and heat smacked me in the face as I stepped out of the Landsing Designs headquarters and shuffled toward my car, getting cold chills and hot flashes from my detox. I thought about going home, but didn't want to face Brianna. We weren't speaking much, and when we were, it was to accuse each other of stealing drugs or lying about it.

I still had no money, and wouldn't start until Monday at best. Even then, I didn't know if I was going to get paid on a weekly or bi-weekly scale. I called Terrorist.

"Listen, punk. You can't keep comin' to me, askin' for favors, if you ain't got no dough." I could hear him spitting into the phone, and then he stopped for a minute.

"Hang on, yo boy Ace needs a getaway driver again, you may be in luck." I really didn't want to be a getaway driver, but I had no choice. I wanted some drugs, I needed some drugs; I needed them very badly.

I swung through Causeway Block and scooped up Ace. This time he was accompanied by two other scruffy looking fellows called Danger and Big Mike. As the three men squished into my vehicle, I couldn't help but think this was a bad idea. I didn't know what I was more afraid of: being a getaway driver for whatever mission they decided I was headed on, or telling these husky drug addicts I was backing out.

The makeshift gang of men was intimidating, and I hastily chose to follow through with my promise to drive them wherever they wanted to go.

"Take a right, then a left…okay, back into this gas station," Ace directed and I quickly obliged. As soon as I had shifted my car into park, all three of them jumped out with lightning speed. Adrenaline shot through my veins as I witnessed them push past customers and pull a gun on the cashier through my rearview mirror.

"Oh my God, oh my God. I can never come to this gas station again." My head was spinning and my heart racing as they hustled back to my car with a bag full of cash. The last time had been frightening, but there had been no guns and I had been distracted by my physical pain. This time I was still suffering from tormenting withdrawal symptoms, but I was more sober than I had been in a while and was trembling with fear.

"Go, go go!" they all yelled, jumping into my car. Snapping out of my thoughts, I slammed my foot down on the gas pedal like it was a cement brick. I don't know how fast my car could go from zero to sixty, but that was how fast we got out of that parking lot. When we got back, they gave the loot to Terrorist, and he rewarded the three of them with a bun and me with just two measly tickets. I couldn't complain. Well, I could have, if I wanted an ass whooping and the drugs I had just earned to be taken away, which I didn't.

"Peace out," I told Terrorist, Ace, Danger, and Big Mike, and I headed back to the apartment with my drugs.

I would ration these two tickets along with the subs I'd

stolen from Brianna as much as humanly possible until I received my first paycheck, if I got the job. With all of the excitement, I had forgotten I needed to be worried that I might not pass my piss test. I knew I couldn't go on playing driver with these dangerous criminals for much longer without getting caught.

Somehow, by the grace of God, I passed the piss test.

"I got the job!" I told Tim and Brandon, after receiving the call the following day.

"Sweet, man, let's celebrate!" Brandon said, tossing me a beer.

Tim cracked open one as well, saying, "Don't fuck this up, man. It will kill Mom if she sees you lose such a great opportunity." He was such a downer.

Brianna was still pouting over not having any drugs, so she refused to play. Apparently she had no knowledge of the whereabouts of her missing subs, which I'd moved from under the mattress to a much stealthier hiding spot.

I couldn't be on a team by myself, so I gave Ace a ring. He wasn't someone I would usually hang out with, but he'd given me his phone number, so I figured why not. I could tell by the looks on Tim and Brandon's faces that having him over was not a good idea. The expressions of shock mixed with fear immediately made me regret my decision.

"Oh, well. It's too late to tell him to go home now," I thought to myself, as we got in position for a pong game.

Ace and I ran the table. The four of us actually ended up having a pretty decent time, until Ace needed to go and I drove him home.

He threw me a ticket for the ride, and in my drunken state I couldn't help but do it all, even though I had vowed to ration my stash until I started getting a steady paycheck. When I returned drunk and faded, Tim and Brandon laid into me.

"Seriously, Ryan! You brought that sketchy guy over here? Now your drug dealer or drug buddy or whatever he is knows where we live. How are we supposed to feel safe sleeping at night? What if you screw him over and he comes after us? And driving drunk again! Really? Do you want a second DUI? What if you killed someone? You're probably going to end up in jail!"

I couldn't even make out who said what; I just blocked them out and stumbled toward the safety of my room. I wasn't safe there either. Brianna was freaking out because she'd overheard I had gotten drugs and I didn't share with her. What was my life becoming? I hated it. I wanted to die, but at least I had been hired at a reputable web design firm.

"I can turn this around," I thought, as I hazily drifted out of consciousness.

———•◆•———

Somehow, I managed to make it to my first day of work at Landsing Designs on time and on enough heroin that I wasn't withdrawing or nodding out. It was perfect. I loved my job. Everyone marveled at my ideas and I got along well with the other designers. Working at Landsing Designs was everything I had ever hoped for in a career. I wished I could enjoy it without the burden of wondering where I was going to get my next drug fix weighing down on me. It was a struggle trying to find either subs or opiates after work every day. With no money, I ended up doing a lot of crazy jobs for Terrorist, Ace, and their buddies.

Before drugs, I was an honest, kindhearted person. I never would have stolen anything from anyone or assisted in any way. But the drugs got me. They steal your conscience; they steal your soul. They have no concern for the person you used to be or you want to be in the future. Everything you cared about gets pushed to the side to make room for your burning desire to find more. Even though opiates were bringing me closer and closer to death every day, I couldn't see it. To me, they were necessary for my survival. Without them, I literally felt like I was dying a painful death.

After receiving my first paycheck, I finally paid rent on my own. My roommates were relieved and my mother was proud. Brianna still hadn't found a job, and her mooching was really starting to get on my nerves. We got along well on payday, when I would bring home an array of drugs to share with her, but I was paid biweekly, and by the end of the second week, we were both struggling hard. When it was time for Brianna, Tim, Brandon, and I to go home for Christmas vacation, I had very few drugs and almost no money. I hadn't bought anything for my family or friends. Normally, if I wasn't in a drug haze, I would have felt like a complete piece of shit, especially for not buying anything for my darling mother—but I didn't feel anything. My mother deserved the world. She gave me presents on top of buying my plane ticket, and all I could give her was a hug, but, to her, that was giving her the world.

# CHAPTER SEVEN:
# Needles

"I can't believe I successfully transported heroin and subs on the plane home. Have I lost my mind?" The small portion of my brain that was still capable of rational thought was telling me I must be completely nuts. I ignored it as usual, masking reality with drugs, not thinking of the possible consequences of my actions. I had lost my ability to think and plan logically. The only thing that mattered was that I had drugs at all times to stay well.

Tim and I have an older sister, Maya. She is four years older than me, and lives in California with her family. I had never met her husband or two small children, and they were supposed to visit for the first time this year. My parents had been out to California numerous times, to visit their grandchildren and to be in Maya's wedding. Tim had also gone for the wedding, but I'd stayed behind, too caught up in the hectic lifestyle of a drug addict and dealer to think about leaving.

Maya used to write me letters. She knew how badly my mother wished and hoped I would get well. I never read any of her letters. I don't know if I was too busy, too lazy, or too scared of what I might find. The envelopes had been piled up under my bed in the room I used to live in at my parents' house. They were gone when I returned. I am not sure if my mother didn't want Maya to accidentally find them and realize I had never opened a single one, or if it was just too sad for her to see so many failed attempts to get through to me sitting on the bedroom floor.

I was really close with my half-brother, but neither of us had ever been close to Maya. There was quite an age difference between her and Tim, but the four years that separated us seemed like a lot more than it was. She left for college when I was entering high school, and hadn't returned since except for the occasional holiday. This had always been hard for my mother, but it was nothing compared to what she was dealing with when it came to me. She longed for Maya because she was thousands of miles away, but she longed for me when I was right next to her, standing so close, yet separated by a vile blanket of addiction. I didn't want to be a burden on her. I wanted to make her proud, like Maya had, but the drugs wouldn't let me. I should have opened all of those letters. I should have quit opiates and all other drugs right then. I was in pretty deep, but not yet past the point of no return.

We were only home a few short days for Christmas break, but I wanted to see all of my friends. I tried to contact Will, my close childhood friend and snowboarding buddy who used to tag along on trips to NYC, but he refused to speak to me. I was puzzled. We hadn't had a falling out that I knew of, but, then again, I couldn't be sure. A good portion of my life was lost to my memory. Curious, I texted some of our mutual friends, who told me he was pissed at me. It had to do with drugs. I had ripped him off in a sale or something. When I first heard that, I was livid for a moment. I had given him so many free drugs on our trips to NYC; how could he possibly think that I ripped him off? My anger quickly faded when I received a text from another old drug connect, Seth, who'd heard I was back in town and wanted to chill.

Seth picked me up at my parents' house on Christmas Eve, because my car was back in Virginia. We went to kick it at his place. I thought about inviting Brianna, but I doubted I would be able to score free drugs from Seth for both of us, so I didn't bother. She was probably doing things with her parents anyway, I told myself so I wouldn't feel as bad. I didn't want to ask him for drugs, but I was starting to come down and my stash was dwindling, so I decided to subtly hint. Luckily, he picked up on it and I didn't have to ask. Seth had inherited a large amount of money, and wasn't as stingy as most people were with their drugs because he always had a constant supply. We plopped down on the raggedy-ripped couch the second we entered Seth's dingy apartment. Everything was like I remembered it: clothes strewn across the floor, the loveseat ripped just like the brown couch we sat on, crusty food and empty beer bottles and cans flung about. Remnants of drugs everywhere you looked, empty script bottles on the floor, baggies in every corner, and even the occasional syringe were strewn about.

"Don't worry about it, bro, it's all good; you're my boy, we go way back," Seth said, as I thanked him for sharing his heroin with me. I watched as he pulled out the little baggy containing the sacred brown powder. I expected him to break me out a line on the table, but instead he pulled out a spoon, some cotton, water, a lighter, and a black and clear syringe with an orange cap.

I'd assumed the needles lying around his house were from other people, but I could see now they were his, and started shaking my head. I was afraid of needles, and never using them was in the set of promises I had made myself when I began using drugs.

"Naw, man, I don't use needles. I'll just snort my line, thanks," I said as he began to take off his belt to use as a tourniquet. He ignored me, and I watched as the belt forcibly compressed his arm and blue veins became increasingly visible. He placed a small piece of cotton on the end of the needle and used it to suck up the murky mixture of water and heroin that floated around in the spoon.

"The cotton is to make sure there is no debris or air pockets," he explained, noticing my confusion. This was all new to me. Sure, I had been using drugs for a fair amount of time, and I regrettably was strongly tied to heroin use, but shooting up was on a whole different level. I couldn't believe my friend was doing this. I felt sick and wanted to leave. I almost excused myself, but then I realized the sickness was mostly my oncoming withdrawal, and Seth had driven me. More importantly, if I left now, I wasn't going to get any of the free drugs he had offered me, so I stayed put.

I watched in horror as the needle entered his blue vein and sucked up bright red blood that fused with the cloudy mixture, then exited back into the vein. Instantly, Seth's entire body went limp with relaxation. He was so faded, I wondered for a second if he had overdosed or died. He hadn't.

"Man, you've got to try it," he drawled, looking up at me.

When I politely refused again, he responded with, "That's alright; if you don't want any, more for me." My heart lurched. He wasn't going to give me some unless I shot it.

"Only dirtbags shoot up. Only junkies use needles. I will never use needles. I hate needles." My head was bombarded with a jumble of thoughts and emotions. I didn't want to do it, I really didn't, but I had to. My withdrawal symptoms were coming on hard, and I knew if I went home, they would continue to get worse and Christmas would be hell.

Seth made shooting up seem like paradise.

"If you think you enjoy your high from snorting heroin, you haven't felt anything yet. Nothing compares to needles. The instant gratification, the rush—it's simply indescribable. You said you're low on supply and don't have much money; well, shooting up delivers an increased effect and is more efficient than snorting. You will get much higher injecting than you would if you snorted it, and you use less of your stash."

My mind and body yearned for the bliss of an opiate high. Since I'd been using, my tolerance had gradually increased. I needed to snort ridiculous amounts of dope just to feel well; an instant high was just too enticing for me to resist. This time, I watched carefully as Seth prepared the concoction of powder and water. I studied everything he did, so I would be able to do it again when I left his house. I wanted to promise myself I would only shoot up this once, but I knew it would be another promise broken.

"Here, I even got a clean needle for you," he said, handing

me the dreaded object fresh out of the package. My hands shook as I grabbed it. He could see me fumbling around and offered to do it for me the first time, so I didn't miss the vein. Normally, I don't like anyone helping me with anything, but this was serious business, and I knew there was a risk of missing the vein, arterial damage, scarring, and more, so I accepted his offer.

The needle neared my arm; I pictured it entering my vein, and held my breath with growing anticipation. The closer it moved toward my vein, the less afraid I was. This shocked me. Whenever I had to get a shot at the doctors, I would flinch, look away, and resist the urge to run out of the room. This time, I wanted just the opposite. I wanted the needle to plunge right in. I could feel the relief from my withdrawal symptoms happen even before the point of the needle broke the surface of my skin.

The instant it punctured my vein, I was knocked over on the couch.

"This is like the first time!" I thought joyously. I had been forever chasing the initial high of opiates so unsuccessfully, I had forgotten what it even felt like and was only using to stay well. I'm not sure how long I was zoned out on Seth's couch, but I thoroughly enjoyed and savored every moment of it. When I was finally conscious enough to have a conversation, I had lots of questions for Seth.

He told me needles could be purchased for less than five dollars at any local pharmacy. Even better, the Vermont Needle Exchange program provided everything you needed to shoot up, free of change. I wondered if there was anything like that in Virginia. I would need to stock up for my trip back. The facility was open from nine to noon and one to five on weekdays, by appointment only, with an exception of drop-in hours on Wednesdays. It was closed for the holiday, so Seth and I couldn't stop by immediately, like I wanted.

We chatted for a few hours, mostly reminiscing about old times, and also discussing drugs, connects, and the struggle. Seth was shocked to hear about my troubles in Virginia, even though he informed me crime was increasing at an alarming rate in Arelington because so many people were addicted and low on cash. Since he had a constant supply of drugs and money, he had never been in the situations I had gotten myself into in Virginia with Ace, Terrorist, and their crew. My stories were not something I was proud of, even then. I almost didn't share them with him, but we bonded over my first time shooting up, and I knew he wouldn't judge me. I was glad to have a friend who was so open and non-judgmental.

It never occurred to me that his relaxed demeanor might have been different if he wasn't constantly high. This friend, who was my boy from back in the day, would rob me if he had to. He didn't because he was the exception, not the rule. He was the addict who had money, but that could change at any time. I wouldn't want to be around if there ever came a day when Seth had used up all of his trust fund money and he was down on his luck. There weren't many people I knew that were more addicted to opiates than I was. In fact, I think Seth was the only one. I shouldn't have been so concerned with the severity of his addiction, but I used it to make myself feel like mine wasn't so bad. We were both addicted, and we both needed a serious change of lifestyle and perspective, but when you're in it, the only thing you focus on is fueling your addiction. You find any way you can to rationalize it to yourself.

———— •◆• ————

"Ryan, where have you been? It's Christmas Eve, and we've been calling your phone for the past hour!" my mother exclaimed when I walked in the door. I was a little taken aback by Maya, her husband, and their two children in the living room with my parents and Tim. The youngest one was a baby. Babies scared me. I don't know if it was because of how fragile they were, or if they were so innocent it was intimidating. Babies know nothing of fear, love, hate, resentment, anxiety, or addiction. They are pure, something I would never be again. I resented them.

"Sorry, I was at Seth's—he has no service," I lied, knowing full well there were a dozen missed calls flashing on my cell phone that I had ignored. I hadn't wanted to speak with my family when I was so high, knowing they would have just blown my buzz.

"We almost hung stockings without you," my mother said. There was a look of longing on her face, like she was begging me to come out of the clouds and return to being the joyful, intelligent young man that was her son. It was as if she didn't even know me anymore. I was lost, and no one could find me.

"You could have, it's fine, I don't care," I said, heading toward my room.

"But Ryan, you love the holidays! Usually you're the first one to get the stockings and decorations out of the basement.

This is the first year you didn't help us decorate the tree!" Everyone was staring at me as my mother and I conversed. The usual warm holiday glow was not in the air. The room felt like thin ice; if anyone spoke, it might break. No one in my family had ever battled addition before. I was the alien in the room. It always seemed like all eyes were on me. Even if I wasn't high, which I almost always was, I knew everyone was thinking that I was or wondering if I was.

It was too much to handle; I just wanted to run to my room and enjoy the rest of my high. I loved being around people when I was doped out, with the exception of my family. As my addiction became stronger, the fading nod that I normally experienced when I was high turned into bubbly excitement. In the beginning stages of opiate addiction, the drugs hit you so hard that you fade out, but as you build a tolerance, they make you feel energized and awake. Usually, after taking enough opiates to cure my sickness and then some, I wanted to frolic, play, party, and socialize; I'd never felt so alive. When my family was around, however, I just felt nervous. I hated being high near my family.

I retreated down the hall. As it turned out, Maya and her family were staying in my old room. There was a crib, a pack and play, and many suitcases that blocked me from entering.

"Where am I supposed to sleep?" I asked, returning to the living room.

"I put our blow up mattress in Tim's old room. You can sleep in there with him. But not until after we hang our stockings," my mother mandated.

We passed around 'Twas the Night Before Christmas, each

reading a section and hanging our stockings, per Christmas tradition. I used to get so much joy out of this experience. My insides would tingle with anticipation for the morning to come, and I would bask in the glory of being a part of a loving family. It was not at all like that this year. Now I only experienced that kind of joy when I was about to score some drugs.

I resented Maya for being so successful. My mother was just as proud of Maya as she was worried for me. Usually I just had Tim to compare myself with, and he always copied me, so at least I felt original, but with Maya around I just felt like scum. Now, seeing my older sister happily married with her healthy, beautiful children and loving husband, I felt a pang of jealousy. She had money to fly from California, unlike me, who had to have our mother cover my travel expenses. I am not sure if she really judged me or if it was just the feeling I got, but every time she smiled at me, I felt like she was laughing at my pain and secretly bragging about how much better off she was. It was probably just my own insecurities, but it drove me nuts.

My relationship with Brianna was on the rocks, to say the least. Neither of us had gotten each other a gift for Christmas. The only thing we wanted was drugs, and both of us were too broke to find enough to share with each other. Then there was the fact that I was newly using needles and she didn't know. Keeping a secret from her made me feel a little guilty, but I didn't feel the need to share this quite yet. It wasn't that I was afraid she would judge me; it was more that I thought she was going to want to try too, and I only had one needle. Seth had let me take the one I used home from his house, and said it was still good for one or two more uses.

Christmas Day blurred by, and I happily enjoyed the plentiful dinner my family had prepared. In the morning, I had successfully shot up in the bathroom for the first time by myself. I locked the door and turned on the shower so no one would be suspicious. It was a success. Feeling relieved, proud, and high, I enjoyed my Christmas while plotting to visit the needle exchange by the city bus as soon as it was open. It was the only thing I had to do before I left. Seeing old friends no longer mattered.

———◆———

Entering the needle exchange office, I prayed no one I knew would see me. How embarrassing. I couldn't believe I was doing this. The light green walls and school-like atmosphere made me feel like I was back in kindergarten. I had to create a unique ID and get a Syringe Exchange Program ID card. This was not the type of card I wanted hanging around in my wallet. After, I was assessed by a nice lady who I felt was judging me, but she must have seen thousands of addicts a day, and most likely had no idea or care about who I was. Vermont was small though, and I feared she might know someone who knew me. If the word got out I was using needles, my reputation would be forever tarnished. I cared about my public persona, and I didn't want anyone who wasn't also banging out to know I used needles.

Since I had to go back to Virginia and wouldn't be able to return to the exchange any time soon, they allowed me one hundred needles in my startup kit, the maximum amount. The package said they were for insulin use only, but everyone at the exchange knew better. Needles were not the only thing provided for free. I also received a tourniquet, gloves, alcohol preps, water in a little tube, and cotton. My stomach plunged to the floor as the lady went over a pamphlet containing information about HIV testing, drug and alcohol counseling, NA (Narcotics Anonymous) and AA (Alcoholics Anonymous) meetings, hepatitis C, methadone clinics, and more. I think this information was supposed to either scare me into not using needles or encourage me to get help, but the free needles in my startup kit were the only things I was concerned with. After the initial shock of hearing the word 'HIV,' the rest just flew in one ear and out the other.

I was sure I would never get HIV or hep C, because I thought I would never share needles. The way the program worked, once you had your initial set of needles, you needed to bring in a dirty needle to receive another clean one. If you brought in twenty dirty needles, you received twenty clean ones. This seemed like a pain in the ass to me, but I assumed the idea behind it was to keep the streets clean. Keep all the trash off the sidewalks. I was part of the trash. A few short years ago, I would have been appalled at the thought of stumbling upon a dirty needle; nothing shocked or disgusted me now. I was immune to society's norms. Things that I once would have considered unheard of became regular to me. A belt was now a tourniquet, and any type of cotton, even just Q-tips, would now forever remind me of getting high. After the first few times shooting up, banging out, or whatever you want to call it, seemed normal to me. I didn't see why everyone thought it was so bad.

# CHAPTER EIGHT:
## Paranoia

"Theft is one of the dead giveaways of addiction." My heart wrenched as I listened to a woman around my age talk about her son. My thoughts quickly darted to the money that had mysteriously gone missing from my purse the week Maya, Ryan, and Tim were home for Christmas. It was only a small amount of cash, and I'd tried to dismiss it as a memory lapse on my part. Perhaps I had spent it and forgotten; maybe I counted wrong when I put it in my wallet to begin with. These hopes that had fleetingly danced about my subconscious were flushed away with the concrete realization that one of my children had stolen from me. Neither of my sweet boys or my darling girl would ever do such a thing. They were brought up religiously and had strong moral values. Family meant the world to them. I didn't want to think of one of my own children as a thief. My heart shattered as I realized that it was definitely my older boy, Ryan, who had stolen from me, his own mother.

Averting my gaze, I cringed at all of the broken mothers in the room, who, just like me, had a son or daughter battling addiction. Not wanting to talk to my friends anymore about the sore subject of Ryan's illness, I had joined a support group. It helped a little to know I wasn't alone, and that Ryan's condition was nothing that I had done wrong as a parent, but it was sickening to see how many innocent mothers had fallen victim to such a distressing fate. I listened as the teary-eyed lady across from me went on to tell how her son had stolen everything from them, from money to television sets, antiques, jewelry, and even one of their cars.

"The addiction happens so quickly, but the signs are so subtle that by the time you notice, your child is addicted and it's too late," another mother wept. I had racked my brain over and over again, day and night, trying to find where I went wrong. If there was something I could have done to change this, it was lost to me. All of these other mothers, mostly from upper and middle class families, clearly loved their children more than life itself. There was nothing we could have done. We didn't know the signs. None of us had known what was coming or what to expect. This horrible drug epidemic blindsided us all.

Although I didn't particularly like to discuss addiction with anyone outside of this comforting little circle, I warned some of my friends with younger children to keep a close eye out for a few signs. Anything I can do to help others avoid this trauma, I will. I pulled the list from my pocket, and jotted down theft as another sign.

# SIGNS YOUR CHILD MAY BE AN OPIATE ADDICT:

1.  Their pupils are pinned out, tiny, like the point of a needle. They don't change size when looking from light to dark. (A normal pupil would increase in size in the darkness.)
2.  Their eyes look tired or droopy, and they occasionally nod out, as if they are dozing off into a slumber.
3.  They don't look you in the eye, and lose interest in activities they normally love.
4.  They get very defensive when you mention any of these things to them, and swear or ignore you altogether.
5.  They're constantly on their phones.
6.  They fidget, sniff, or twitch their nose a lot.
7.  They scratch themselves often.
8.  They can't stay anywhere for long periods of time, and are always running off to go somewhere or making excuses to leave.
9.  Their moods can dramatically change over basically nothing in a short period of time.
10. They have track marks. These usually look like little red dots, bumps, or skin irritations, and are found over veins, most commonly in the arms, but also in all other areas of the body, from shooting up.
11. They have anxiety when they didn't before and are very irritable.

12. Loss of appetite and excessive weight loss.
13. Theft. They steal things from stores, strangers, friends, and family.

I'm sure there are many signs that I am still missing. I learn more facts every day that no mother or sane person should ever have to.

I imagine my son will stick a needle filled with a potentially deadly substance into his veins today, probably more than once. The thought makes me shudder. My life is encompassed in a hazy cloud of dread. I try to push the constant worry of where he is and if he's alive out of my thoughts. I care so much, but I can't let this obsession ruin me. I know worrying won't help, but it is impossible not to. With every fiber of my being, I yearn for a day when I don't wake up nervous that I will receive that dreaded phone call or knock on the door from the police, telling me my son is deceased.

The staggering voice of yet another mother breaks my thoughts. "My son went to rehab three times. I would breathe a sigh of relief when he was there. I would think that my sweet little baby was safe tonight—but you are never safe from addiction. I am lucky that he is now in jail and not dead, but the story of how he got there is beyond embarrassing. His girlfriend, also a recovering addict, had been clean from drugs since delivering their newborn. She had custody of the child, my darling granddaughter, and decided to give my son another chance when he was released from rehab the third time. Not even a day later, they were pulled over for erratic driving. The officer noticed they were faded out of their minds, and held them until he got a search warrant. Upon searching the vehicle, they not only found heroin, needles, and various prescriptions in the car, but there was a bag of heroin in my granddaughter's diaper. The diaper was on her." She choked out the last words before exploding into a watery fit of salty tears. The women on either side of her gathered her in a warm embrace. I studied the complete strangers hugging, brought together by horrific tragedy. The bond between the people here gave me hope.

"What a disgrace to her entire family. How horribly awful for the baby; I hope she's in good hands now," I thought to myself, thanking God Ryan didn't have any children.

Addiction is such a distressing thing to watch. People who once had hobbies, dreams, jobs, aspirations, and lives wither away. Their addiction becomes the only thing they live for. As much as I am sure the addict suffers from physical, mental, and emotional pain, the suffering of the loved ones feels almost greater. We have to endure the pain of watching our sons, daughters, and lovers get taken over by their disease, and there is not a damn thing we can do about it. Addicts are the most illogical people on the planet. They don't see things the same as they did when they weren't addicted. Extended opiate use changes their brain chemistry, and the pain they inflict on those around is completely lost to them. Their addiction takes over. It eats their body and their soul. Most addicts are so deeply in denial, they don't even realize they're physically and mentally deteriorating right before our eyes. No matter what we do or say, we are only bystanders, watching as our loved ones slowly die in front of us.

I've noticed Ryan, an already tiny person, has gotten skinnier, and he has some small red blotches on his face that he swears is just normal acne.

I bring this up when it is my turn to speak, and the other mothers, girlfriends, daughters, brothers, sons, and fathers of addicts in the group nod along. Opiate addicts are like walking dead people, evil shadows of their former selves. You never see an opiate addict who lives to be old. There are a select few that make it out the other end alive; the rest quickly end up dead or in jail. I pray Ryan can beat this. Every morning, every night, every second of every day, I hope and pray for my baby. It has to come from him. There is nothing I can do until he sees through my eyes; most addicts never recover enough to reflect, but Ryan is smart and so special. I will never lose hope.

Although there might not be much more I can do for my own son at this moment, being a part of this community of suffering has opened my eyes to the spreading epidemic of heroin abuse in our beautiful town. As the next section of the meeting begins, an official from the Department of Health steps up to the podium.

"As you may have seen on the fliers, today we are offering a two-hour training on the use of naloxone, or Narcan, an opiate antidote that can reverse a heroin overdose. Anyone who wishes to participate in this free session will learn how to identify and treat an overdose, and will receive a kit containing two doses of Narcan, along with a prescription for additional doses and a certification of training. I highly recommend this session; each of you have been affected by the widespread heroin issue in our community, and this training could save so many lives."

I watched a small number of people shuffle out of the room. The idea of overdoses would have been too much for me to handle such a short time before; my heart went out to these people, who just need space from believing that their loved one's problems could possibly reach such a dire point. Coming to these meetings has given me the strength to face the worst, and I want to be prepared to save my son's life, to save any addict's life, if I'm ever faced with such a terrible situation.

They began by teaching us how to identify an overdose, and differentiate it from someone who is just very high. Since opiates are depressants that work on the central nervous system, they slow down breathing and heart rates. Too large of a dose, which is highly variable according to a person's tolerance and the purity of the product, will cause breathing and the heart to stop completely.

One of the key differences to identifying many overdoses is the person's ability to respond to outside stimulus. If a person cannot respond to light shaking or loud noises, it is best to treat the situation as though it is an overdose. None of the techniques they were teaching us would be harmful, and I focused my notes on the actions I can take. The key, the trainers said, is to not leave someone alone if you are concerned. If the person is conscious, you should keep them awake, watch their breathing and heartbeat, and try to get them to walk around with you. They also covered stimulation techniques like sternum rubbing, which should cause enough discomfort to rouse someone who is very high. They stress how rare it is for someone to instantly die when they overdose, and how critical it is to respond quickly.

Next, they trained us in rescue breathing and the recovery position. If someone is not breathing, or is breathing very shallowly, you need to put them on their back, tilt their chin up, pinch and plug their nose, and blow two regular, even breaths into their lungs, watching to make sure their chest rises. You need to repeat this every five seconds for a minute, and then put them into the recovery position and get your Narcan. To put a semi- or unconscious person in the recovery position, you should check their airways to make sure there is nothing physically blocking their breathing, and lay them on their side, supported by bending their knees (like a more relaxed fetal position pose). Their face should be turned to the side, to ease breathing and stop them from choking on vomit.

There is injectable Narcan and nasal Narcan, and I was relieved we were going to be issued nasal Narcan. We practiced putting together the delivery system, which involves an atomizer, needleless syringe, and the cartridge of naloxone. Once these are all assembled, you need to tilt the person's head back and spray half of the Narcan up one nostril, and half up the other. Since Narcan only works to knock the opiates out of the opiate receptors of the brain, it does nothing for anyone who is not currently on opiates, so we were even able to use some expired kits to practice on each other. We were warned that after being roused with Narcan, the person who you've revived may not realize what is going on. They also may be very irritable because the opioids were just stripped from the opiate receptors in their brain, resulting in an intense onset of withdrawal.

I'm happy I learned so much during this training session; having my kit and certification is very empowering. I can't go back in time and change anything, but I can be as prepared as possible to help my son. With the emotional support, education, and training these meetings give me, I feel like I can make a real difference in the lives of my loved ones and community.

## Chapter Nine:
# Death

Things went pretty well the first few weeks I was back in Virginia. I made it to work on time, wasn't sick, and Brianna had gotten enough money from her family on Christmas to buy her own drugs and keep her quiet. She wasn't opposed to me using needles, but preferred not to, so I didn't have to share.

My boss chose me to go on a business trip to Oregon with him because of my superb photography skills. A high profile client wanted custom photography done for the website we were designing. That meant getting on a plane. I wasn't afraid of flying, but I didn't want to make a habit of transporting drugs in the air. I might have just gotten lucky when I didn't get caught bringing stuff home for Christmas. Very strategically, I wrapped my heroin stash in plastic wrap, along with a few needles. Then I squished the plastic wrap containing the goods into a shampoo bottle, and filled it with shampoo carefully squeezed out of another bottle to put in my checked bag. I knew it would be messy to undo, but I couldn't risk getting caught or being away on an important business trip with my boss and feeling sick.

Luckily, the trip was a success. Oregon was beautiful. The

client loved my photos, my boss was proud, and I didn't get caught smuggling drugs on the aircraft. The only torturous part was the return trip. Our last returning flight was delayed and I had run out of my stash. I faked sick, and thankfully my boss bought it and wasn't the least bit suspicious. Everything was normal when we returned, and I prayed it would be awhile before I had to go away for business again.

A coworker from Landsing Designs named Chris befriended me. Chris was also an addict. I knew it as soon as I saw him. He had only been employed a short time longer than me and was already on the brink of getting fired. He was a skinny fellow and his hands were always moving, even when his body wasn't. He would look well one day and sickly the next. He was often late to work and I heard him throwing up in the bathroom stall on numerous occasions.

Many addicts are able to function within society for years before anyone even notices there is something wrong. Chris had been an addict for a long time; I could tell by his appearance. I wondered how he had gotten the job. He must have gone through a hellishly painful detox and used cleansing kits to pass the test, like I had.

One day we were outside, smoking cigarettes together on break. I'm not sure when or where I picked up the nasty habit, but smoking cigs was just another gross addiction I had fallen victim to. I didn't bother hiding my cigarette use because it was far more socially acceptable than heroin, especially in the south. It broke my mother's heart to see me smoking, but she knew she had to pick her battles. Drug addiction was a much larger problem than cigarette smoking, so she never bothered me about it.

Chris looked like he was hurting pretty badly. I am sure he knew I was also an addict, but we had never spoken about it.

"Bro, I'm dying over here. I need to get some stuff quickly, can you help me out?" he asked. It was our last break, and we only had two more hours of work. I was still feeling pretty good and didn't want to get fired over him. He said he didn't have a car and needed a ride to a connect's spot or something.

"Sure, I can help you if you can make it 'til three; we only have a little more time 'til the end of the work day, and I'm really in the zone with this design," I replied as we walked back inside.

He nodded to the bathroom and said, "Get me when you're done. I'll be in there."

I thanked the Lord I wasn't feeling like he was. I could sympathize and wanted to help, but not at the expense of my job. I needed all the money I could get. Even at twenty dollars an hour, I was just barely getting by.

"Where we headed?" I asked Chris, as he struggled into the passenger seat of my Impreza after work. He instructed me out of the parking lot and down a few blocks, toward the lower income side of town.

We pulled up to a small shack, and he asked me to wait in the car. This guy was pretty lucky I was helping him out like this. I didn't know this neighborhood and wasn't sure what I was up against. If anyone rolled into Causeway Block like this, uninvited, they would get shot.

Chris returned, but he was not alone. My back door opened, and a trashy looking girl flopped herself in. Her skirt was so short her ass cheeks were hanging out the bottom of it, and her bright pink G-string was visible from the top. The shirt she wore looked more like a tattered push-up bra.

"What's with the hooker?" I wondered, but didn't say anything out loud.

"Hi, handsome, here's my card," she oozed, handing me a business card with a girl on a pole. She worked as a stripper at one of the underground clubs.

"Sorry about the chick, man, this is the deal. The only way my boy would hook it up was if I brought her home. She lives right down the street from me. You can drop me off, and then drop her at her spot on your way home. Thanks so much for doing this," Chris gushed.

"I better get some shit out of this too," I demanded.

"Yea, yea, my bad, here," he said, handing over a little baggy with a hard black chunk in it that looked like a rock.

"What's this?" I asked, used to my heroin in powder form.

"Black tar heroin, bro. It's fire," Chris answered.

I dropped him off just around the corner, and he gave me directions to drop off the prostitute. It was only a few minutes further down the road, and in the direction I was going. I was pleased with the reward of heroin Chris had given me and couldn't wait to try it out, so I said my goodbyes to him and agreed to drop off the prostitute.

She slunk into my front seat and pulled a needle out of somewhere.

"Where did she get that from, up her butt?" I wondered to myself. She had no purse and was wearing virtually no clothes, yet somehow managed to store everything she needed to shoot up.

"Can you wait 'til you get to your spot?" I asked her, not really comfortable with her shooting up in my car. "What if we pull up next to a cop at a red light?"

"Don't worry, sweetie," she slurred, clearly intoxicated.

I turned away and kept my eyes on the road. I could see her insert the needle out of the corner of my eye, and I fought back an overwhelming urge to pull over and get high myself on the side of the road. Her body went limp, as Seth's had when I first watched him shoot up.

"That black tar heroin must be some good shit," I thought to myself, expecting her to come to at any minute. Something was different.

"Hey, girl. You alright?" I asked, hoping she would respond, but the feeling in my gut told me she wasn't going to. I changed my route and pulled off the main street, into a parking lot behind an old abandoned liquor store. My pulse was racing, adrenaline shot through my veins. What had Chris gotten me into?

"That bastard, I should never have helped him out!" I thought, checking for the girl's pulse. I felt nothing. She wasn't breathing. What could I do? I dragged her limp body out of my front seat onto the pavement and smacked her in the face. Nothing. Panicking, I opened the water bottle I had on the floor of my car and dumped the entire thing on her head. Her lips looked purple, her face pale; she didn't breathe or move. An eerie silence filled the air. Cold chills ran up my spine, even though it was a pretty warm day for winter in Virginia, especially compared to the freezing Vermont weather I had just returned from. I was pretty sure she was dead, but I wasn't sticking around to find out. I had to get out of there.

I drove a few blocks away in the direction of my house, then pulled over on the side of the road to shoot up. I had to do something to calm my nerves, anything to get the image of her lifeless corpse staring up at me out of my head. Pulling a fresh needle out from under my floor mats, I began to prepare my kryptonite, using a lighter to heat the spoon to break up the tar. Stirring it a bit with the plunger from another syringe, it started to separate, making the water a brownish yellow color. My hands shook with fear and anticipation as I aimed at a vein. Thankfully, I didn't miss.

"Damn, this shit is GOOD! No wonder that bitch died," I thought to myself as I floated in and out of consciousness, enjoying the blissful high. I was in such a fog, I nearly forgot the incident that had just occurred.

Finally bursting out of my relaxed state, vivid images of the dead prostitute invaded my memory. Shuddering, I decided it was time to go home. Glancing at the clock in my car, I noticed it was almost seven. It couldn't be. Had I really been nodded out on that stuff for almost three hours? Maybe the girl was alive. I had to check. I really didn't want to go back to the scene of the crime, but I needed to know. If she wasn't dead, I would feel so relieved. I didn't kill her, but I was with her when she died, and I had done nothing. That had to be illegal and was definitely immoral. I had never seen anyone die before, or even a dead body at an open casket. This was my first encounter with death, and I hoped it would be my last.

The sun was beginning to set, so I flicked on my high beams to get a good look as I drove past the abandoned liquor store. Not wanting to draw attention, I didn't pull up too close. Sure enough, I could see her body still lying flat out on the pavement.

Should I have hidden her? Thrown her in the woods? Buried her? She didn't have an ID, and I didn't even know her name; there was no way I was pulling back into that parking lot. I didn't want my fingerprints to be on her any more than they already were. Sure, we were in a sketchy neighborhood, but I couldn't believe no one had reported her yet. I wondered when the cops would find her, and hoped that her death wouldn't be linked to me in any way. She had clearly died from an overdose. Too high to worry anymore, I focused on getting home without nodding out and crossing any medians.

"Should I tell Chris?" I wondered as I walked into work the next morning. I decided it was better not to, and didn't get the chance anyway. Chris had been fired.

It wasn't too long before I heard from him again, though. When addicts get desperate, they will go to any lengths to get their fix. They contact people they hardly know, set up their friends, and use other people's drug dealers because they owe their own money.

In this case, Chris owed money to all of his dealers. He swore he had money to buy some drugs, but he couldn't go through his connects, because he owed them and he didn't have enough money to pay back what he owed and take some home.

I hit up Terrorist first, to make sure it was legit if I brought a buddy with me when we rolled through the block. He said that it was cool, as long as I vouched for him.

"He worked with me, and we've hung out a few times. I don't know him too well, but if he causes you any trouble, I'll take responsibility," I responded.

Giving Terrorist my word was a big deal, and I made sure Chris knew he was not to get out of the car. I begged him to just give me the money and wait for me outside of Causeway Block, but, like most junkies, Chris trusted no one, especially a fellow user. The only reason I had agreed to help was that he promised to give me half of what he picked up. He said he had enough for a bun, and getting half of that for free was an opportunity I simply couldn't pass up.

Scooping Chris up from his spot we cruised to the block. When we pulled up to Terrorist he handed me the stuff. I passed it to Chris and held my hand out for the money. Suddenly, I felt a hard cold object pressed up against my ribcage. I looked at Chris.

"What the fuck!" I spat, when I confirmed he was pressing the barrel of a gun into my ribs.

"Drive this car now, or I will pull this trigger and blow you to pieces." Chris meant business. I slammed my foot down on the gas pedal and took off.

"Fuck, fuck, fuck. I'm so screwed. Terrorist is going to murder me," I thought.

His attempts were much quicker and more literal than I had expected. I heard a loud bang, and my rear windshield shattered all over the backseat. Then I felt the wind from another bullet barreling past my left shoulder. I had to get out of there. Chris was hanging out the window, shooting back at Terrorist, Ace, and their gang.

"What a psycho! What the hell is going on?" I thought, too freaked out to analyze the situation. All I could do was drive. My banged up vehicle whipped through the block, not stopping for anyone or anything. I burst out onto the main road with no regard for oncoming traffic. Luckily, I escaped without causing an accident or getting a bullet to the head. My car was destroyed! My mom and Don were going to kill me when they found out, that is, if Terrorist hadn't literally killed me first.

Once I had gotten far enough away from Causeway Block that I could actually catch my breath, I turned to Chris, who was shaking his head.

"Sorry, man, I didn't have the money. Here's your half, like I promised." He handed over half the bundle, and I snatched it up before telling him to get the fuck out of my car. We were in a decent neighborhood, and he could walk or take the bus home. He could get run over and die, for all that I cared. I was livid. Chris understood how pissed off I was, and didn't ask for a ride home. We both knew we would never speak again.

Immediately, I called Terrorist. I had to, for a few reasons. If I didn't make peace with him, he was never going to supply me with drugs again. I also had a strong gut feeling that if I ignored him, he was going to kill me, or have one of his crew members do it for him.

"You fucking dumb little bastard!" Terrorist screamed into the phone.

After minutes of him yelling at me and me begging and

pleading for forgiveness, he said, "You're going to have to work pretty damn hard to make it up to me if you want to live. You're lucky your little punk ass friend doesn't know how to aim, cuz if he shot one of us, neither of you would have made it out alive."

I told him I was willing to do whatever it took, and that I was no longer speaking with Chris. He had seen that Chris had a gun to my ribs and set me up, but I think the only reason he chose to forgive me, if you can even call it that, was because he could use me.

Whenever Terrorist needed something, I came running. I committed more crimes and ripped more people off than I am comfortable admitting to over the next few weeks, until I had paid Terrorist back with interest.

"You're so fucking stupid. You're going to die. Those crazy junkies know where we live, you idiot!" My brother and Brandon let me have it when I got home, after they saw my battered car and hounded me for information. I told them I was set up and it was all good now, but they weren't having it. They didn't want to listen to anything I said.

Eventually, Tim walked into his room and locked the door, not wanting to deal with the situation any longer. Brandon continued to ream me a new asshole. I eventually got so fed up, I said, "Shut up, or I'll fuck your sister when she comes to visit." I knew I shouldn't have said it, and immediately regretted it, but it just slipped out. Brandon's sister was supposed to visit from Vermont. Tim and I frequently joked about hooking up with Brandon's sisters. He would joke back, saying he was going to hook up with our mom, or that Maya's kids were actually his instead of her husband's, but this time we weren't joking.

"I deserved that," I thought, as I felt Brandon's fist smash against my jaw. I could taste the blood pooling up in my mouth. I wanted to fight back, but I was in the wrong and Brandon was stronger than me. Before the drugs, I could have kicked his ass, or at least put up a good fight, but now my body was brittle. I turned away and retreated to my room.

Brianna wasn't there. She wasn't anywhere to be found. Most of her belongings still lingered around my room, but her suitcase and favorite clothes were gone. I didn't want to ask Tim and Brandon where she was, so I just passed out.

In the morning, I learned she had moved home. I wondered if she was going to quit opiates on her own back in Vermont, and if she would be successful. I felt no sadness at her departure; I was just a little mellow and felt alone.

The drug supply was running low again, and I needed to think fast. I had been slacking off at work. I showed up late and sick whenever I wasn't able to fund my habit. Most of the work I was doing for Terrorist was just to pay back my debt and stay alive.

Brianna had taken a flight back to Vermont, and it had been a few weeks since we spoke. She wanted nothing to do with any of us. She owed Brandon money for utilities, and he had tried to contact her numerous times without success. I hadn't spoken to Brandon since he punched me in the face, but as the two of us were eating toast together in silence, I got a crazy idea that broke the ice.

"What if we sell Brianna's car?" I said to Brandon.

"What do you mean? We can't do that," he responded.

I was already putting it on Craigslist. At first I meant it as a joke, but then I thought we could really do it. She clearly wasn't coming back for it. What was I supposed to do, let it rot in the yard and take up a valuable parking space?

Within minutes, Brandon's phone started ringing.

"I wonder who is calling me; I don't answer numbers I don't know," Brandon said, putting his phone down.

"Gimme that. It could be someone from Craigslist," I said as I grabbed the phone.

"What the fuck, Ryan? You used my phone number to sell Brianna's car?" I had meant to make up with Brandon and I had just pissed him off more, but I needed the money.

"I'll split the cash with you," I offered, taking the call. I could hear him mumbling in the background that I was an idiot and he didn't want anything to do with cash from a stolen car, even though its rightful owner owed him money.

I used to be like that, moral and righteous. Now who was I? I didn't even know. I was just an innocent bystander to the drugs that controlled my body. No longer was I concerned with right and wrong. The car sold within minutes, and I had to take the ad down from Craigslist because Brandon's phone kept blowing up with interested parties.

"Damn, I should have sold it for more," I thought as I counted the crisp bills and the car's new owner happily drove away. I had money to buy drugs, and that was all that mattered. Heading to the block I grabbed some dope, and retreated to my room to indulge.

# CHAPTER TEN:
## Tim

A loud thud came from Ryan's room that caught my attention as I sat on the living room couch just outside his door, playing PlayStation with my roommate Brandon.

"Hey, Brandon, maybe we should check on Ryan; he hasn't left his room in three days," I said with a little concern.

"You check on him, he's your brother," Brandon replied. I knew he wasn't just trying to be cold; we were both afraid of what we might find.

Tentatively, I knocked on Ryan's door and pressed my ear to it. I heard nothing.

"Ryan, if you don't answer, I'm coming in," I called out, expecting to hear a faint "Go away," but there was nothing. Slowly entering the room, I was taken aback by its filthy appearance. Ryan was slightly obsessed with cleanliness, and always kept his bedroom neat and tidy, with his shoes and hats in a line and his shirts all hung and color coordinated. That was not at all the scene that I had just walked into.

My brother was badly into drugs. It hurt me to see him struggling, but there was nothing I could do. The more I tried, the more he lied and pushed me away. He was the same way with our mom. Every time she Skyped with me, I could see tears in her eyes and her lip quivering when she asked how Ryan was. I had even taken to telling little white lies to make the situation sound slightly better than it was, because there was nothing we could do and I hated to see her suffering.

Ryan's girlfriend, Brianna, had lived with Brandon, Ryan, and me in our second story apartment in Virginia. The two weeks prior to her departure back home to Vermont she had been sleeping on the couch, so I knew they had not been getting along. Before that, Brandon and I could hear them scream and argue through their bedroom door almost nightly. We just turned up our music, played beer pong, and attended class at the local university. School was the reason Brandon and I had moved down here, but it wasn't for me. We both had decided to drop out and work full time after this semester. It was a decision neither of our mothers were very pleased about, but next to Ryan we were angels and could do no wrong.

Amidst the array of clothes, rotting food, and CDs, I spotted Ryan's gun. I knew he had one and had wanted to get a gun myself, so I wasn't too shocked. Next to the gun, there was something else that caught my eye—a needle. Not a sewing needle, a needle used for injections. Ryan had a long-standing pill addiction, I'd recently caught him smoking crack and knew he'd started snorting heroin, but I had no idea he had gone to needles.

I stood in stunned silence. I needed to talk to him or do something; I wasn't going to let this go any further. I would tell him he was a liar, and that the sneaky behavior had to stop.

Somehow, I would make him go to rehab. I didn't know how I was going to do that, but I was determined. I didn't want to lose my brother (any more than I already had). After the initial shock of seeing the needle wore off, a feeling of dread hit; there were many things in the room, but one thing I didn't see was Ryan.

Quickly scanning the room, I noticed his bathroom door was closed.

"Ryan! If you are in here, open this fucking door right now!" I screamed, pounding on the door. Brandon appeared in the bedroom door behind me to see what all the fuss was about. He had known Ryan since we were kids, and I could tell by his facial expressions that the messy state of Ryan's room was a shock to him as well.

"Dude. You have to help me get this door open. I don't know if Ryan is in here or not, but we need to find out," I said in a hurry, pointing at the needle on the bed. I didn't want Brandon to know that my brother had stooped so low that he was using needles, but if he was behind that door, I needed Brandon to know how serious it was.

"I know; he has a stash under the floor mats of his car. I watched him shoot up the other day. It's absolutely awful; I couldn't bring myself to tell you. He had me promise not to," Brandon told me.

My head was dizzy, and I felt nauseous. My own half-brother, who I had always looked up to, was shooting up, and my best friend since birth, now my roommate, had known and didn't tell me. There was no time to think or argue until we found out if Ryan was behind that door.

Brandon noticed that I was in such a state of shock that I hadn't moved, and pulled his ID out of his wallet to card open the bathroom door. We entered the front door of our house like this more often than we used the keys, but the bathroom door wouldn't budge. It was one of those doors with a little pinhole that didn't come with a key. I looked down and noticed some of Brianna's stuff on the floor by my feet. A hairpin was falling out of the makeup bag, among the many things she had left behind when she jetted off to Vermont.

Springing into action, I snatched up the pin, lunged over to the door, and inserted it in the tiny hole. Hearing a click I pushed the door open a couple of inches before it stopped. I heard a thud, and realized something was blocking the door. Brandon ran over and helped me push it in. The heavy mound of clothes that blocked the door was on Ryan's limp body.

The color was drained from his face. He looked like a ghost. I noticed a belt around his arm and a needle sticking out of it. Panicking, I ripped the needle out of his arm, splattering blood everywhere. I listened for a heartbeat—nothing. I felt for a pulse—nothing.

"This can't be. Ryan can't be dead; I need to save him," I thought to myself. Normally, I would be grossed out by even the thought of giving my brother mouth-to-mouth, and I had no idea how to do CPR, but I attempted for a few seconds that dragged by like agonizing hours. Brandon was in a panic, shaking Ryan and trying anything he could think of to help.

"Dump some water on him!" Brandon suggested. Even though Ryan weighed only slightly over one hundred pounds, his body was dead weight; we didn't want to lose precious time by trying to lift him into the bathtub. I grabbed a glass off his bathroom sink and quickly filled it with cold water from the tub. In a panic I dumped the entire thing on his face. Then I heard Ryan gasp for breath, and his eyes slowly fluttered open. Letting out a sigh of relief, I looked over at a pale Brandon, who shook his head and walked out of the bathroom.

"Tim? What are you doing in my bathroom, why am I all wet?" Ryan mumbled in a slow and drawn out slur. I wanted to hug him, cry, and punch him in the face, all at the same time. I was relieved he was alive, but almost too furious for words. He didn't even realize what had happened. He knew nothing of the pain and suffering he was causing me, our family, and everyone else who cared about him. Selfish and ignorant, that's what he was.

"You just died. We saved your life, you fucking junkie. Why don't you clean yourself up," I spit out the hateful words, almost instantly regretting them. What if he did die, and that was the last thing I ever said to him?

"I'm sorry, Ryan, our whole family really loves you and Brandon does too. It's tearing us apart to see you like this. You need to hear it how it is, or else you may never change. If you don't change soon, you're going to die, and I really don't want that."

I had said enough. I never share my feelings, and this day had gotten the best of me. It was time for me to lock myself in my room for a few days.

# CHAPTER ELEVEN:
# Ashley

On my knees gasping for breath, I clutched the white porcelain rim of the toilet bowl in the bathroom of Landsing Designs, withdrawal symptoms coming on full force. No matter how hard I tried to fight it, I couldn't shake the pain. Vomit, vomit, dry heave, vomit, dry heave. That was my morning. Drooping lifelessly over my pile of puke, I noticed it was streaked with blood.

"What is wrong with me? Why am I throwing up blood?" I wondered for a brief moment. My worry was placed on the back burner, as another wave of sickness took over my shaky, limp body.

Without saying anything to anyone, I took off for home. There was no way I could survive the day at the office.

Pushing open the apartment door, I prayed Tim and Brandon were out so I wouldn't have to explain why I was home early. What I found was the polar opposite of what I'd hoped for.

"Mom, Don, what are you doing here?" I mumbled, shaking and looking down.

"Ryan!" Mom exclaimed, coming toward me for a hug. I pushed her away, saying I didn't want to be touched, and tried to walk out of the room. Tim stopped me.

"You're not going anywhere, Ryan. Look at yourself," he demanded.

"What the fuck, leave me alone. Why the hell are they here, why didn't you warn me?" I fumed.

"They're here for you. I called them. They flew here because we're having an intervention for you. If you don't stop this behavior, you're going to die for real, and none of us want to see that."

I looked up at the nervous and caring faces of Brandon, my mother, and Don. It was unlike Tim to call me out in front of my mother, and very unlike him to have summoned her from Vermont.

"They must think I'm worse than I really am; I'll be fine if I can just lie down and get some subs," I thought, trying again to retreat to my room.

This time, it was Don's voice that stopped me.

"Ryan. Your mother and I flew all the way here because we're very worried about you. Don't walk away from us. We need to figure out what to do. You're ruining our relationship, because all your mother does is worry about you. I wish I could calm her down or help you, but you refuse to open up to us," he said sternly.

I was infuriated. What an asshole. Feeling like I was near death, trembling and shaking from severe withdrawal, the last thing I needed was to listen to him.

"You're not my father and you never will be, so why don't you just shut the fuck up and fly back to Vermont. I'm not talking to you," I said, scooting into my room and slamming the door.

"Get out here, Ryan, stop being a pussy. We're all here for you. You need us, and you know it," Brandon said, knocking on my door. I said nothing and lay shriveled up, clutching my stomach, soaking my bedsheets in a freezing sweat.

The door opened and I kept my eyes shut, but could tell by the gentleness of her step that it was my mother who had entered. She laid a hand on my shoulder and sat in silence for a while.

Finally, she spoke. "Ryan. More than anything in the world, I want to see my beautiful little boy again. I know your eyes are shut, but I have two pictures here, one of you before you started taking drugs, and one of you at Christmas. Although the differences are small to someone who doesn't know you, I can tell you've completely changed. I want the Ryan back who isn't constantly suffering. Where is the Ryan who was so full of life?"

I moaned in pain and said nothing.

"You can get through this. I'm sure it's difficult to deal with this pain and admit what's happened to you, but it's not nearly as difficult as spending your whole life running from it. You may feel vulnerable, but you can't give up on love and joy. We're your family, and we all love you so much and want to see you succeed. You're a strong, powerful young man, and I know you can beat this darkness and discover your own light. We're all standing behind you."

"I love you, Mom, but I'm sick. Can you and Don just go away?"

"I figured you might say that. Don told me I was wasting my money, buying a plane ticket here. I bought a one-way, so you could dictate when I went back home, but I would really like to stay and help if you'll let me. You can come home with us and go to rehab," she offered.

"Mom. Go away. You can't help me. I don't want to see Don, and I don't need some stupid intervention. There is no way I'm going to rehab. I can't believe Tim and Brandon let you come here," I muttered, barely able to speak.

"I'm sorry, Ryan. I just love you so much. I was hoping there was something I could do," she whispered. I could tell there were tears in her eyes. I felt guilty, but the guilt was nothing compared to my physical pain. I wanted to die.

She sat beside me for hours, saying nothing, and then finally rose when Don knocked on my bedroom door. He whispered something to her, and then she returned to my side.

"I love you, Ryan. I wish I could help. Please call me if you need anything or want to come home," she said, and then tiptoed out of my room.

I lay in agony all night, barely able to move. In the morning, I glared irritably at my phone, which had two missed calls from Landsing Designs. Without showering or changing my clothes, I struggled to the car and headed to work. If I lost my job, I would never get out of this agony. As soon as I entered the building, I got the overwhelming urge to vomit. Running to the bathroom, I just barely made it to the stall. Blood again. I hadn't eaten anything since the day before and was feeling very weak on top of my dope sickness.

When I finally mustered up the strength to leave the bathroom, my boss was standing there waiting.

"Ryan. Will you please follow me to my office, we have to

talk." His solemn tone told me this was not a question. I didn't have a choice. I slunk along behind him, expecting the worst.

Usually I was a master of talking myself out of difficult situations. Since getting addicted, I had learned to read people, preying upon their weaknesses to convince them to do what I wanted, either by making them feel sorry for me or persuading them that giving me a second chance was a good idea. I hadn't been able to do this with Dr. Jones back in Vermont, but I'd slowly been getting better at it. When you're an addict, persuasion, deceit, and trickery come naturally to you. Addiction strips you of your morals and leaves you with these evil skills. You will do anything to survive. Drugs kill you slowly. First, they kill your pain, then they kill your joy, hope, body, and brain, and finally, they take away your judgment, morals, character, and destroy your soul. If I hadn't been suffering from such extreme withdrawal that morning, I believe I would have been able to talk my way out of being fired, but I was in so much pain that I could barely talk.

"I regret having to let you go very much. You have real talent. It's a shame you can't get your act together, Ryan." My boss's words stabbed into me like daggers. Losing my job meant no more cash flow, no more paychecks, and no way to buy more antidotes to cure my daily pain.

I left the office and headed straight to the Virginia walk-in clinic. I had no money, but I was still on my parents' health insurance until I was twenty-six, and I hoped they would be able to give me something to ease the pain.

It was surprisingly easy to obtain a script for subs. I bubbled over with excitement as the orange pills touched my palm. I snorted an entire pill and was able to function again, cursing myself for not thinking to visit the health clinic earlier.

Upon returning home, I flung open our apartment door; I was taken aback when I saw two girls in my kitchen. Brandon and Tim never had girls over, so I wasn't expecting it. I had completely forgotten that today was the day Brandon's girlfriend, Melany, and his sister, Ashley, were scheduled to arrive for their visit.

"Uh, hey," I said, as I entered and immediately retreated to my room.

Ashley was stunning. We were next door neighbors and had gone to high school and college together, but we were never in the same classes and didn't have friends in common. I knew what she looked like from pictures on Brandon's Facebook, and I'd checked out a few of her snowboarding shots, but she'd moved out of her mom's house a long time ago, and I hadn't seen her in person in years. Once I had gotten into drugs, I had stopped going over to Brandon's to play basketball like I used to when we were younger.

No one knew I had been fired, and I aimed to keep it that way. I had joked about banging Brandon's sister, but she was way out of my league. She had long blonde hair that fell in loose, gentle curls almost to her waist. Her eyes were sparkling blue, with naturally long and surprisingly dark lashes. The pear shape of her body, with a tiny waist and big hips and ass, made my insides tingle. I had to get up the courage to talk to her. What did I have to lose? She wasn't going anywhere for a week, and I had nothing else to do.

Exiting my room, I tried to avoid staring at her perky breasts popping out of the top of her tiny pink bikini, and addressed Brandon first.

"Wanna get some beers and play a little pong?" I asked. Before Brandon could even respond, Ashley opened my refrigerator and pulled out two Coronas.

"We just stopped at the store; here, take one. Wanna be my pong partner?" Ashley offered, handing me a cold Corona.

"Sure, let's kick Brandon and Melany's asses!" I responded, cracking the beer open with my lighter, marveling at how she had talked to me first. This couldn't get any better! For a brief moment, I forgot about opiates. I forgot about addiction. I just relished the fact that this gorgeous girl had given me a free beer and wanted to be my partner in pong. Ashley was about 5'2, which was perfect; I wasn't very tall, and being with small girls made me feel dominant, similar to the way drugs gave me confidence.

The two of us made a fabulous beer pong team. We smoked Melany and Brandon three times in a row, and Brandon and Tim twice. Ashley and I joked and laughed the entire time. I didn't feel nervous. She was open, honest and funny. Best of all, she knew my family, had heard about my troubles with addiction, and still wanted to talk to me. Throughout the week, the two of us became much closer. I felt as if we had been intimate for a lifetime, and we hadn't even kissed. The connection was like no other. Hearing how she had also attended the same snowboard camp as me (only a different summer), and then returned every year since made me want to get back on a board. We bonded over a love for snowboarding, our families, and an unreal sexual attraction. I knew she felt it too, but she was leaving at the end of the week, and I was supposed to stay in Virginia for a few more months, until our lease was up, and maybe longer.

We swam in the pool, visited the ocean, went out to dinner with Brandon and Melany, grilled, and played basketball and beer pong. The subs, rationed as much as possible, kept me from feeling sick, and I started to believe I could live a normal life again. The only time Ashley and I disagreed was when I lit up a cigarette.

"Ew. That's disgusting. I am allergic to cigs and I hate them. If you're going to smoke that, I'm going to wait for you across the street," she said to me as we walked to the Quick Stop to buy more beer.

I was shocked. I had never been spoken to by a girl like that before. Normally, I would have ignored her and smoked it anyway, but there was something about Ashley that made me want to impress her. I really wanted her to like me, enough that I put out my cigarette and threw away the pack.

"Great, another addiction I have to kick," I thought to myself, but Ashley was the perfect distraction. Sure, I still thought about opiates and cigarettes while she was there, but I only did subs to stay well. Each day, I took less and less of my script, hoping to wean myself off completely and turn back into the person I really was, the one Ashley could love.

We talked about our pasts, our families, our friends, our hopes and desires for the future. The two of us were laughing and talking, lying in the grass outside my apartment, and she made me play a game of truth or dare. When I chose truth, she asked the dreaded question.

"Have you ever shot up?"

I really wanted to impress this girl, and I intended to fully recover and never shoot up again.

"No, I haven't," I replied. I expected to see a look of relief on her tanned little face, but instead the corners of her mouth turned downward, and she let out a disappointed sigh.

"Ryan, I really like you, but I value the truth. I would rather know the horrible truth than be lied to. I've had some pretty shitty, dishonest, and abusive relationships in the past, and I didn't even know how bad some of them were because my boyfriends would lie to me and hide things. I would much rather be alone for life than associate with people who lie to me."

I felt a surge of guilt. "How does she know I was lying? Did my face give it away, or is she just guessing I'm lying and trying to call my bluff?" I wondered. Hoping for the latter, I continued, "No, seriously, I haven't, why do you think I'm lying?"

"My brother told me you hide needles under the floor mat in your car. He said he watched you shoot up the other day. I love my brother more than anything in this world, and he shouldn't have to see that. I came down here not really expecting to like you. Our mothers asked me to find out how bad your addiction was, and to let them know if I thought there was anything they could do to help or to stop you. Up until right now, I really liked you a lot."

I wanted to cry. I wanted to run away. I really wanted to shoot up some potent heroin, right that very second. I must have looked pathetic, because Ashley gave me a hug. Wrapped in her arms, I finally felt I could be honest.

"I'm sorry I lied to you. I just really like you, and it's embarrassing to admit that I have shot up before. I know what happened to your dad and your brother, and even though Brandon never talks about it, I can tell how much it affects him, so this must be really hard for you too." I choked back tears.

Ashley's father and her older brother James had both passed of opiate addiction, right around the same time I started my relationship with drugs. Her parents were divorced and James had lived with their father, so Brandon, Ashley, and their younger sister were not very close with either of them, but I couldn't imagine losing a sibling or my mother. Being so young when my dad passed, I had no conscious memory of it. Even though I resented Maya for having such a perfect family and Tim for having his father alive, I could never imagine them passing.

"I never want to end up with someone like my father," Ashley said. "I always think of the Game's song lyrics, 'Like I needed my father, but he needed a needle,' and I promise myself that I will never put my kids through that. I really want to have a family someday, and every child deserves a father who is there for them and doesn't choose using needles over being a parent. I'm sorry, I'm rambling."

I had only been talking to Ashley for a few days, and I already felt like I was in love with her. I wanted to be the father of her children, and I wanted to be there for her instead of having my life run by needles, pain, and suffering.

"I'm sorry, Ashley. It's a lot harder than it looks. My entire life has gone downhill." I spilled my stories of my car getting shot up in Causeway Block, doing jobs with Ace and his crew, and everything else, except for the prostitute dying in my car. I even told her I had been let go from Landsing Designs and I was deathly afraid to tell my mother.

It felt great to have someone to talk to. Sure, Ashley had never been through any of my troubles, like some of my previous girlfriends had, but she had experienced some tragic events. She'd survived her parents' divorce and the death of her father and brother, all without turning to drugs. Instead of feeling judged or looked down on, I felt inspired by Ashley. She gave me new hope that there might be better things in my future—but when she mentioned how scared she was for a scheduled surgery on her knee, the only thing I could think of was what she might get prescribed, and how I could convince her to give them to me.

Shoving those thoughts out of my mind, we moved onto lighter topics and engaged in joyful conversation until we had finished all of our beer. I shared hiking, canoeing, and camping stories from the past. She told hilarious tales of her friends from back home, including one about her best guy friend, whom she called Good Vibes, calling Dominos for a pizza at 11:55 p.m. on New Year's Eve and then getting the pizza for free when it arrived at 12:15 a.m., because he complained that he'd ordered it last year. We were both pretty tipsy, and neither of us should have been driving, but I offered to drive us to the store. It was close enough that we could walk, but in my drunken state, I decided I would pick up some crack in Causeway Block. I don't know how I thought I could do this without Ashley knowing; the alcohol had clouded my judgment.

"As long as I don't get opiates, I'll be fine," I thought, as I texted Terrorist and he agreed to trade me a few of my subs for a small rock of crack. We grabbed the beer from the nearest gas station, and I headed off in the direction of Causeway Block. Ashley and I discovered we had yet another thing in common: we both had the exact same taste in music, and neither of us could sing well at all, but we both loved to anyway.

"Hangin' round downtown by myself, and then there she was..." We belted out song lyrics, flying down the street toward my awaiting dealer. Ashley was very intoxicated and we were involved in heavy conversation when I pulled up to Terrorist. We exchanged drugs in a matter of seconds, and I quickly pulled away. Ashley didn't even see the exchange, but she saw me pull up to Terrorist and knew something was up.

"WHAT THE FUCK, RYAN! Are we in Causeway Block?" she screamed at me.

"No," I lied yet again, not wanting to fuel her anger.

I saw her look out her window and notice the street sign, and my stomach dropped.

"Ryan, you lying piece of shit. That sign said Causeway Block. The only thing my brother told me when I said I was visiting was not to let you take me here. I said of course I wouldn't, and here I am. Bring me back right now, and don't speak to me the rest of the time I'm here. I hate you!" she screeched.

I didn't know what to do. I wished I had gotten heroin instead of crack. I was no longer in the mood to smoke it.

"I just tossed the drugs out the window," I lied again, hoping to make her happy. She didn't respond. When we got back to the apartment, she grabbed a pair of my shoes and headed to our community workout room.

"Who the hell works out when they're that drunk, and why did she have to take my shoes?" I wondered. I guessed she didn't have anywhere else to escape to.

"Ryan, what the fuck did you do to my sister?" Brandon approached me and sent Melany after Ashley to make sure she was okay.

I almost started crying. What the hell was wrong with me, were drugs really so important to me that I would ruin everything in my life to get them, time and time again? Brandon ripped into me hard when I admitted I had taken Ashley to Causeway Block.

"Dude, if you wanna be a fuckin' lowlife junkie, ruin your life, and get your car shot up over some stupid drugs, then so be it, but leave my sister the fuck alone. You almost died in that development not long ago, and you bring MY SISTER there?" He raged on, cornering me in the kitchen and almost knocking me into the stove.

I really liked Brandon as a friend and as a roommate. Given his situation with his father and brother, I knew he was extremely emotional when it came to drugs and the safety of his family. I started bawling. I couldn't help myself. Tears streamed down my face like a raging river, and I could not get them to stop. I thanked the Lord the girls were not here to witness this. I think Brandon was shocked to see me cry, because he was quick to apologize.

"I'm sorry, man. I just really care about my family, after all we've been through," Brandon said, backing up and patting me on the shoulder.

"I know. I'm a horrible person. I won't talk to your sister anymore, unless she wants me to, and I will never bring her anywhere near drugs or trouble again," I sniffled and headed to my room.

I spent the next day nursing a hangover with subs in my bedroom. I desperately wanted to see Ashley, but I was still too afraid and embarrassed to face her. She was supposed to leave to go back to Vermont the following morning, and I still hadn't even gotten her phone number. It would have been easy to ask Brandon for it, but I only wanted to get it if she wanted to give it to me. It was almost midnight and I couldn't sleep. I was working up my nerves to go out into the living room to see if she was still awake when I heard a light knock on my door. I quietly opened it, overjoyed to see Ashley standing there with two beers in her hand.

"I am still mad at you, but I couldn't leave without a proper goodbye," she said, walking past me and sitting down on my bed. I joined her, and we talked for hours, only stopping to venture to the kitchen for snacks and beers. Sitting at the kitchen counter, I must have apologized a thousand times for my behavior the evening before, and I think she knew I was being sincere.

"Hey, let's go in the hot tub," she said, grabbing my arm. The pool in our neighborhood closed at ten and it was nearing three in the morning, but there was no way I was going to resist.

I hurried to my bedroom to grab my bathing suit and when I returned, she was already in a skimpy bikini, swaying drunkenly around and clutching two towels. We each grabbed a few Coronas and snuck out into the darkness. The gates were locked. I almost turned around.

Ashley laughed at me and said, "We have to hop the fence, silly."

I hoisted her up, thankful she was so light, and then lifted myself over, and we slipped into the hot tub.

Sipping Coronas and gazing at the stars, I had the intense urge to kiss her. She was leaving, and I didn't know if it was a good idea, but I decided I needed to try anyway.

As I started to move toward her, she must have had the same idea. She grabbed my head, pulled me close, and whispered, "Ryan, I really like you," before pressing her lips gently on mine. Our half naked bodies pressed together, dripping with warm water, and her tongue softly massaged mine. I had to find a way to keep this girl; I never wanted to let her go. In the moment, I stealthily untied her bikini top; I'm sure she noticed, but she didn't pull away. It fell into the dark hot tub water, and I could see its outline floating by the pale light off the moon. I then tried to untie the bottom part of her bathing suit, and felt her hand block me.

"You took me through Causeway Block, and you lied about it. You also lied about shooting up," she said, as if she needed an explanation for shutting me down.

"I know, I'm sorry. I got carried away," I apologized, helping her put her bikini top back on.

I sat back down in the hot tub and had just pulled her onto my lap when we saw a spotlight shine at us.

"Hey! Who's there? You kids, get over here!" We heard the shouts of our neighborhood watch, and it was time to bolt. We scrambled to grab our towels and shoes, scaled the fence, and booked it back to the apartment before we could be identified.

———◆·———

I was filled with dread the following morning. Ashley departed back to Vermont, and loneliness enveloped my soul, while the desire to take opiates came creeping back in. I knew I had to do something to distract myself, or I would start looking for drugs. I needed to get out of Virginia. Locking myself in my bedroom, I started to pack. Hundreds of colorful t-shirts, baseball hats, flip brim hats, sunglasses, shoes, and pants sat piled on my desk. I had enough clothes to dress about a hundred homeless people in style, with shoes and sunglasses to match.

"Damn, I have a lot of clothes; how am I going to get everything home?" I wondered. On the way down to Virginia, we had gotten a U-Haul for beds, dressers, and other large furniture, but I had no money for the way back. I didn't want to just bail on Tim and Brandon, but the longer I stayed in Virginia, the more trouble I was bound to get into. Ace and his crew were going to rob the old Keller mansion just outside of Causeway Block for Terrorist next week, and I was supposed to be their getaway driver. I needed to get far away before that happened. Exhausted from packing and staying up all night with Ashley, I snorted a few benzos, drank a beer, and passed out on my bed.

After snoozing for a good forty-eight hours, I woke up

and decided to text Ashley, to see if she had made it home okay. I had given her my phone number, but she had yet to text me. I was never the first one to text a girl. They always contacted me first. I wondered for a brief moment if I should wait, but I didn't play games. The worst she could do was tell me not to text her anymore.

I typed out, "Hey... how was your flight? Make it home okay?" I felt a nervous twinge as I hit send, adrenaline shooting through my veins. It was very uncharacteristic for me to feel like this over a girl. The anticipation felt similar to the feeling I got when a heroin-filled needle was about to enter my tied off veins. That sensation was a thousand times better and more intense than this, but it was in the same family. Both drugs and Ashley brought me joy and allowed me to escape from my own mind.

Less than ten seconds later, I heard my phone buzz. Quickly flipping it open, I read, "I died. My plane crashed." I didn't really know what to make of this. I sat with a quizzical look on my face, staring at my phone, trying to think of a response, when it buzzed again.

"Just kidding, it's about time you texted me. I got surgery on my knee and I'm stuck sitting in a recliner all day with ice packs around my leg. The pain pills they gave me made me so nauseous. I wish I was back in Virginia," her text read.

I wished she was back in Virginia too, or that I was in Vermont with her and the pain pills. I wondered what she got. There was no way she would let me have any, but maybe I could take some from her script without her noticing.

"God, Ryan, you've really got to snap out of it!" I thought to myself. There was no way I could get high today, because I'd taken some Suboxone right when I got up, but even the mention of any type of painkillers heightened my senses and filled my brain with a sense of longing. It was hard to describe; I was yearning for something so badly that I knew would hurt me. It was like wishing I could spend time with someone I loved so much, but I couldn't, because they were dead. I pictured myself crushing up the little pill, mixing it with water in a spoon, injecting it into my tied off arm, and relishing in the warm, carefree, blissful high. I felt so strongly about my love and desire for opiates that I was comparing not being able to get drugs to a dead loved one. There was something seriously wrong with me, but I didn't see it.

"Virginia blows. I might come back early. What did they give you for pain meds?" Send. Damn. I shouldn't have asked that, Ashley already thought I was a junkie. My phone buzzed again and I was expecting to get bitched out for asking about the pills, but I was pleasantly surprised.

"You should come back early and keep me company. I really want to go kayaking and I need a buddy! The pills are something called Dilaudid, tiny and orange with a two on them, but they make me so sick. I also have to take a miniscule sugar pill type thing so I don't puke. I sold a few to my sister's friend for two dollars to help her bad back. I may just throw the rest out." My heart lurched when I read the last bit. She might throw out Dilaudids! That was a sin.

"Don't throw them out. I can get you at least ten dollars per pill when I get back," I sent.

"Really? I have seventy! That's $700! I could really use that, since I can't bartend with my knee," she replied.

Shortly after, she sent another text. "When are you coming back to Vermont?"

"Your guess is as good as mine," I thought. I knew I was supposed to stay until the lease was up and return with Brandon and Tim, but I had no career and would much rather spend time with Ashley than do jobs for Terrorist, which would inevitably result in a relapse.

"I don't really know. I think I might leave now," I responded.

"Awesome! We could go kayaking tomorrow!" she answered. What a crazy girl; she had just come out of surgery and wanted to go kayaking with me. It was a match made in heaven; I loved outdoor activities. With that in mind, I loaded up my car.

"What are you doing, Ryan?" Brandon asked, as he pulled in next to my Subaru in our community parking lot. I was shoving the last of my belongings into my car, duct tape covering the bullet holes.

"I'm peacin' out, dude. I can't stay here anymore. I'm probably wanted for more than one thing—the TVs, Brianna's car, the corner store—and my buddies want me to do a bigger job for them next week that I shouldn't do." I shut my door, and Brandon put up his fist for a pound.

"Nice job, bro. It's good to see you making smart decisions. Stay safe on your way home, and remember, if you hurt my sister, I'll kill you—but watch out for her too, she's a wild one."

I smiled, picturing Ashley's lightly tanned face and sparkling blue eyes. Brandon knew I really liked her, and this was as close to having his blessing as I was ever going to get.

"Thanks, see you in a while. I couldn't fit all of my stuff, so I hope you guys don't mind loading it in the U-Haul for me on the way home. Tell Tim I say bye."

"Will do." He gave a quick wave, and I was off, thanking the Lord I had a large stash of Adderall to keep me alert for the long drive. I was going to make it without one stop.

———•———

"Ryan, what are you doing here?" My mother smothered me with hugs and kisses, a genuine look of shock on her face as I pulled into her driveway the following morning. I had taken a bunch of Adderall to stay up, and driven all night from Virginia to our home in Vermont. I was worn out from the eleven-hour drive.

Her hugs felt nice, but I brushed them off. I wasn't deserving of such affection from the woman who had done so much for me, just to watch me throw it all away. I went into my old bedroom to lie down. She nicely offered to unpack the car for me, but added that Don had mentioned taking it away when I returned from Virginia. I rolled about restlessly in the dark room. It was my intention to take a nap, but my mind had other plans. I felt uncomfortable with my thoughts; I was upset and unhappy, and I couldn't put a finger on why. My legs kept relentlessly twitching. I wanted to get high, but I had taken some Suboxone not long ago, and for the first time in a while, I had no opiates in my possession.

After flailing around, trying very unsuccessfully to get

some rest, I decided to text Ashley, who was staying with her mom after her knee surgery.

"Hey, what's up? I decided to leave Virginia last night and I made it home. I'm next door at my parents' house." Send.

I flicked open the blinds, and sunlight splattered about the room. Squinting my eyes, I picked out a clean shirt from the neat pile of clothing my mother had carried in from the car.

"Damn! You drove all night? Good thing you didn't fall asleep! I can't believe you're still up, do you want to kayak?" Ashley's text flashed on my screen.

I couldn't believe I was still up either. I had taken a decent amount of Adderall, but I guessed I would still be awake even if I hadn't. Sobriety, or at least abstinence from opiates, came with many horrible prices. One of them was insomnia. I hated it. I was constantly tired, but could never sleep.

"Hell yea. Come get me," I sent back. My mother had agreed with Don's idea to take the car, and they'd seized it for an undisclosed amount of time. I wasn't happy about it, but I had a feeling Ashley would drive me around, and it was a good thing I didn't have access to a quick and easy way to visit Seth or any of my other VT connects.

Ashley showed up in no time, driving her mother's pickup truck with two kayaks hanging out the back. I wondered how she had gotten them into the truck with crutches. Noticing my quizzical look and sensing my curiosity, she offered an explanation.

"My mom put them in; I helped her, hopping around on one foot," she laughed. I pictured the comical scene, and wished I'd looked out the window to watch. Then I realized I would be the one helping her take the kayaks out of the truck once we got down to the boating access.

My mother came outside and struck up a conversation with Ashley. I could tell she was relieved I had chosen to go kayaking with someone she knew, rather than getting scooped up by a random person who was most likely a drug friend.

"Ryan quit cigarettes too!" I heard Ashley gleefully exclaim to my mother, who nodded approvingly. I knew she was much more worried about the drugs. I was sure she was grateful that Ashley had enforced me not smoking, but worried that it might be too much to quit at the same time I was giving up opiates. I winced as I fought back a craving to smoke a butt. Quitting smoking was not as difficult as staying away from opiates, but cravings were cravings, and they were no fun.

"I'm allergic, so I told him if he smokes, we can't hang out," Ashley quipped to my mother.

I needed to get out of there. I wanted to shoot up and smoke a cigarette and blow it in both of their faces, but then Ashley smiled at me.

"You ready?" she asked, making my nerves tingle and butterflies dance in my stomach. It was the first time in a while when butterflies had signified a positive feeling. My cravings ceased, and I helped her into the driver's seat of the automatic truck, taking her crutches and putting them in the back with the kayaks.

We waved to my beaming mother and took off toward the lake.

"You shouldn't be driving if you're on Dilaudid," I told

Ashley, even though I had driven on them and countless other drugs almost daily for years.

"I'm not on Dilaudid; you told me I could get ten dollars each for them, and I figured I might as well save them and keep the money. I can deal with the pain anyway, it's not that bad." She grabbed my hand and launched into a story about her surgery and how she was sad she couldn't drive her car, because it was standard.

"This girl is badass; she drives standard and doesn't use painkillers after surgery, even when they are prescribed to her!" I was amazed by her. Grabbing my phone, I went to work, texting people who would want to buy her script. Even though I had been gone for almost a year, I had all seventy accounted for within fifteen minutes.

"Let's go to the Stars parking lot when we're done here, and I'll get you the money for your script," I told her. She obliged, saying that she would have to join me for the transaction, so she knew I didn't sneak one for myself. I yearned for one so badly, but even being able to sell them brought back a little of the rush and calmed me down. I tried not to think about it as we shoved our kayaks into the deep blue water.

Ashley was saying something about how beautiful the day was and how she was so happy I had come back early as we paddled out into serene Lake Champlain. The sun was out, birds were chirping—but all I could think about was selling Ashley's script. If I couldn't get high, I at least needed to deal. Maybe I could make some money again and save it this time; that way, I could take Ashley out, instead of her driving my sorry ass around. The idea was inviting, but mostly because I longed to hold a little orange pill bottle in my palm, even if I couldn't indulge in its contents. My mind raced. I wished I had bought a beer to bring out on the water, but I had no money. I didn't know Ashley well enough to ask her to buy me one on the way over.

"You should have said something, I would have picked up some beers. I almost suggested it, but I didn't want to have to pee when we were in the middle of the lake," Ashley said, laughing.

I must have been thinking out loud. Either that, or she read my mind. Ashley was like that. We had a special connection. It was strong and elusive; I couldn't put a finger on what made us so compatible, but we were both equally drawn to each other. I think Ashley might have been drawn to my addiction more than she was conscious of—as if saving me was a desperate attempt to save her late father and brother. I didn't mind. I wanted this beautiful creature to save me, but the problem was, at the time, I had convinced myself I didn't need saving.

After struggling to get the kayaks out of the water and into Ashley's mother's truck, my feeble arms trying to make up for Ashley having to hobble around on one leg, we headed to the Stars parking lot.

"Isn't this kind of a sketchy place to be meeting people? Especially with kayaks hanging out of the truck?" Ashley questioned, as we pulled in to meet my first custy.

"Naw, not at all. The more out in the open you are, the less sketchy it is. People don't expect you to be dealing drugs right in the middle of a packed parking lot, and so many cars pull in and out in a day; it's really perfect," I informed her.

One by one, my long lost acquaintances popped up to the passenger side window of the truck and slid me cash. I stealthily passed them the correct amount of Dilaudid and sent them on their way. A look of disgust creeped onto Ashley's face as the quality of the people coming up to the truck quickly declined. It had been less than a year, and these people I once called my friends were almost unrecognizable. Their faces were either deathly thin or puffy and enlarged on skeleton bodies. Their stench radiated off of their unwashed bodies and into the vehicle. I had only been using needles a short amount of time and had a superb immune system, so I didn't look too bad. I was ridiculously skinny and had a few small scars from injecting, but I had yet to be homeless and I kept up with my personal hygiene.

"Ew. You talk to him? That guy looked like he hadn't showered in weeks. His hair was disgusting, and I'm pretty sure I saw blood running down his hand. Gross," Ashley said, after the second to last custy had left.

I shrugged, "He didn't look like that last time I saw him, but he's just dirty. Everyone does this shit; the guy who's supposed to get the last few is an elementary school teacher," I said, as if I needed to defend the type of people I associated with.

"What the fuck. That's even worse. I don't really feel comfortable with this, Ryan. I'm so glad you didn't have these scumbags meet up at my apartment," Ashley said.

I brushed off the insult to my friends and turned to my window to see my last customer.

"How you doin', bro?" I asked him.

"Good, dude, just got married, still teachin' kids. Life is

alright," he sniffed. I reluctantly handed him the remainder of Ashley's script and pocketed the cash. He thanked me and took off.

"I wonder if his wife knows! I can't believe he does that stuff and teaches kids!" Ashley exclaimed, as she sped out of the Stars parking lot, in a hurry to leave the whole episode behind.

"He's alright; he doesn't teach high, and he just snorts them," I responded, to which Ashley gave me a knowing glare. There was no getting anything past this girl; she had lost two family members to addiction, and knew well that just because someone wasn't shooting didn't mean they weren't on a fast track to death and destruction.

I pulled the gigantic wad of cash out of my pocket and handed it to her.

"I'm glad that's done, and it will never, ever, be repeated again. Now, where do you want to go to dinner?" she asked me, with a twinkle in her eye.

I learned fast that Ashley loved to eat and was good at managing money. We ate at restaurants all over town, went to the drive-in movies, and drank a good deal of alcohol that summer. When it was over, she still had some of the money. I was amazed. I could have burnt through $700 in an hour, easy.

To date, that summer was one of the best summers in my life—except for my two-week sprint at rehab. I was clean, from opiates anyway, when I returned home from Virginia, and I don't know how I let Ashley convince me to go to rehab.

"Do it for your mother, please," she begged me, over and over again. I wanted to say no, I did say no, but she wouldn't let it go. Finally, I reluctantly agreed to be subjected to two weeks of utter torture. After a few weeks of waiting to be admitted, I sat beside my mother in the car. We turned onto the long dirt road to the rehab center, and I instantly regretted my decision.

"I want to go back. I'm fine. I really don't need this," I begged, anxiety taking over. I didn't know what I was going to do for two weeks without even a beer or a benzo. Complete sobriety scared the shit out of me. It left me alone with my inner demons; there was no way I could escape from myself.

"It's okay, Ryan. I'll visit Sundays, and come to all of the NA and AA meetings they allow visitors at, and call you every day," Ashley reassured me from the backseat. Nothing she could say would take away the fear that gripped my entire being. I wished I could be at peace with myself, but there was no calming my heart. At that moment, there was nothing that I wanted to do more than cut open a bag of heroin with a razor, and mix it up in a spoon to inject into my veins.

I felt a buzz in my pocket and pulled out my cell phone for the last time before confinement. I was nearly as afraid of being without my phone as I was of going without any type of drugs or alcohol for at least two weeks. The length of treatment depended on my evaluation and the length of my detox; since I was clean from opiates going in, that was sure to shave some time off.

Flipping open my screen, my jaw dropped at Brandon's text.

"Your boy Ace and his buddies are getting sent to death row, dude. Just saw it on the news. I guess they tried to rob the old Keller mansion, fucked up bad, and burnt the house down. Mr. Keller burned to death inside, and now they're all going to die by lethal injection for second degree murder."

"Damn," I muttered out loud as I reread his words; the reality was sinking in that I was supposed to be with them. If I had stayed in Virginia, and been the getaway driver as planned, I too would most likely be on death row.

I tried to hide this from my beloved travel companions, but Ashley snatched my phone. This girl didn't mess around. I watched her face scrunch up with concern, and then her jaw dropped in horror when she made the connection. I would soon be dead if I hadn't come home early to see her. I knew my mother was overcome with a burning desire to know what the text said, but neither Ashley nor I offered, and she didn't ask.

## Chapter Twelve:
# Rehab

Upon arrival at the secluded rehab center, I was checked in and searched, as was my luggage. Instantly, I was reminded of my dreadful weekend at CRASH. That was only a weekend, and I was able to use my phone after nine in the evening. Exquisite OxyContin had also gotten me blissfully through—not this time. I couldn't bear the thought of sobriety for two weeks, combined with detachment from my prized cell phone. Having a limited amount of phone time and sharing a cord phone attached to the wall with numerous strangers was sure to make rehab feel even more like jail than it already did.

"Just one more kiss?" I begged, parting with Ashley as they dragged me away for drug testing. Apparently physical contact was also frowned upon at rehab.

"Of course it is," I thought to myself, turning my head for one last look at Ashley, who was gazing fondly at me with encouragement in her eyes.

"She thinks it's going to be okay, because it's not her that has to go through this, it's me," I thought begrudgingly, as if it wasn't my own fault I was there to begin with.

From the uncomfortable beds, dismal walls, lack of outside communication, and limited food choices, to the endless anxiety, fear, denial, and frustration, rehab was just as bad as I had imagined.

The first evening, a speaker came to talk to us. Our melancholy bunch funneled into the main room where we had meetings and ate our meals. There were rows of hard blue chairs set up facing a small podium. The speaker droned on and I blocked most of it out, wishing I could be with Ashley, enjoying life. One thing he said suddenly caught my attention, and I snapped out of my daydream.

"I was petrified of needles. Whenever I had to go to the doctors for shots as a kid, I would hide. If you told me ten years ago I would shoot up numerous times daily in the hands, arms, neck, even in between my toes, I would have told you that you were nuts."

I stared up at the thirty-something year old man in front of the withered group of recovering addicts I sat among. I could relate. Nothing scared me more than needles—unless they contained some kind of drugs, preferably opiates. The longing for a high drove you to overcome any fear, because it allowed you to escape the emptiness of sobriety and the deadening sickness of withdrawal.

"Getting high allowed me to beat my demons, one day at a time, but they always returned, gathering strength like an army fighting against me. Being an addict is a full time job. It leaves you no time for a real career, social life, or family. You're constantly chasing the high or running from sickness, with no regard for the consequences. In the brief moments during my ten-year battle with drug use that I managed to be sober, I still couldn't fathom what I had done to my life. So many opportunities that I could have embraced were destroyed.

I was in and out of jail, and would probably be dead right now if it wasn't for my last offence. I was up against some pretty hard time, fifteen years. I had the choice to successfully complete an intense two-year sobriety program, where I was drug tested every day and had to attend counseling sessions. I hated it, but it was better than fifteen years of jail time. If it hadn't been so long, I most likely would have gone back to using. I still battle my addiction every day, but toward the end of the second year, I really grasped the depth of my situation. I broke out of the haze. Everything I had been through was real, not just some sick dream. Most of my friends were dead or had disowned me because of my addiction, and I had caused my family members irreparable emotional scars. I finally realized I couldn't have the euphoria and the rush without a casket.

Luckily, I had not been put in an early grave, but most of my friends who have overdosed did so right after coming out of rehab. Their tolerance was slightly lowered, and they were craving the feeling of the warm, welcoming hug only achievable by injecting opiates. Even if someone had warned them it would be their last rush, I believe they still would have done it. I would like to think that at least one of you young people sitting before me will follow through with recovery, and not join my dear friends in heaven... or hell." He brushed back a tear as his speech came to a halt.

There was a brief moment of awkward silence, and none of us made eye contact. We were all thinking, "The others could die, but it would never happen to me." Our captor thanked the speaker, and it was time for bed.

Tossing and turning, I wished for some sort of relief. Finally rising from my bed, I plodded down to the nurses' office and pleaded for something. To my surprise, I was granted a single trazodone to help me sleep.

"I don't usually do this, but since you were clean from opiates when you came in, I am allowing this just once. It will not be repeated, so don't come ask tomorrow night. You must take it now, orally, in front of me," the nurse instructed. It wasn't much, compared to what I was used to, but trazodone was used to treat depression, anxiety, and sleep disorders, so I hoped it would do me some good.

———◆———

Adrenaline rushed through my veins, and they bulged out as I tied my arm off. They were so welcoming, thick and blue. My heart pounded out of my chest as I watched my roommate slice open a tiny bag of precious heroin with a razor. I wondered how he had gotten it into rehab, through the violating searches. I watched as he prepared a concoction with a spoon stolen from the dish pit. We had chores that had to be done at rehab, and he had been assigned to dish.

"Genius," I thought. Leaning forward, begging for just a small taste, I pushed Ashley's disapproving frown and my mother's weeping eyes from my thoughts. The speech from earlier in the day and deadly overdoses flashed through my brain, taunting me.

"It won't happen to me, I'm a beast," I thought to myself. My roommate passed the concoction to me, revealing he had also managed to sneak in a clean needle. I held it to my tied off arm, just seconds from puncturing the vein. Suddenly, I toppled over; the prized needle flung from my grip and across the room. Ashley was on top of me. My stomach lurched, and I wondered how she'd gotten in here. She beat me repeatedly; her fist with a sharp ring slammed my face again and again.

I woke up, gasping for breath. My face hurt, as if the beating from the dream somehow translated into real life. I was shocked, disturbed, and disappointed, all at once.

"That damn trazodone. Those things always make me have crazy dreams," I thought to myself. I spent the rest of the early morning tossing and turning sleeplessly until rousing time at seven.

The only things that kept me sane during my forced stay in that desolate prison were visits from Ashley and my mother, meals, and free time. Originally disgusted at the limited meal selection, I steered clear of food, but as my appetite returned after a long vacation, I branched out and tried a few new things. Soon, I was shoveling down more meat and vegetables than I had in years and enjoying every second of it. Our free time was limited, but they did allow us to go outside for activities. It had been a long time since I had handled a basketball. It brought me back to before the drugs, when Tim, Brandon, and I would play pickup games in Brandon's driveway with other kids on our street, without a care in the world.

I shot—swish—and smiled; I still had it. A few other fellow rehab inmates joined me on the court, and we played a short pickup game. Energized by the physical activity, I momentarily forgot where I was. Stealing the ball from a tall, skinny, scruffy-looking kid, I went in for a layup. I heard a swift pop as my arm rose above my head, followed by an intense pain. My teammates cheered as the ball flew effortlessly through the net, but I could not rejoice.

Doubled over on the pavement, I clutched my arm.

"What happened to me?" I wondered, grabbing my shoulder and shoving it back into place as I headed inside to see the nurse.

"You appear to have dislocated your shoulder. Hopefully you won't need surgery, because you've checked into rehab they will no longer prescribe you any painkillers at the hospital. Lots of physical therapy and abstaining from any sport that uses your arm or shoulder should help," the nurse advised.

My mind quickly flew to snowboarding. I had really wanted to ride, but I was nervous. Now that I had hurt myself playing a simple basketball game, my dreams of getting back onto the mountain seemed even further away.

"Great. I was just starting to get excited to get back into sports, and now I can't play. What the fuck," I vented.

"I'm sorry, Ryan, I see this happening here frequently. Your drug addiction has worn down your body, and you're more susceptible to injury," she informed me. After discovering this, getting back on a board didn't seem like such a great idea. A part of me really wanted to try it anyway, but my shoulder was now compromised. Snowboarders use their arms a lot for balance, and who knew how my legs would hold up. They felt weak and achy from lack of painkillers. The scar on my femur from years ago still felt fresh, and I hadn't been on a board since the accident.

"Fabulous. More pain. Drugs have really ruined my life, and they're all I want," I thought, feeling trapped in unfathomable torture. At least Ashley and my mother were visiting that day. Even though it wasn't a Sunday, when visiting hours were held, NA and AA meetings were open to the public, and it was meeting time.

"Hi, my name is Ryan, and I am an addict." I should have said an alcoholic-addict, but admitting one problem at a time was enough of a step for me. Even as I said it aloud, in front of a group of people who were also clearly in trouble and in denial, I couldn't believe myself.

I hated the way they made everyone identify as an alcoholic, an addict or an alcoholic-addict. This was not how I identified myself. Not who I was. When I looked in the mirror, I saw myself as I was before drugs—a smart, talented, good-looking guy with a bright future. I didn't notice the small changes in my appearance, or if I did, I convinced myself I didn't. Still partially in denial about the effects of my addiction, I was only there to make my mother and Ashley happy. I didn't belong in here with these lowlifes.

Ashley sat to my left, clutching my hand, and my mother to my right, desperately trying to conceal the tears welling up in her eyes. I was blessed to have such wonderful people in my life and desperately wanted to show them that this was not who I was, but even as I sat in that chair over thirty days sober and finally through detox, all I could think about was getting high. Not just heroin either—I craved a drink, some Adderall, cocaine, opiates of any kind, maybe even some crack... anything to escape from the deathly frightening dark tunnel of sobriety that surrounded me.

"I am not here. This is not real. I need a quick fix, something to make this okay. Why did I ever agree to this? I'm fine," I thought to myself. The rules of rehab said otherwise. When the meeting was over, Ashley and my mom would leave and I was required to stay, unless I somehow got high.

If you got high in rehab and got caught, you were kicked out, which sounded amazing to me, but I didn't want Ashley to leave me, and my mom had spent her hard-earned money to send me here.

"I can do this," I thought to myself. "Only a few more days."

One of the only things that calmed me was music. Certain songs would bring me back to the days when I was getting high without a care in the world. I was overcome with a rush of feelings that didn't come close to an actual high, but relaxed me momentarily, then brought on a strong craving for whatever drug I associated the song with. We weren't allowed to listen to music in rehab; it was considered a trigger. No triggers were allowed. What kind of hell was I in, and how did I manage to get myself there? Over and over again, I asked myself these questions; the only answer I could come up with was that it must have been an awful mistake. I didn't know how my mother could have been so mistaken, I was fine.

The meeting ended all too soon, and we were forced to say our farewells. I cherished the moments Ashley and my mother were in my presence, also slightly resenting them. They were the reason I was subjected to this torture, but it was only because they cared so deeply for me. I gazed out the window, watching as my mom's maroon Corolla disappeared down the long dirt road, holding back tears. I felt lost and empty, when I should have felt truly blessed.

## CHAPTER THIRTEEN:
# Promises

Finally, my imprisonment at the dreaded rehab center came to an end. Before discharging me, one of my captors encouraged me to get a sponsor. I politely refused, but she handed me a pamphlet with a list of names and phone numbers.

"All of our sponsors are graduates of this very rehab center, and volunteered to help anyone who is dedicated to recovery," she explained.

Glancing down the list, I spotted Brianna's name. Apparently she had gotten her act together after leaving Virginia. "Good for her," I thought, shoving the pamphlet in my bag and heading for the door.

Ashley was waiting for me, beer in hand. I had used my persuasive powers to convince her to pick one up.

"I really think you should stay sober from everything, like they told you to in rehab. I will quit drinking with you, if you would like," she offered, hesitant to hand me the beer I had begged for during our daily phone calls.

"Hell no. That's insane. I'm giving up all opiates, and I quit cigarettes. You can't possibly be serious." I snatched the beer from her hand, giving her a playful grin. A half smile spread across her face, but I could tell she was still slightly reluctant.

"If my father hadn't gone back to drinking, I doubt he would have gone back to opiates; same with my brother. I wonder what it would be like if they were alive today. I couldn't bear to see the same thing happen to you…" Her voice trailed off.

For a second, I felt slightly guilty. Obviously, this girl was so head over heels in love with me that she was allowing me to manipulate her into supporting my drinking. When I popped open the beer, the fizzing sound was like music to my ears. It ran down my throat in cold, refreshing gulps. Blocking out Ashley's rambling about how I should get a sponsor to help me stay clean, I pounded it down. My body felt a warm, tingly glow, similar to the feeling I got from opiates, but very bleak in comparison. There was nothing that compared to the warmth in my chest that spread through the rest of my body when I shot up. Finally, I snapped out of the daydream, nestled my head onto Ashley's shoulder, and tried to reassure her that I was going to be just fine without a sponsor.

"I'm not going anywhere. I'm invincible. I don't need anyone, except you, to help me. I'm never going back to opiates. You are my opiate now." I could feel her body loosen and relax with this response, but she still insisted I consider getting a sponsor. I agreed to think about it just to get her to leave me alone.

I was still in shock over how much this girl liked me. All of my other relationships were centered on drugs. My sex drive had lain dormant for years. To my other girlfriends and my past self, drugs were far better than sex. In the short time I had been back in Vermont, Ashley and I had made love numerous times prior to my rehab sentence. For the first time, I really enjoyed sex, but it was still nothing compared to the euphoric numbing and energizing rush of heroin.

Ashley's knee was healing surprisingly fast, and I was still in awe of her for dealing with the aftermath of surgery without the assistance of painkillers. She held my hand skillfully, shifting her car at the same time, as we drove back into town toward splendid nights filled with dancing, bonfires, swimming, traveling, camping, love making, and laughter. I wish I could relive that summer over and over.

—— • ——

"Gross, Ryan, are you really going to snort molly again? Remember how much it made your nose bleed last time? When you snort it, you're so fucked up that you don't know what's going on. Then you start coming down when I'm still rolling and it's no fun. Just drink it, like I do," Ashley said, stirring the white powdery crystals into a shot glass filled with orange juice.

"I just roll mine up in a tiny bit of toilet paper or a capsule and swallow it," our friend Nina chimed in.

I wanted to snort it. Snorting was the closest thing to shooting, which Ashley had strictly forbidden me to do. Time and time again, she reminded me that if I wanted to remain her boyfriend, I would not use opiates, I would not smoke cigarettes, and I would not use needles.

Grabbing a shot glass and filling it with orange juice, I

mixed in the molly. Supposedly it was pure MDMA, but you never really knew what people mixed drugs with. Out of the drugs Ashley allowed me to do, molly was my favorite. It delivered a more consistent high than ecstasy pills, which were sometimes speedy, sometimes dopey, or somewhere in between. Our dealer, Eric, always had the same stuff, and he sold it for a decent price. We could get a gram for seventy dollars. I would buy at least that, then sell a few tenths for fifteen or twenty dollars each and make my money back, plus some. Ashley and I also got to roll for free. I was extremely thankful she let me roll, but we both quickly built a tolerance to molly. It wasn't addictive like heroin, but we needed more and more of it to feel the same effects.

Ashley didn't want to do molly all the time, only for dubstep shows and special events. I enjoyed doing it as much as possible, and sometimes I could convince her to do some with me just to go to the bars or play on the playground down the street.

Swings and slides were amazing when rolling. The wind whipped past me on the swings, and I could feel every muscle in my legs as I pumped myself higher and higher into the sky. Slides felt like rollercoasters, and my legs were so light I wanted to run, jump, and dance. Nights when Ashley and I rolled, we would ride our bikes to the bars, which felt so inexplicably amazing. I wanted to keep riding past downtown Arelington and into the night, never stopping until I came down from my high. That particular evening, Ashley, Nina, her boyfriend, and I were pre-gaming for a Nero concert at the local auditorium. We pounded back beers, laughed, and talked while we waited for our molly to kick in. It never kicked in at the same time for all of us, but once the first person started rolling, I would become elated with anticipation.

I grabbed my water, suddenly preferring it to beer as my roll started.

"Too bad molly isn't good for you. I never want to eat when I'm rolling, and I always want to run around. What a great way to diet!" Ashley said, as she walked towards me, slowly lifting one leg up and then hopping back onto the other with a loopy smile on her face. I grinned at her fondly; she was such a cute girl, and I loved her so dearly.

Nothing had been able to keep me from opiates for so long. It had only been a few months, but to me, that was a lifetime. There was no way I could do opiates, because Ashley and I were together all the time. I had never felt this way about a girl before. Usually my girlfriends would annoy me and I would want some space, but not Ashley. I just wanted to snuggle her all day. We were one of those couples that disgusted other people. We had weird little inside jokes that no one else understood, and would frequently draw each other pictures or send text messages randomly with reasons why we loved each other.

One day, I received a text that said, "You're weird. You smell good. You get along with my friends. You make me feel special. You never judge me. You make me laugh. You're sexy." Included with the text was a picture of a seal floundering around on its belly. That's how I often looked when I was hungover, and Ashley liked to point out the similarity.

I smiled at the memory and glanced up as she hopped toward me, engulfed me in a huge hug, snuggled her face into my chest, and then looked up at me, grinning, and said, "Hi."

I was feeling weightless from the drugs, and felt my love for Ashley bursting out of my body and morphing into hers. She was my soulmate. All of my other girlfriends had used me for drugs, and Ashley wanted to protect me from drugs. We had only been dating a few short months and I already wanted to marry her, but there was this intrinsic fear lodged deep inside my conscience that I would not be able to stay away from heroin and that Ashley would eventually leave me.

I pushed that fear aside for the moment, and relished in the elation of my roll. Pressing my face right up to hers, squishing her little nose with mine, I replied, "Hi," and we pulled ourselves together into a passionate kiss. The room slipped away; we weren't concerned that our friends were present. The only things that mattered were our bodies and souls, deeply entwined.

Finally releasing from our tight embrace, we piled into my car (which had been returned to me upon my successful completion of rehab) to drive to the concert. We definitely should have walked, but it was cold out and I loved driving. Revving up the engine, my tires spun as I quickly shifted from first to second gear. I was one with the car. It felt like my arm was extending from my body into the shift knob and down into the transmission; my arm was a part of the car.

"Ryan, slow down!" Ashley's voice of reason broke my spell. I lifted my foot from the accelerator and pulled into a parking space. This girl really had a hold on me. She was right; I didn't want to drive around and possibly end up in jail. I wanted to go to the concert and dance the night away with my beautiful girlfriend. We held hands and ran with Nina and her boyfriend toward the crowded doorway. I double checked my pockets for my backup stash of molly and felt satisfied and happy for the first time in a while. I wanted to grow old with Ashley. She really got me. We both loved the outdoors, and I could be my true weird self around her and she would respond with something just as crazy. Despite her glowing beauty and intelligence, I never felt judged by her. Ashley made me feel like I was wonderful and nothing less. She believed in me.

"And you keep telling me, telling me that you'll be sweet, and you'll never want to leave my side, as long as I don't break these...promises, and they still feel all so wasted on myself..." Nero's lyrics blasted out into the auditorium, and I felt Ashley's warm, sweaty body against mine as she pulled me close. My heart wrenched as she promised to never leave me as long as I didn't go back to opiates or needles. I held her tight, our bodies swaying to the beat, my shaky vision jittering from the molly. My legs felt light, my body limber. There was nothing I wanted more than to stay there dancing with Ashley forever and never break my promises to her, except for heroin. I wanted heroin more than anything, and it plagued me every day. When I was with Ashley, especially when we were rolling or getting drunk, my cravings for opiates were not as great. I experienced elevated levels of dopamine and serotonin from the MDMA, but also from just being with Ashley alone. I was so attracted to her that, even after a few months of dating, a single kiss from her would result in an adrenaline boost.

Back at Ashley's apartment after the concert, I stretched

out on her spacious memory foam bed, sipping a beer. After a long night of dancing, followed by barhopping and then skinny dipping in the nearby lake, I still felt energized. Ashley and I had continued taking molly throughout the night, despite her protests that we should probably stop. I smiled fondly at the memory of her bottom lip curled down, making a pouty face.

"We're going to feel like shit tomorrow," she protested, but I disregarded her statement. Despite the negative consequences, I just couldn't give up the temporary pleasure. I felt the same way about heroin, which was why it was so impossible to quit. My vision shook pleasurably from the molly. I was so deep in thought I hadn't even noticed Ashley leave the room until my thoughts were interrupted by a knock on her bedroom door.

"Come in," I called, staring at the door with needy anticipation remembering she'd suggested role play. The door flung open and Ashley strutted in, her blonde hair up in the sexiest pigtails and makeup done to perfection. Her tiny top only covered her nipples, which I could see poking through the thin white fabric. Her navel was barren, with the exception of a glittering blue diamond bellybutton ring that matched her blue plaid pleated skirt and sparkling flirtatious eyes. She looked hotter than any schoolgirl I had ever seen in porn, and she was all mine.

"You wanted to see me, sir?" she asked, with a seductive look on her face.

"Yes; you've been a bad, bad girl," I scolded, my arousal impossible to hide.

She stepped closer to me and dropped a pen on the ground. Slowly, she turned around, bent over, and picked it up. I could see up her tiny blue schoolgirl skirt, and I gazed at the lacy black underwear that clung to her shapely behind. Thin black straps fastened the underwear to fishnet leggings that outlined her athletic legs. My body tingled with anticipation. I couldn't wait to peel them off her. Ashley rarely ever wore heels, but in the bedroom I fully enjoyed watching her long, gorgeous legs in sexy black stilettos.

"I know. I've been so bad. What can I do to make it up to you?" Ashley gushed, sweetly taking another step forward and dropping to her knees. She skillfully unfastened the belt I now used only to hold up my pants, and swiftly removed my jeans and boxers in one motion. My thoughts escaped me briefly. I couldn't help but picture the belt fastened deliciously around my arm as a tourniquet, ready for the deadly substance that delivered calming warmth and pure bliss. The ecstasy was starting to wear off and I yearned for opiates.

My attention was soon brought back to the moment, as I felt Ashley's soft wet lips against my hard shaft. Her tongue slid up and down and then circled my erect head, slightly sucking, teasing and pleasing me all at once. She held my gaze with the most erotic look on her face; she got pleasure out of sexually pleasing me.

"I hope that was satisfactory, sir," she said, standing up. Was it ever! I pulled her on top of me and yanked her forcefully down by the pigtails. She straddled me slowly, moving back and forth, taunting, making me crave more. We kissed passionately, gazed into each other's eyes, and then she flounced out of the room.

The best thing about sex with Ashley was the passion. The

intensity of our attraction made everything seem clearer than anything else in my life had been in years—like I had come out of a fog. When we made love, we could both feel our love for each other radiating from our bodies. Neither of us had ever felt like this before. I knew, because we had discussed it. We discussed everything. I waited anxiously for Ashley's return, and recalled a conversation we'd had a few days back.

"I don't know what it is about you, but when I'm around you, I always want to have sex. It's like you bring out a side in me I didn't know existed. I think it's because I feel so comfortable with you, like you would never judge me," I remembered her saying.

"Me, judge her! Is she kidding?" I had thought. I was in love with a sex goddess who had a good head on her shoulders and returned every ounce of my love; the only thing that would have been better was if someone could magically make heroin that wasn't bad for you and wasn't addictive and was free. Of course, that would never happen.

The door burst open again. Ashley returned in shiny stiletto black boots laced all the way up to her knees. On top, her breasts were poking out of a terrifically short police uniform. A police baton was fastened to her side, and a shiny black cop hat took the place of her pigtails.

"Mr. Landry. You are in some serious trouble," she threatened, taking out her stick. Was she going to beat me? Ashley and I had only been together a few months, and our lovemaking had spanned from the usual bed sex to bathroom sex, sex on the beach, public sex, and even sex in a treehouse—but this was my first experience with role playing, and I wasn't quite sure what to expect.

She placed the baton on the nightstand and pulled pink furry handcuffs from her bra.

I sat up, only to be shoved back down. She grabbed my hands one at a time and expertly fastened them to her bed. I lay transfixed as she grabbed her phone and switched on some seductive music. She picked up the baton from the nightstand and tapped me lightly on the nose with it.

"Be still," she whispered. I was in awe.

"If you're good and take your punishment, you can spank me with this later. If you move or speak before I say so, I will spank you," she continued.

I froze, my blood pressure rising from desire. She slowly and seductively danced in front of me, stripping off one article of clothing at a time. She tossed her police hat; it spiraled like a Frisbee and then landed directly on my face. I wanted to move it, but my arms were tied. I almost asked her to, but I remembered her threat and desperately wanted to be the one to do the spanking. I had never been spanked, and the thought of it didn't turn me on. Spanking her, however, was a treat I couldn't pass up.

Luckily, it wasn't long before the hat was lifted from my face, and Ashley was dancing above me, naked.

Moments later, my pants were off and I was inside her at last. It felt a little strange, having sex while my arms were handcuffed to a bed, but the splendid thrusts of her athletic body moving up and down on mine took my mind off the handcuffs.

"Your turn," she said sweetly, removing the cuffs. As soon

as my hands were free, I flipped her over, forcefully throwing her legs behind her head. I had never felt so powerful and turned on; the built-up longing to touch her while I was cuffed exploded out of me, and I had new found confidence. Suddenly, I realized why she had restrained me.

In all my relationships, I'd had sex and I'd fucked, but I had never made love. I hadn't known the difference before. The difference wasn't how it was done, it was the feelings that were involved. They were unimaginably powerful. I would gladly go another five years having mediocre sex, or even no sex, if I knew I could have passionate sex just one more time. Luckily for me, that summer was filled with steamy, loving, needy, and kinky sex.

After giving her a delightful spanking, it was my turn to leave the room. A few uncomfortable minutes passed, while I stood at the door, naked with an erection. Then I heard Ashley call, "You may enter."

She was seated behind her desk, in a business suit and short plain heels. Her hair was in a simple braid; she wore reading glasses, and appeared to be engrossed in a novel.

"I suppose I should have dressed better," I said awkwardly, standing in front of her naked.

"No. You're dressed perfectly. I cancelled all of my meetings. Come help me into the same outfit you've got on," she said, placing her book down and walking around to the front of the desk.

I lunged at her, and she met me halfway in a luscious embrace. My hands shook from lack of sleep and the come down from the drugs, but I couldn't feel them. Hungrily I removed her business suit, glasses, and heels, and hoisted her naked body up onto her desk, pushing its contents onto the floor. She wrapped her legs around me, and we made love for hours.

Molly, like heroin, makes it hard to come, but I finally released myself into her, collapsing from my orgasm. We fell to the floor panting, de-clothed and intertwined.

"I love you," she breathed, and I said it back. For a precious moment, opiates were banished from my thoughts. Leaving our mess of outfits strewn across the floor, we finally climbed into bed just an hour before sunrise.

I dreaded sleep, because I knew it would not come to me without the help of some type of substance. Sitting up alone, I pounding beer after beer and admiring Ashley's soft tanned body and beautiful face as she peacefully slept. I took some melatonin, a supplement that was supposed to naturally induce slumber. Ashley had bought it for me, hoping it would help me conquer my insomnia, but it was no match. I felt more connected to her than to any other human being on the face of the planet, but there was still a huge barrier between us. I feared my addiction would drive us apart.

I switched the music on Ashley's phone. "You love me, but you don't know who I am. So let me go, let me go." The lyrics ate away at my subconscious as I stroked Ashley's hair. She smiled in her sleep. I desperately didn't want to let her go. I wished I could have her and heroin, but I knew I had to choose.

Ashley was the healthiest addiction I had ever had, although she didn't come close to heroin. The sex was phenomenal.

Her kinky tendencies and love for role playing, combined with brains, cooking skills, and love for the outdoors, were a dream come true—but heroin was better than a thousand orgasms.

# CHAPTER FOURTEEN:
## Relapse

Summer sadly came to an end, and Ashley returned to Arelington College to complete her final semester. She had double majored in marketing and public relations, which resulted in her taking an extra semester to complete a second internship. She also resumed her bartending job at one of the local sports bars a few nights a week. I was devastated. Ashley kept my opiate cravings at bay. She was my anti-opiate serum, and I knew the more time I spent away from her, the more likely I was to give in to the tempting force of my addiction. I should have started to look for a photography or web design job and thrown myself into work, but I was scared. Remembering how quickly I had failed the last time I had a full time job, I didn't want to commit to a serious career until I was positive I wouldn't return to using opiates. I doubted that such a time would ever exist.

During that fabulous summer, I had been with Ashley every second of every day, with the exception of rehab. My addiction to her, paired with alcohol, MDMA, Adderall, and benzos, had kept me distracted from my own mind, entertained, and more at ease with life than I had been in years. The people I had surrounded myself with were mostly Ashley's friends (and she had many), but they all went back to school or pursued full time careers when that summer came to an end. I was left alone.

Ashley pushed me to apply for jobs or to even post a Craigslist ad to see if I could score any freelance photography gigs, but I convinced her to let me have one more year of fun before committing myself to a full time career. I washed dishes at a restaurant a few blocks from Ashley's apartment a couple days a week so I could have some cash of my own. Ashley had been letting me live at her place for free. She paid for everything for us, which made me feel like shit, but not bad enough to get my act together and send out my resume.

Time alone is a horrible thing for a recovering addict. As soon as Ashley got up to go to class, I would hit up everyone in my phone to chill. Unfortunately, the only people who responded were the junkies. Everyone else had something better to do on a Monday at eight in the morning than kick back a few cold ones.

One of the responses was from Amanda, a girl I used to hang out with in high school. She was one of my long time custys who I hadn't spoken to in a while. She didn't know I was clean. It wouldn't have mattered if she had known; I am sure she would have asked me for the dreaded favor anyway. Addicts quickly get to a point where they don't care who they use in front of.

"Ryan! Yes! Let's hang out! Beers on me if you help me bang out." Staring at the text on my screen, I knew I shouldn't reply. Being around someone who was on opiates would be torture enough, but actually tying her arm off and poking the needle into her skin was dangerous territory. I felt goosebumps rise up on my arms, despite the warm fall temperature.

A tingling of excitement shot up my spine as I typed back, "Sure, come over, I'm at Ashley's spot."

The phone rang, and I jumped up in surprise. It was Amanda, calling for directions. Of course. How could I have expected her to know where Ashley's spot was? We hadn't seen each other in years, and she'd never been friends with Ashley.

Anticipating Amanda's arrival, I paced around the apartment, knowing Ashley wouldn't be pleased if she ever found out I drank with a girl in her house while she was in class. Thanking God she didn't have roommates, I dug my power hour CD out of my car and grabbed two of Ashley's shot glasses from the kitchen. My hands shook with excitement and fear. Just the thought of being in the same room with opiates provoked inexplicable feelings of burning desire—longing, wanting, needing.

After what seemed like an eternity, Amanda arrived at Ashley's front door, droopy eyed and faded.

"Did you do it yourself?" I asked, opening the door.

"No, man! I need you to do it. I'm too scared still, I just started shooting. I snorted one on my way over, to kick the withdrawal." She smirked, holding up a bottle of miscellaneous pills and shaking it in front of my face.

"Let me see that. How did you get all these?" I asked, my pulse quickening from touching the orange bottle, sans label. Anyone who sells their script knows to peel off the label, to avoid getting caught for distribution. This bottle was a collection of various wonderful drugs. I spotted the Dilaudid right away, some were 2s and some were 10s. I gazed in wonderment at her glorious collection. Placing them down on the table, I thanked God I couldn't afford one, since I hadn't gotten my first paycheck from the restaurant yet. Snatching up the beer Amanda had bought for me, I cracked it open, downing the entire thing in a matter of seconds. It was a bad idea. I couldn't be around these delicious drugs without doing them. I wondered if Amanda would notice if I snagged one. Maybe she would even give me one for helping her shoot up.

"Got them all for free. I work at a nursing home, and they leave scripts lying around all the time. There is also this trash bin, where you're supposed to discard any drugs that are no longer needed or fell on the floor or whatever, and I take from that daily. It's amazing!" she gushed, almost stopping my heart. Had I heard right? She'd gotten the pills for free.

"Do you want one?" she offered before I could even ask. Ashley's disappointed face flashed before me, but I held out my hand.

"Do you have a clean needle?" I felt a pang of guilt as I uttered the words. The past few months were the longest stretch of time I had ever gone without opiates since the beginning of my addiction. Was I really going to break my clean streak?

"I will go right back to being clean after this one time, and Ashley will never know," I thought to myself. Craving the temporary relief of getting high blurred my vision of the future consequences. I resented my constant battle with anxiety. I needed to feel the welcoming relief from pain, the sense of control and warming calmness to distract myself from my own mind.

"I just picked up some new needles at the exchange today," Amanda said, proudly extracting them from her purse with a few other miscellaneous items. "I just need a spoon; do you have one I can borrow?"

"Ashley has spoons in the kitchen. I'll go grab one, but you'll have to take it with you. I'm sure she would notice the burn marks on the bottom and question the shit out of me if I put it back." I jumped up and ran to the kitchen, trying to recall a time in my life where I was more excited about anything. I couldn't.

Savoring every moment, I crushed up the precious pills and mixed them with water in the spoon. Every part of the process aroused me. Amanda demanded that I take care of her first, because she wasn't sure how messed up I would be after injecting myself, given that I had been clean for months. Thinking back now, I wonder if she felt any guilt or remorse about enabling and even encouraging me to enter back down the dark path of addiction.

I assume she just wanted me to join her, with no regard for my future or health. Addicts don't like to be alone. They don't specifically aim to bring others down with them, but they enjoy the camaraderie of indulging in their bad habits with others, and prefer it to using alone or in front of someone who is not. She didn't apologize, and at the time I didn't expect her to, but I fiercely resent her for it now.

I secured her pink belt tightly around her thin bicep, restricting blood circulation and causing her thick beautiful veins to bulge out of her arm. Swiftly, I filtered the solution through a small piece of cotton into the syringe and poked it into her vein. It was so easy to hit. I could tell she hadn't been shooting up long, and I was envious. Even during my months of sobriety, I would catch myself admiring the veins of strangers, wishing mine were as prominent as they used to be. I felt a slight pop as her skin broke, letting the needle through and causing her body to go limp with relaxation. I hurried to remove the belt from her semi-conscious body and fasten it to my own arm; the only thoughts in my mind were of getting high. I could think of nothing else, not even that Ashley's last class for the day was scheduled to end in a half an hour, and college courses frequently ended early.

I must have been in a daze for at least twenty minutes. Ashley's car pulling into the driveway woke me with a jolt. I clumsily swiped the drug paraphernalia from the coffee table into Amanda's purse. She was still zoned on the couch, her eyes fluttering open and closed. I had to get her out of there.

"Amanda, wake the fuck up," I hissed.

She struggled to lift her eyelids, tilted her head, and said, "You're welcome, Ryan. That was some pretty good shit, and you're not being very grateful."

"Thanks, but Ashley's here; you have to get out of here, now!" I dragged her weak body off of the couch and quickly ushered her toward the door.

"Text me later. Ashley can't find out about this," I mandated, waving farewell just in time. I heard the backdoor fling open, and simultaneously shut the front door behind Amanda. If Ashley had seen Amanda, she would have immediately been suspicious that I had relapsed and possibly even cheated. That was the last thing I wanted. Unwelcome at my parents' house because of Don's resentment for my addiction, I would have been out of a place to live if Ashley had kicked me out.

"Ryan! I'm home! What a long class, I really hope you don't want to drink tonight!" she shouted as she entered the house. I walked over to meet her, giving her a dopey smile and warm hug.

"You look happy," she said, studying me with a quizzical look.

"I'm just glad you don't have to work tonight. I can't stand being alone. If you don't want to drink, we don't have to. Let's get some ice cream and watch Netflix," I said, joyfully taking in her shocked grin.

Staying clean from opiates was a constant struggle, and I had guilted Ashley into drinking, doing molly, and taking Adderall with me on almost a nightly basis. She was drained and wanted to stop. Ashley craved sobriety like I craved drugs; it was mindboggling. Unable to understand how she was sick of getting drunk nightly, I begged and begged her to join in. I didn't want to be drunk around her alone, because I thought I would embarrass myself, but on opiates everything was different. I felt relaxed and energized. For the first time in months, I knew I was going to get a good night sleep. Withdrawal didn't even cross my mind, because I didn't think it would be that bad after a single use.

After a quick trip to the supermarket and a home-cooked meal, Ashley and I lay in bed cuddling. We split our two favorite kinds of Ben and Jerry's ice cream and watched the show Weeds on Netflix.

"I don't understand why you won't let me sell weed. I hate

weed now, haven't smoked in years, and wouldn't even want to smoke it. I could make so much money and buy you things." I nagged Ashley time and time again to let me sell in my spare time. Watching a show about marijuana dealing reminded me of how much I had enjoyed the life of a drug salesman. I understood why she wouldn't let me sell harder stuff. She was worried I would get addicted, and she didn't want scumbag addicts around her house, but weed was harmless. Selling it would help take my mind off of the anxiety, and the money would be nice.

"Ryan, I love how sweet you are, but I don't need things and I don't need money. What would make me happy is to see you get a job you enjoy in web design or photography, staying away from drugs altogether. You could help out with rent and start a career you that makes you happy; don't you want to do that?" She wasn't budging.

I flinched a little as she added, "As long as you're not getting high, I don't see why you would even need the extra money. Because of me, you live for free."

Luckily, she didn't notice, and I decided to drop the subject. I couldn't risk upsetting her and having her find out I was high.

"Okay, I'm sorry. I love you, kid," I said, sweetly smiling up at her and then nuzzling my face into her neck. She smiled back, laughing at me for calling her kid when she was the more responsible one, and shut off the computer. We finished our ice cream and drifted to sleep.

My much needed slumber was rudely interrupted by aggressive pain all too soon. Ashley was rising for a full day of courses followed by a night shift at the bar, and I didn't have any plans until I was scheduled for dishwashing at the restaurant at two in the afternoon. I had wanted to sleep the day away, but the pain was intolerable.

"Why am I withdrawing from opiates? I only shot up once!" My angry thoughts screamed at me, inquiring what I had gotten myself into.

"Have a good day, babe, I love you," Ashley said, sweetly kissing me on the cheek. "I'm so glad you slept last night; you fell asleep before me, it was amazing! I'm so happy for you," she included, adding piercing guilt to the physical pain stabbing me in the abdomen.

"Uhhhhhh," was all I could muster as a reply. I felt like death.

"Are you okay, cutie?" she asked, concerned with my response. I had to make her believe I was fine. If she knew I had slept and then felt sick, she would instantly know I had gone back to drugs. Ashley had a lot of experience with addiction from watching her father and brother suffer before their deaths. I kept forgetting she wasn't an easy girl to trick.

"I'm fine, just tired; have a good day." I struggled to get the words out and buried my head deep into the pillow, mentally willing her to leave so I could text Amanda.

As soon as I heard the door slam shut, I reached for my phone.

"Come over now. Need help. Desperate," I painstakingly typed out. After a few minutes with no response, I sent out a mass text to everyone I knew in Vermont who might possibly have had opiates of any kind.

My phone flooded with an overwhelming number of

responses. It was so easy to get opiates, easier than buying cigarettes or even gum, because a lot of dealers would deliver to your car, work, or doorstep. My only problem was lack of cash. I had to go into work to get my paycheck.

Arriving at work a little early to pick up my check, I planned to tell my manager I was sick and unable to work.

"Our lunch rush has extended into the afternoon, the dishes are piling up. We really need you. You clearly feel well enough to get your paycheck, so you must feel well enough to work. I will let you out early, but we really need you right now. If you want to keep your job, help us through this rush and then you can go."

My manager's words chopped through my heart like a dagger. I had been living in hell since I had woken up, and I couldn't stand the thought of a few more hours of this torment. I almost walked out with my paycheck, but I knew Ashley would investigate the reason I lost my job. I feared she would discover my relapse, so I reluctantly slunk back to the dish pit. After about twenty minutes, I had a revolutionary idea. I waited until a cute little server was mucking off her dishes so I would have a witness, and pretended to slip and fall.

"Ouch! My back!" I yelled, grasping my spine and pretending I was unable to move from the floor.

The server ran to get my manager, who decided I was allowed to go home.

Finally! I had the money for drugs and freedom at last! I limped from the restaurant, clutching my back for emphasis. Extracting my cell phone from my pocket, I had to decide which of my numerous connects I could cop a bun from. I didn't want to get more than one bag of heroin. I still wanted to find some subs and get clean again before Ashley found out, but I told myself I could just sell the rest or use it for backup if needed. My gut told me it would all be needed. The first text I read was from Amanda.

"Sorry I didn't respond earlier. Seth has this shit called TNT. It's fire. You have to try it. Heroin mixed with fentanyl. So potent, you only need a tiny bit to get high."

Disregarding the other twenty some odd responses in my phone, I quickly answered her.

"Word. Let's meet up now. I need to get down."

The sound of my heart pounding in my chest was unnervingly loud as I rushed to meet Amanda at Seth's house, rolling through stop signs, running red lights, and only stopping to quickly cash my paycheck. I didn't know much about fentanyl, but I did know it was used for chronic pain and would delightfully and dangerously enhance the effects of heroin.

My Subaru screeched to a halt in front of Seth's place, and I bolted to his cracked open door.

"Sup, buddy?" I entered without knocking and made my way over to join Seth on the couch. His longtime girlfriend, Mary, was huddled up on the loveseat with a needle protruding from her arm. Looking up in a silent greeting, he motioned for me to sit. Seth was faded every day of the week, but today he looked particularly out of it. I returned my gaze to Mary, who still hadn't moved. She looked a little different, but I couldn't put a finger on how.

"What's up with Mary, bro, she alive?" Despite my desperate

urge to focus on getting my fix, I felt a little weird getting down while a possibly dead friend was just across the room.

"Naw, she's good. She's pregnant, so the shit hits her harder," he mumbled.

"Pregnant? What the fuck!" I was in shock. Seth couldn't even take care of himself; how was he going to take care of a baby? My moral compass was quite off track because I'd been blinded by my compulsion to get high, but even I was worried about the unborn baby inside Mary—and I hated babies. Seth didn't seem concerned. The poor innocent child was going to be born addicted to opiates, if it survived to that point. Was that what Seth wanted for his son or daughter, or was he so gone he hadn't even put that together? Thoughts rushed through my head, and I thanked God I wasn't going to bring a child into this fucked up world any time soon. I knew that if I did, Ashley would give it the best care humanly possible, even if I was a deadbeat dad. I shuddered, shaking the thoughts from my cluttered brain. I wanted to be a father someday, if I could get my shit together, but right now I just wanted to get high.

After handing Seth one hundred dollars, basically my entire paycheck, I stashed nine of the bags and opened the tenth with trembling fingers. Seth was my boy; one hundred dollars was a deal on a bun in Vermont. If I could travel back to NYC like the old days, I could get it cheaper, but the markup wasn't nearly as profitable as oxys had been, and I had lost contact with Black when they stopped making 80's. Since I had been back in Vermont, Ashley had filled my time with exciting and alluring non-opiate activities, so the thought of traveling to NYC to see if

I could find any heroin connects hadn't crossed my mind. I flirted with the idea as I gleefully watched the murky brown powder enter the syringe through the tiny cotton filter that prepped it for my waiting vein. There was no way I would be able to pull off trips to NYC without Ashley knowing, and our relationship would inevitably end. I decided against it. I could push dope small time here, and hopefully turn enough of a profit to feed my habit without Ashley noticing. That was, if I couldn't wean myself off of heroin with subs again.

My vein gave a glorious pop as the needle entered, and warm fuzzy clouds hugged my body and soul. The world around me drifted into a perfect blur of blissful calamity. I had no problems, no worries, no fear. Flitting in and out of consciousness, I enjoyed a breathtaking high.

Three hours had passed when I finally came to. Mary was stirring and had removed the needle from her arm (either that or it had fallen); I spotted it resting in a tiny pool of blood on the floor beneath the loveseat. Seth was still in a daze. I wasn't sure if he had shot up again since I had been there. Three hours had flown by!

I looked up with a jolt as the door flung open unexpectedly. The noise momentarily brought Seth back to consciousness, and I was startled to see Will standing at the door. He cringed when he noticed me, and addressed only Seth, requesting some dope. He was a shadow of himself, with baggy and torn clothes; I almost didn't recognize him as the same Will who had joined me on so many carefree trips to NYC in college and braved the sketchiest terrain on the mountain back in the good old snowboarding days. I desperately wanted to know why he had such a problem with me, but his body language made it clear it wasn't up for discussion.

Seth handed him a bag, and he sat down on the couch, as far as he could get from me. Then gathered a spoon, cotton, water, and syringe without so much as glancing in my direction. Seth slumped back over, nodding out, and I closed my eyes, drinking in the relaxation. I'm not sure how much time passed, but it only seemed like a few seconds before I felt Seth shaking me.

"Ryan, look at Will. I think he's fucking dead."

His words pulled me out of my happy place, a womb-like bliss, into the harsh real world. Weakly pulling myself off the couch, I froze, staring at Will. He was foaming at the mouth, or maybe he just vomited on himself a bit—I couldn't tell which. His eyes were a dull lifeless grey, and his lips and fingertips were blue.

"Will! Wake up! What the fuck!" I shouted, shaking his corpse-like body. He made no movements.

"We've got to get him to the hospital," I urged Seth, who looked at me skeptically. I lifted up one of his arms; it was heavy and cold. There was no way I could carry him to my car solo. I dropped the arm, and gravity pulled it quickly back to the couch with a lifeless thud. Now I started shaking Seth.

"Dude. He's either dead or he's going to die in your house. He's our friend; we need to get him help, or at least get him the fuck out of here!" I was now shouting at Seth, which roused groggy, pregnant Mary. She looked up at us silently and then dozed back off.

"Too bad I don't have any Narcan," Seth grumbled, reluctantly helping me drag Seth to my Impreza.

"What's Narcan?" I inquired, struggling as we stuffed Will's limp body in the backseat of my car. I slammed the door and hopped in the driver's seat, demanding Seth come with me.

"It's a life saver. Narcan reverses opiate effects and brings people back to life when they've gone over the edge. If he has overdosed, it's what the hospital will use to save his life. It would be handy to keep some around, but it's not as easy to get as dope. Rumor has it that they just started handing it out at the needle exchange, but I haven't been in a while and I never really thought I would need it," Seth mumbled, glancing behind us. Will's eerily still body tumbled off the backseat and onto the floor as I careened around a bend in the road.

The light up ahead turned yellow; I could make it if I sped. Praying there wasn't a cop at the intersection, I drove the gas pedal to the floor, just barely making the light. We'd have been screwed if we got pulled over. Ashley would have been so upset and disappointed if she ever found out this happened. She would have broken up with me, kicked me out, and my family would have stopped talking to me, for sure. Things at home had just started to get better. My mother was beside herself with joy that I had completed rehab, was dating Ashley, and had gotten hired at the restaurant. Tim had started to hang out with Ashley and me a good deal, and even my stepfather and I had a few decent conversations lately. I was risking ruining everything, but with a dying friend, I didn't really have a choice. I suppose I could have just left Seth's. Had he been a stranger, I would have, but I knew

Seth wasn't going to take him to the hospital. He would have died for sure, if he wasn't dead already anyway.

Minutes later, I sped up to the emergency room entrance of the local hospital, bypassing every parking spot and slamming on the breaks right in front of the hospital door.

"Put your hood on and help me get Will out of the backseat, there are probably cameras," I instructed Seth, rushing out of the car and yanking on Will's lifeless limbs. With Seth's assistance, I was able to discharge Will from the rear seat in a matter of seconds. We left him lying on the ground, jumped back into the car, and hauled ass out of there.

"Thank God silver Imprezas are really common around here and I didn't have my front license plate on. I really hope that's not on the news," I gushed to Seth, who seemed like he could really care less.

"I don't need the heat on me. Let's just get back," he said, never looking me in the eye or showing any emotion. Glancing in the rearview, I saw a group of people in hospital scrubs rush outside and gather over Will's withered body. I hoped he would be okay; then again, he hadn't spoken to me in years. He had some sort of drug-related grudge against me, so his fate didn't concern me too much; at least I had tried to help.

My phone buzzed in my pocket. It was Ashley.

"Hi," it read, with a picture of peanuts from the bar arranged in the shape of a smiley face. I grinned; I loved that girl so much. She was bored at work, sending me cute smiley face photos, and I was off dragging a possibly dead body to the emergency room and defying her wishes in more ways than one.

"No opiates and no needles and I will never leave you." Her words stung my subconscious, accompanied by pangs of guilt; I brushed it off, readily welcoming another spoonful of brown powder upon returning to Seth's. After my stressful afternoon, all I wanted to do was fade away.

Hours passed as Seth and I sat in silence, nodding out on the couch. Eventually, as my eyes drifted open, I could make out a knot in the wooden table that resembled the shape of a heart. Snapping a picture on my smartphone, I sent it back to Ashley with a text message heart emoji. I was hours late, but at least I'd responded. I was prepared to use the "I didn't want to bother you while you were working" excuse, if she asked why it took so long for me to get back to her text.

The daytime hours had slipped away, and I could see the moon shining outside Seth's window. I knew Ashley wouldn't be home from work until after two in the morning, when the bars closed, so even though it was late, I had time. Seth rose and meandered to the kitchen, returning with two beers. Just what I needed.

"Awesome. Thanks, man," I said, popping the top of the cold Corona with my lighter. As I sipped the beer, the crisp taste brought me momentarily back to the night at my Virginia apartment in the hot tub with Ashley. I longed to go back so I could relive the past summer. It was the only time during my young adult life that I was actually able to have fun and interact with people my own age, instead of constantly chasing the high and running from withdrawal. I missed it. I shouldn't have turned back to heroin, but with Ashley away, the cravings were too intense. I was lost without her loving distraction.

"Because I'm stronger on my own." Lyrics, followed by the womp, womp of dubstep music, sounded through Seth's speakers as we sipped our beers. I was stronger on my own, because, without Ashley, heroin was with me. When I was alone with heroin, I was the most powerful, carefree person alive.

"What's up, bitches!" The slurred voice of Sean, a high school classmate, broke my thoughts. He entered Seth's miniscule apartment just as we all had, without knocking. I wondered if everyone coming in was so concentrated on getting high that they forgot to knock, or if they just expected Seth to be so faded they would have to let themselves in anyway, so there wasn't a point in knocking. It was probably a little bit of both.

I hadn't even known Sean and Seth knew each other. Sean and I had never been friends, but we were in the same classes in school for as far back as I could remember. I'd met Seth through friends of my first girlfriend Layla. Sean had a beer in his hand that clearly wasn't his first.

"I heard you got some fire shit. TNT or something? I wanna try that shit now, man," he slurred to Seth.

"Damn. Good news travels fast; how much you want?" Seth smiled, pulling a few bags out from under the couch cushions for Sean to inspect.

"Just a ticket. That's all I can afford for now, but word on the street is that's all you need." I could barely make out his slurred speech. Seth didn't appear concerned that he was stumbling over his words, and gladly sold him a ticket.

"Don't do it here, bro. We've already had one hospital visit, I don't need another one," Seth warned.

"Whatever, I don't care if I die. I want to die anyway. I'm so sick of this bullshit of a life. Every day withdrawal, no money, lies, hurt, pain, suffering, want to see my son, not allowed, can't, why," he rambled on and on, placing the bag in his pocket.

"Dude, I don't think you should do that tonight. You're too fucked up, and that shit's strong," I echoed Seth's warning. Sean promised he would refrain from taking it until he was sober, but kept saying over and over that he didn't care if he died and didn't know why we were so concerned.

"I'm out. Party at Jeremy's, you fuckers wanna join?" he slurred, stumbling to the door. I wondered how he was going to get to Jeremy's; a party sounded appealing. With a head nod to Seth, who was helping Mary tie off her arm again, I stepped out into the night with Sean to check out whatever was going on at Jeremy's house. God forbid I stayed at Seth's and was there when his pregnant girlfriend overdosed, which I figured was bound to happen.

I wasn't sure if Sean had walked over to Seth's or if his ride had abandoned him, but it was a good thing for him that I had decided to join him on his quest. It was too far for someone who was clearly blackout drunk to walk on his own. Sean stumbled over himself and nearly fell twice getting into my passenger seat.

I felt my phone ringing in my pocket, and prayed it wasn't Ashley saying she was out early. I dug it out and checked the name on the screen. Amanda. Shit, Amanda was supposed to meet me at Seth's hours ago. I had completely forgotten!

"Ryan! You're alive!" Her troubled voice sounded muffled through the phone.

"Of course I'm alive, Amanda. Where are you and why didn't you meet me at Seth's?"

"I was going to! I decided to snort some of that TNT before heading over, and I just woke up!" she exclaimed. She rattled on and on about how good it was, but said she probably would have died if she had shot it. Eventually, she hung up, but only after begging me for a ride to Jeremy's party.

Changing my course, I headed back into town to get Amanda. She was only a few minutes out of the way.

"Dude, I can't believe you shot that shit and lived!" Amanda was still in awe as she hopped in the backseat of my Impreza, giving me a quizzical look and greeting Sean as she entered. She knew who Sean was from high school, but she clearly hadn't been expecting him to be hanging out with me.

"I picked him up at Seth's; he's the one who told me Jeremy was having a party," I explained.

"Party, don't care if I die," Sean grunted from the front passenger seat.

Ignoring him, I turned to the back to face Amanda as we came to a red light.

"That TNT shit is fire, you were right. Seth and I got so faded off booting just a tiny bit, but it almost killed Will." I launched into a detailed recounting of the earlier evening's events. Amanda's jaw dropped in horror when I told her we had left Will at the ER doors and bolted.

"What else could we do? Stay with him and get busted?" I inquired. She shrugged and agreed I had a point.

We arrived at Jeremy's parents' large house, which was

guarded by trees and a beautifully landscaped lawn. Jeremy still lived with his folks, in an affluent development. They traveled a lot, so he threw a lot of parties. They were usually ragers, but when I pulled up to the house, there were only a few cars scattered along the driveway. Sean sat up straighter and squinted his eyes.

"Bullshit party, where is everyone?" he muttered, climbing out of the car.

I followed him reluctantly, with Amanda behind me. Jeremy was nice, but not one of my close friends, and as far as I knew he wasn't into opiates. His brother used to sell oxys back in the good old days, but, to my knowledge, neither of them used. If I was going to spend my evening sitting on a couch, I would have preferred to do it at Seth's, where I could have shot up in the open if I so wished.

Glancing at my phone, I saw it was already almost one in the morning; Ashley would be out soon.

"I might as well just hang here and have a few beers 'til she texts me," I thought to myself, ringing the doorbell with Sean and Amanda by my sides. Sean was good friends with Jeremy, and I'm fairly sure Jeremy knew about his struggle with drinking and opiates. He didn't look particularly pleased when he opened the door and saw the three of us standing before him.

Sean said nothing, hit him on the shoulder, and entered the house.

"Hey, man, Sean said you were having a party and he needed a ride, so we brought him over. We can head out, if you want?" I greeted Jeremy with caution, not wanting to upset him in case his parents were home.

"Naw, it's all good. Come on in. I was going to throw a rager, but my mom called and said they'd be home early in the morning. I didn't want passed out kids and beer cans strewn all over the house. There's just a few of us chillin'; you're welcome to stay for a little bit." He opened the door wider, motioning for us to step in.

We heard a cheer as we entered the house.

"We're watching football. We TiVo'd the game from earlier because none of us got to watch it; do you want a beer?" he generously offered, motioning to a fridge full of Heineken, Corona, Magic Hat, and various other brands. I grabbed a Long Trail Triple Bag because it had the highest alcohol content, thanked Jeremy, and chose a chair in the living room.

Football wasn't my thing, but drinking free beer was. I cracked open the top with my lighter and took a sip. Ashley had recently been questioning why I carried lighters.

"If you're not smoking cigarettes or doing drugs, why do you need a lighter?" I could hear her question again and again, never satisfied by my answers, "To light candles, start fires, or open beer."

I couldn't wait until Ashley was out of work and I could snuggle up in bed with her, but I was dreading the morning. Even though I had a decent stash in my car, I was worried about how I was going to shoot up in the morning without Ashley finding out. There were two bathrooms in her apartment, but neither of the doors locked. Ashley would frequently walk in when I was in the bathroom, and I knew she would question me if I told her to stay out.

"Hey, where'd Sean go?" Jeremy asked, coming back from the kitchen with another beer.

"Bathroom, I think," Amanda replied, without looking up from the television. She was into football and wanted to see the outcome of the game.

"He went to the bathroom almost an hour ago. I thought he left. I'm going to go check and make sure he's okay, he was pretty drunk," Jeremy thought out loud, heading off in the direction of the closest bathroom.

My droopy eyes lifted a bit when I heard Jeremy pounding on the bathroom door from down the hallway.

"Sean, open up! You've been in there a long time, are you okay? If you don't come out, I'm kicking this door down!" he hollered, hitting the door with his fist harder and harder. Rising in a daze from where I had sat lost in thoughts of Ashley, I started to piece together what was going on. I should have immediately known when Jeremy said Sean had been in the bathroom for nearly an hour. Shit.

"Can someone go outside, around back, and look in the bathroom window? I don't want to kick my parents' door in unless it's a real emergency. He could just be passed out drunk," Jeremy requested in a panic. Without hesitation, I slipped my shoes on and darted around the back of Jeremy's house. Dragging a patio chair over to the window, I boosted myself up and peered in.

My insides hardened with guilt and regret. Sean had mentioned not caring if he lived or died, and I had let him out of my sight, wasted, with Seth's potent heroin. He had said he wasn't going to use it until morning, but I should have known better. Trusting a drunk junkie is one of the most deadly mistakes one can make. I felt bile run up my throat; without warning, it shot out of my mouth and ran down the dark green siding on Jeremy's house. I was glad no one had joined me outside.

Looking at Sean, I was almost certain he was deceased. I left the patio chair where it was and rushed back inside, trying to push out the image of his lifeless body flopped over in front of the bathroom door. The needle, still in his arm, was visible from the window, and he was white as a ghost. The floor was covered with what appeared to be a mixture of puke and blood. With a weak stomach and shaky legs, I pushed past Jeremy, extracted my driver's license from my wallet, and briskly carded the door. Jeremy looked at me in shock as it popped open an inch and then stopped.

"Call 911," I said, leaning all of my weight against the door to open it enough to let myself in. Although unlocking it with my ID had been a breeze, Sean's weight was a substantial force for my brittle limbs to fight against. Amanda and the few others who were still there helped me open the door while Jeremy dialed 911.

Frantically, I checked Sean's pulse. There was none. He wasn't breathing.

I felt a buzz in my pocket. Ashley.

Her text read, "Closing the bar now. Leaving in five mins. Love you, babe, can't wait to snuggle," complete with smiley face and a heart.

Fighting the urge to vomit again, I grabbed Amanda, and

hastily apologized to Jeremy. We raced to my car before the cops and rescue team arrived.

"Shit. Sean's dead. I shouldn't have let him take that dope from Seth! I had to get out of there. Sorry for making you leave so quickly, but I can't risk being around when help arrives, Ashley might find out. I'm sure it's going to be all over the news." I was rambling, but it was the only way I could deal with what had just happened. Seeing someone I'd known for years dead before my eyes was different than witnessing the death of some stripper I barely knew. The drug problem in our town was spiraling out of control, and I was caught right up in the middle of it.

"It's all good. My mom is already on my ass, thinking I'm doing drugs. I don't want people knowing I was there either. I'm glad you're my ride home and I had an excuse to leave. Guess I won't be shooting the rest of this stuff, just snorting it," she said.

We drove for a few minutes in silence, and I flinched when we had to pull over to let an ambulance go screaming by. It was undoubtedly headed for Jeremy's house, to attempt to revive Sean.

"How did you get out of working today anyway?" Amanda asked, changing the subject in a failed attempt to distract us both from the reality of Sean's death. I launched into a detailed explanation of my fake slip and fall, and Amanda responded with a fabulous idea.

"You should get workmen's comp. Then you will get paid for being out injured, and you won't even have to work."

I couldn't believe I hadn't thought of this myself. When I was in rehab, I had heard stories of other addicts pretending to slip and fall at work, so they could get paid and not have to work for their money. We reached Amanda's house, and she agreed to help me with the paperwork for worker's compensation the following day. The only problem was that this meant I had to tell Ashley I hurt myself. Lying to Ashley was not something I wanted to do, but it was better than telling her the truth. If I told her the truth, she would leave me, and I would be devastated.

My stomach filled with anxious butterflies as I neared Ashley's apartment. Speeding up the hill and into her driveway, I kept my eyes peeled for her car. A wave of relief washed over me when I realized I had indeed beaten her home. I was not in the mood to explain my whereabouts, and I had to pretend I had a hurt back.

Letting myself into Ashley's apartment, I rushed up the stairs and stashed some heroin and supplies to shoot up way behind shampoo, hair straighteners, a blow drier, and various other things she had under her bathroom sink. Then I changed into sweat pants, took off my shirt, cracked a beer I'd taken from Jeremy's fridge, and slipped into Ashley's bed. I took care to leave only her light blue heart-shaped nightlight glowing next to the bed. I didn't want her to examine me when she arrived. I feared she would notice the subtle track mark on my arm, or make me look from the light to the dark and back again to see if my pupils changed size. For a minute, I thought about pretending I was asleep, but I knew that would raise a red flag. Even though it was nearing three thirty in the morning, I never slept sober, and Ashley knew it.

A few minutes later, she flounced into her bedroom, look-ing as cute as ever in her tight jeans and skimpy bartender top. I sipped my beer and greeted her, noting silently how lucky I was that she hadn't arrived any earlier. The night would have turned out very differently if she'd beaten me home.

"I'm so glad you're not begging me to drink with you. I'm exhausted," she said, stripping out of her clothes and joining me in bed. When I was clean, I needed Ashley to drink whenever I did, but now that I was enjoying the lingering effects of the miraculous heroin Seth had sold me, I could causally sip a beer without asking her to drink, no problem. I finished my beer and reached over Ashley's bare chest to place it on her bedside table. My heart lurched when she grabbed my arm.

"What is that?" she asked in an accusatory tone, pointing to a tiny red bump professionally lined up over one of the veins on my arm.

"I don't know," I said, scratching at it with feigned confusion.

"Don't act like you don't know. I've been watching it for a few days, and it hasn't gone away. I really hope you're not shooting up, Ryan." Adding my name at the end for emphasis, she gave me a worried yet hopeful glance.

"I'm not. It will probably go away soon. Don't worry. If I was shooting up, don't you think I'd try to hide it a little more? There are plenty of places I could shoot up that would be far less obvious. It's probably just a skin irritation." My response seemed to satisfy her tired mind, but I knew I was going to have to be more careful; she was going to investigate, for sure.

The next morning, I was rudely awakened by the loud buzzing of Ashley's cell phone on the bedside table, combined with a fierce onset of opiate withdrawal.

"Damn, I do not miss this. Thank God I stashed some stuff in the bathroom," I thought to myself, using every ounce of energy I had in my feeble body to rise from Ashley's bed and head toward the bathroom. I hoped her phone would distract her and she wouldn't come to see what I was doing, but the flu-like symptoms were hitting me so hard, I didn't care about anything but feeling better, even if it was at risk of getting caught.

"Oh my God!" I heard Ashley exclaim through the paper thin walls, as I injected the murky mixture into a more discrete vein in between my toes while leaning on the bathroom door to prevent her from possibly entering. By the tone in her voice, I could tell she had discovered something important. The next thing she would do was find me to share it with; she told me everything. Clumsily, I rushed to clean up my mess, washing off the spoon I had taken from Ashley's kitchen and hiding my stash beneath the sink for a second time. Thankfully, she had many spoons of all shapes and sizes, and had not noticed any missing.

I glanced at myself in the mirror. My pupils were pinned, my eyes droopy. I looked faded—there was no way around it—but the afflictive feelings of withdrawal had been lifted, and I was feeling good. Splashing some water on my face in an attempt to look a little less high, I plodded back to Ashley's room to see what she had discovered. In my dazed state, I didn't even think that it might have been something related to me.

I didn't even have to ask what it was. As I entered, she was already moving toward the door to find me. It was a good thing I hadn't nodded out for hours, like I had before off of this really good stuff.

"Becca's cousin Sean died last night! Heroin overdose! He was found dead in Jeremy's bathroom!" she practically screamed.

The buzzing that had awoken me minutes earlier was a text from Ashley's good friend Rebecca. I had forgotten she was Sean's cousin.

Panic filled my body, breaking through the bliss of my high. I cringed at the gruesome memory of finding Sean dead on Jeremy's bathroom floor, and silently prayed Ashley wouldn't find out I had been there to witness it.

"I'm so glad you don't do that shit anymore! That could have been you!" Ashley gushed, enveloping me in a gigantic bear hug.

I clung tightly to her, glad she couldn't see my face. If she only knew how true her last statement was. I had done the same heroin that killed Sean and put Will in the hospital. It could have been me, and it might be me in the future. The thought of the remaining stash of the deadly heroin, tucked under Ashley's sink and hidden in the spare tire in the trunk of my car, crept into my consciousness. I brushed it away. Ignoring reality was so easy when I was high, but it was hard to ignore Ashley. She was bursting with emotion. I was in control of her happiness, and I was on the fast track to mess it up. I had never felt so guilty about being loved in my life.

Squeezing her tightly, I vowed to look for some Suboxone when she left for work and get rid of the heroin stash, longing for the summer days when she was with me every minute of every day. I couldn't control myself; addiction was in control of me, and was not showing any signs of surrendering. To stay clean, I needed constant looking after.

Luckily, Ashley evidently mistook my worry for empathy, and attributed my droopy eyes to lack of sleep; either that or she knew deep down, but was in denial. She rushed around, getting ready for class, and I retreated back to bed. I hadn't even told her my back was hurt yet, but I wasn't so sure this was the right time.

When the weekend had arrived and I told Ashley about my back, she insisted I stay in bed. Telling her might not have been such a good idea; she was like a concerned mother. Luckily, I still had some dope stashed, and I was able to sneak off and get high every so often, or I would have gone crazy. When I was sober, I was so anxious that lying in bed would have been an awful punishment, but now it was welcoming.

Ashley and I watched Netflix and ate. My chest clenched with fear when she mentioned she'd had trouble finding a spoon for her cereal, but luckily she didn't think twice when I said they must all have been dirty. "I should probably try to find some replacement spoons," I thought, but I was too high to really care. I relished in knowing that I was going to be paid—not much, but it was better than nothing. I mentally noted that I should thank Amanda for the brilliant idea and for making all of the phone calls to get me compensation for my fake injury. Ashley examined my arm, where the track mark had slowly started to fade. I tried to read her expression as she ran her hands along my vein. Her face was scrunched up, and her eyes darted along my arm and up to hold my gaze. I could tell she wasn't convinced I was sober.

"I want you to take a drug test," she stated.

I acted shocked and appalled.

"Seriously? You don't trust me? That's pretty shitty. Relationships are built on trust, and I thought we had a good relationship, but if you can't trust me, apparently we don't," I sputtered, my mind racing, wondering how quickly she could get a drug test, and if I would have time to detox if she somehow forced me to take it.

Her expression softened a bit, but it was still clear she wasn't pleased.

"I love you very much, Ryan. It's not you that I don't trust, it's your addiction. I watched my dad and my brother go through the same thing you are, and their paths lead to death. Now that Sean is dead and Will is in a coma, I am more worried about you than ever. I know you and Will used to be good friends, and that the three of you graduated high school together," she whispered.

"How do you know Will is in a coma?" I questioned. Seth and Amanda had both informed me earlier in the week via text, but somehow Ashley had also gotten ahold of the information. Each time she found something out, I stiffened in fear that she would discover I had again succumbed to addiction.

"Becca told me, and it was in a few local news articles that covered Sean's death. The heroin they did was laced with fentanyl, and I'm sure it will cause more deaths. They've already arrested one of the dealers after setting up a controlled buy, but I'm sure there are more. I can't believe how stupid people are. It seems like so many people we know are either dead, in jail, or will die soon. What inconsiderate assholes, selling stuff that could possibly end someone's life!" she ranted.

I stayed silent, resisting the urge to defend the dealer and the dead addicts. I didn't want to blow my cover, but I wanted Ashley to realize that she was judging too harshly. It wasn't their fault.

When Monday rolled around, I was almost out of my dope stash.

"Shit. I meant to sell some of that shit and get some subs," I thought to myself, shaking my head as I mixed the remainder of the beloved death serum carefully in the spoon in Ashley's upstairs bathroom. She had finally just left for class.

My senses heightened with anticipation as the needle drew nearer to my vein. Shooting up in inconspicuous places had proved to be difficult, but I quickly perfected the skill and went from narrowly missing my vein to being able to inject in even the most miniscule vein without error. Embracing the euphoria, I sunk to my knees on the bathroom floor. All worries were replaced by a rush of happiness and relaxation; the feelings of warmth and well-being took over, replacing my sickness and fear.

I'm not sure how much time passed before I rose, but after basking in the hazy glory slumped behind the closed door, I hopped up with a sudden burst of energy. My first unemployment check had not yet arrived, and I had already burned through the bundle I'd bought from Seth. Broke was not an option for me. I fished my cell phone out of my pocket, glad my mother still covered the bill, and started hitting people up.

In just minutes, I had enough custys to cover the cost of another bun and have some leftover cash. I sped off to Seth's to pick up.

"Dude. You know I don't usually front," Seth said, when I arrived without cash.

"Yea, but check this out: I can show you everyone who wants to cop some. I'll more than make my money back within the hour, and come right back to pay you," I bargained with pleading eyes.

"Just this once and only cuz it's you, but I'm going to need your watch and your laptop for collateral," he countered.

"You're kidding me, right? You need my fucking laptop? You've known me forever, bro, I'll be right back."

"And when you return, your laptop will be right here," he said, not budging.

I let out a huge sigh and removed my watch. Luckily, I had my laptop in the car and didn't have to return to Ashley's to grab it. When I re-entered the house after snagging my laptop, Seth had my dope all prepared and ready to go. I mumbled unenthusiastic thanks and sprinted to the car.

My phone was exploding from needy messages and I set to work, meeting up with junkie after junkie in back alleys, trashy apartments, and public parking lots. Meeting up with people who needed heroin or crack was always a simple task. They're ruthless when you're dry—blowing up your phone, showing up at your house and work, hoping you'll have something—but at least you can always count on them to be ready and waiting when you set a time to meet up.

Even though many of the people I met up with had been my classmates or friends just a few short years ago, I was still very cautious with them. Every gun I'd ever owned that hadn't been stolen, I'd sold for drug money. Ashley would flip out if she ever found me with one, but I did carry a knife, just in case one of the people I sold to felt the need to rob me. I shuddered, pulling into Stars to meet a particularly sketchy custy, Robby, thinking about how I'd driven to meet him in this very parking lot a few years back.

He had jumped into my passenger seat that day immediately, thanking me for meeting up.

"I'm so grateful you could meet me. You don't even know, I'm so sick," he whimpered.

I had grabbed my backpack and fished out an 80. He lunged at me, snagging the backpack out of my lap with one hand, chucking it on the floor just out of my reach, and pushed me back against the seat with the other hand. I dropped the pill and grabbed at his wrist.

"What the fuck are you doin', man?" I asked, so shocked and high that it took me a minute to realize what was happening.

Slumping down in my seat, I desperately tried to reach for my backpack, where my 9 millimeter laid waiting, but I was stopped by a switchblade neatly slicing my tee shirt. The more I struggled to reach for the backpack, the greater the pain in my sternum. I was trapped. Robby gave me a final shove and fled, with my backpack in hand. Bright red blood leaked through my shirt and I winced. I couldn't really feel my physical pain, but I was beyond startled and resentful that he had taken my bag containing four 80's and my gun.

That memory still seemed fresh in my mind, but not meeting up with him didn't even occur to me. Just like not returning to Causeway Block after getting my car shot up wasn't an option. My brain didn't function normally. Drugs and money were more important than physical safety. To me, they were physical safety, protecting my feeble body from the inevitable extreme suffering I would endure if I was unable to get down.

Meeting up with Robby last on purpose, I stashed the money from my other custys behind the plastic casing for my speakers in the car. Since Seth had my laptop, the only other thing he could possibly take from me was the ticket he was buying, and I was willing to take that risk over a measly twenty dollars.

Robby was looking scruffy, as usual, when I pulled up. All the doors were locked, and I only rolled the window down a crack.

"You know you can't get in, bro. I don't have shit but this ticket anyway," I said, holding it in view, but slightly out of reach.

"I told you I'm sorry for that, man, I was in a really tough place," he grunted, producing a dirty bill from his pocket and sliding the twenty through my cracked window. I briefly considered driving away without handing over the ticket, to get him back for robbing me years ago, but I didn't want to risk getting my car shot up again. I couldn't have junkies after me without raising Ashley's present suspicions, and I knew I had to be extra careful if I was going to keep up this double life.

Robby eagerly snatched the ticket through my window and scurried off. I wondered where he was headed. It didn't look like he had a home or even anywhere to shower, but that was not my concern.

Now I had more than enough cash for a bun. Bursting with positive energy, I weaved through the city streets back to Seth's spot.

Seeing my laptop still intact on Seth's cluttered coffee table upon letting myself into his place, I breathed a sigh of relief. He was slumped over on the couch half-conscious, his normal stance. Slapping him in the face with a stack of twenties, I roused him from a drug-induced slumber. Noticing an unopened bottle of prenatal vitamins resting on the grimy surface of the coffee table next to my laptop, I wondered where Mary was. I didn't know much about pregnancy, but she probably should have been taking those vitamins and definitely shouldn't have been shooting up. Feeling relieved I was born a male and couldn't get pregnant, I reimbursed Seth for the bun I had bought that morning, and negotiated with him to get the most out of the rest of my cash, stashing five dollars away for gas.

After getting my fix and zoning out on Seth's couch for a while, I remembered Ashley had invited our mothers over for dinner that evening. Scratching my face and gathering my belongings, I tried to say goodbye to Seth, but he was too far gone.

I continued to scratch on the drive back to Ashley's. Opiates make you itchy, but in a good way. It's difficult to describe. I enjoyed the itching, because scratching felt so good, I never wanted to stop. It was so rewarding.

I almost didn't notice that Ashley's car was already in the driveway when I pulled in. I wondered what she was doing home, and pondered where I should tell her I was. I would have been totally paranoid she was going to realize I was high, but I was so faded it didn't occur to me that my behavior might look suspicious, until I opened the back door.

"Where have you been?" Ashley's tone was shockingly

soothing compared to the ominous look on her face.

"She knows. Shit. Shit. Shit. She knows. No, she doesn't. How could she possibly know?" The thoughts flooded my clouded head. I racked my brain, thinking of possible ways she could know; not coming up with any, I decided to play dumb.

"I was at a friend's. You're home early," I said, as calmly as I could. I noticed her hands were trembling, and my stomach dropped to my feet.

"Why is she acting so calm if she knows?" I thought to myself, trying to read her expression.

"Class got out early. We need to talk after dinner."

I shivered at the crisp anger conveyed with her body language. This was a big deal. I knew Ashley better than any girl I had ever been with, or any friend I ever had, and I could tell she was beyond pissed. There was no way this conversation could wait until after dinner. If she was going to leave me, I needed to get out immediately. There was no way in the world I was going to sit through an entire dinner with our parents wondering about such an integral part of my future.

Stepping inside, I removed my shoes and shut the door. Facing Ashley, I took her hands. She tried to turn away from me and go back to her cooking, but I wouldn't let her.

"If you have to talk to me, I want to do it now. I can't sit, worrying about what you have to say, all through dinner. I can tell by how you're acting that it's bad."

"Are you shooting up, Ryan?" she asked in a trembling voice. My suspicions were confirmed; this was about heroin.

"No. I told you that. Look, my arm has even healed," I said, holding out my arm. The red mark that I had sworn was not a track mark was starting to look like normal skin again.

I breathed a sigh of relief as she studied my arm, mentally thanking myself for shooting up in between my toes and in other much less obvious areas.

"Please don't lie to me. I can forgive you if you tell me the truth, but if you lie, I am not sure that I can. I really love you, and I want you to feel like you can come to me for help and not hide your problems from me," she continued on, making me more and more nervous with each second.

I had to make a decision. I needed to either come clean or continue my lie.

"I promise, I am not shooting up," I said again, and tears welled up in her eyes.

"Then where have all the spoons been going?" she spat angrily.

I started to respond with the first thing that popped into my head, but she turned on her heel and hurried out of the kitchen. I could hear her quiet sobs as she padded up the stairs toward her bedroom.

I wondered if I should go comfort her, or get angry with her for not believing me. I decided to take the angry approach; I had to make my lie believable, or I would be kicked out for sure.

"Shit. How did I get myself into this mess? I need to convince her I'm not shooting up, and then stop again for real. This is destroying my relationship and my life," I thought to myself, heading toward the stairs to confront her.

She was marching back down the winding staircase as I was

about to head up. Fury was etched across her beautiful face, and her eyes burned holes in my deteriorating soul. I looked down for a second, embarrassed and grief-stricken that I was responsible for evoking these harrowing emotions in such a sweet girl.

Then I saw it. There was something in her hand. It happened so quickly, I am not sure if I heard her accusing words first or recognized the objects she held.

"If you promise that you're not shooting up, then how do you explain these?" she shouted, holding up a fistful of dirty needles, tainted with my blood.

I halted dead in my tracks, unable to stop the sudden rush of tears that came streaming out of my eyes. I considered lying and saying I was getting rid of them for someone else. I knew she wouldn't buy it, and she would probably have the blood tested to prove that it was mine. Denial was no longer an option. I had to face reality and pray she wouldn't leave me.

"Where did you get those?" I muttered through tears.

"I got out of class early, excited for our dinner, and thought I would get some laundry done before I started cooking…" Her voice trailed off and she let out a sob.

I immediately knew where she had found the needles. How could I have been so stupid?

"I thought I would be nice and wash some of your clothes too, and when I checked the pockets, I felt something hard in the side pocket of your pants. My heart sunk when I felt it. I don't know how I knew what it was going to be, but I just knew. I opened up the pocket and pulled out one of your socks, filled with these." She sniffled, holding up the needles.

"Are you going to leave me?" I whimpered.

"You have a lot of explaining to do after dinner," she said.

"I'm not staying for dinner if you're going to leave me," I threatened.

"I won't leave you if you promise never to shoot up or do opiates in any form ever again, and back up that promise by letting me drug test you every single day for the rest of our relationship." She held me with her piercing gaze, as if she expected me to argue, but I was relieved. I needed to stop anyway, and this would give me the motivation to quit for good. Ashley wasn't leaving me!

Still crying harder than I would like to admit, I gathered her in a loving embrace, never wanting to let go.

"I'm sorry you had to see those. I was going to get rid of them tomorrow and get some subs before you found out I had relapsed. I will explain everything to you after dinner. I'm so sorry for lying to you. I just really didn't want you to leave me. You don't understand how hard this is." I sniffled, clutching her tightly.

"After losing my father and my brother, do you think this is easy for me? Go set the table for dinner. You better act happy and polite when our mothers arrive," she retorted, pushing me away with tears in her eyes.

As I began to set the table, I heard her mumble something about how if I had gotten a sponsor and put more energy into working the program, I probably wouldn't have relapsed, but I pretended I didn't hear.

The past few months have been the best in a while. Ryan successfully completed rehab, and seems really happy with Ashley. I've started to see glimpses of my beloved little boy, the one I knew before the drugs. Ashley invited her mother and me over for dinner this evening and, of course, I was delighted to join. However, when I arrived at the door, I wasn't greeted with the usual smiles and hugs. Something was wrong. The tension was palpable.

"Can you please pass the butter?" Ashley asked Ryan, with a strained smile. He obliged, and I watched her carefully butter her corn and then cut into her expertly cooked bacon-wrapped filet. The dinner was mouthwatering, but it didn't sit right in my stomach, because my worry for Ryan had returned with full force.

"Is he using again? Will Ashley leave him if he is? Is she suspicious of him using, but unable to confirm it? Has he lied to her or stolen from her?" The possibilities swarmed through my mind, making it increasingly difficult to engage in pleasant conversation.

Based on their body language, I guessed Ashley was mad at Ryan for something, and I just prayed it wasn't drug related. I was fairly sure he hadn't cheated on her. My Ryan was a loyal boy, but

I had seen how much drugs had changed him in the past. If he was using again, I certainly wouldn't put anything past him.

When I first found out about Ryan's habit, I was in denial about the severity of it. After finally coming to terms with how horrible his addiction was, I tried to be there for him as much as I could, but I'm not sure if I helped or hurt the situation. Moving only made things worse. Rehab seems to have helped, but that was only because of Ashley. I would have liked him to go to rehab of his own free will, but I knew he never would have.

It had gotten to the point that my worry for Ryan was ruining my marriage and my relationship with my two other lovely children. Don said I was becoming more distant and spending too much time at support groups. He also hadn't been thrilled when I paid for Ryan's rent in Virginia for the first few months, about the money I'd spent on our plane tickets for the attempted intervention, and that rehab had been so costly. Maya was frustrated with me for not taking her advice and moving on.

"There is only so much you can do, Mom. If you keep worrying about him, trying to contact him all the time, and giving him money, you're going to lose your mind. I also hope you realize that you're enabling his drug-seeking behavior. You should cut him completely out of your life for now. As long as you keep paying his phone bill, letting him have his car, and responding to his beck and call, he will continue to use you. I know it will hurt, but it may be your only hope." She lectured me time and time again in our Skype chats and phone conversations. Tim didn't say much, but I could tell from his silence that he was slightly resentful that I focused so much of my energy on Ryan.

When I really thought all was lost, Ryan started dating Ashley and stopped using opiates. It filled me with hope. Sitting at the dinner table, I could feel that hope slipping away.

## CHAPTER SIXTEEN:
# Guilt

"I can't believe you're going to make me take these every day," I said, as Ashley carried boxes filled with hundreds of opiate tests into her apartment.

"Just consider yourself lucky that I found a way to buy these in bulk for only around a dollar a piece, because they're almost sixty dollars for one at the drugstore, and you're paying for them," she snapped, and I felt another pang of guilt mixed with anger and resentment.

If I hadn't loved this girl more than life itself, I would never have agreed to taking drug tests, much less paying for them. Deep down, I knew I was also doing it for myself. My opiate addiction led me to a dark place where I didn't want to be. Ashley kept reminding me that I was lucky I wasn't on the streets, and I would lose my car, my dignity, her, my family, and everything else if I didn't do as she said. Even though I wanted to get clean, I resented her for making me, and was frustrated with her for being right. I hated being wrong, and even though I knew doing opiates was dangerous, I had myself convinced I was invincible.

"There's no point in taking one now, it's going to be dirty," I said, as she stacked them in her bathroom. "Since I am quitting for good, can I please get high one more time? I won't do heroin, I promise; I just want to do one Dilaudid, and I want you to be with me, so you can see it isn't that bad," I begged her, trying to remain calm when she faced me with a shocked expression.

"Please, I feel really sick, and I have no Suboxone to start my detox now. I swear on my life, I will detox tomorrow and find some subs to help. I'll let you drug test me every single day for the rest of my life and I will pay for it. I will even get a full time job in six months, if you let me just relax and sell weed for a little bit." The shocked and appalled expression remained splattered across her face, and I thought she wasn't even going to respond.

"You're kidding me, right? You want me to watch you shoot up? And you want me to let you sell weed for six months before you start applying for web design or photography jobs?" she repeated in a stunned whisper.

"Yes. If I sell weed, I can help you pay your rent, and it will keep me busy while I get used to being sober again. I hate weed and never smoke, so it won't be dangerous for me to sell it. If you watch me shoot up today, I can find some subs and start detoxing tomorrow. In six months, I will actively apply for career-oriented jobs until I'm hired, and you can drug test me as long as you want. I really want us to have a good future together and get married; I just want six months to have fun before I start a career. I need to know for myself that I can stay sober, and you will know too, because you'll be drug testing me."

"No way. I'm not watching you shoot up, that's disgusting. Go find some subs now or detox without them; as for selling weed, you're still employed as a dishwasher, and you got to be out of work and paid while your back healed, if it was even really hurt to begin with. Clearly you're well enough to go back to work, and that will be enough," she rejected all my propositions.

"Well, I'm getting something either way. I can't be sick, and my sub connect doesn't get another script 'til tomorrow. If you wanna break up with me over that, then I guess our relationship really doesn't matter that much to you. If we can get through this, a happy marriage with no drugs is in our future; I just need to get this out of the way. Are you coming with me or not?" I countered.

After pausing for a long time, she finally nodded, with tears streaming down her face. The marriage card worked with her every time. For the first time in my life, I had actually found a girl I wanted to marry, and I was using it against her to get my way. It was wrong, but it was the only way I could get her to agree, so I couldn't help it.

"Okay. Let's get this shit over with. I can't believe I'm actually agreeing to this. I love you so much. I want to have a future with you and to see you succeed. If this is what it takes to get this out of your system before we can have a normal, happy life together, then fine. You can sell weed to keep busy for only six months and get high this one last time, but I want it in writing, too," she demanded.

I thought it was a little bit weird that she wanted me to write down and sign a piece of paper saying that I would never touch opiates again, let her drug test me daily, stop selling weed, and apply for full time employment in six months, but I gladly did it—because it meant I would get to shoot up one last time!

A half an hour later, we were meeting some of my connects to snag a Dilaudid in a church parking lot.

"I can't fucking believe I'm here, doing this, instead of in class," Ashley muttered, as she put together a PowerPoint presentation for one of her marketing classes in my passenger seat.

I didn't see what the big deal was. It looked like she was still getting her work done to me, but Ashley rarely swore, and I could tell by her tone of voice and body language that she was still beyond pissed.

My connects finally pulled up, looking apprehensive because I had a passenger. It turned out they knew Ashley from college, so it was fine she was with me, but she shot them an evil glare.

"I think your girl is mad, bro," the guy whispered, handing me the Dilaudid and departing back to the car, where his junkie girlfriend waited.

The words went in one ear and out the other. I didn't care if Ashley was mad; this was my last time shooting up opiates, and I wasn't going to let anyone or anything ruin it.

"You're going to do this right here?" Ashley questioned with an appalled look on her face.

Fumbling around in my glove compartment, I grabbed my driver's manual to crush the pill and a baggy filled with other items I needed to get my fix. Ignoring her question, I realized my lighter wasn't in the bag.

"Shit. I need a lighter. Do you see my lighter anywhere?" I asked.

"Ryan. What the fuck. I don't want to be seen with you,

this is disgusting and embarrassing. If you have to do this one more time, can we at least go back to my apartment, please?" she begged, her voice trembling with annoyance and fear.

I still had no response for her. The only thing I was concerned about was finding my lighter so I could get this process going. Flinging things all about, I searched the car in a panic. Finally, I felt something small and hard under my seat. Stretching my arm under the seat as far as it could go, I was able to extract the item.

"Yes! My lighter! Thank God!"

I cheerfully set about preparing my illegal concoction, not fazed in the least bit that we were in the middle of a church parking lot in broad daylight and Ashley was close to having a panic attack.

"You'll see. It's really not that bad," I reassured her, as I removed my belt from my waist and securely fastened it around my bicep.

"Not that bad. Seriously, Ryan? You think it's not that bad because you've been doing it for a while and you're friends with a bunch of junkies. For normal people, it is worse than that bad— especially for me, someone who is in love with you and has had to deal with the pain of losing my father and brother to this very same thing. I hate you right now for putting me through this. I really regret saying this was okay. Can we please just go home, and you can sell that stupid pill back to some other junkie?"

I blocked her voice out; the excitement was too real. I was just seconds away from my last glorious high ever, nothing she had to say mattered. It was just me and the needle; I was in the zone.

Accurately hitting my thin vein right in the center, I felt a refreshing pop. The color drained from Ashley's face as my blood mixed with the water-Dilaudid solution in the syringe. I barely noticed her negative reaction; it didn't faze me. The mixture entered my bloodstream and I felt instant bliss. Ashley's approval was no longer needed. I closed my eyes and breathed in relaxation.

"See, that wasn't so bad, was it?" I asked Ashley, opening my eyes. A simple Dilaudid wasn't nearly enough to make me nod out or look faded enough to scare her, so I was hoping she would be okay.

"Not that bad?" she shouted, almost in tears. I pulled out of the parking lot and headed toward her house, hoping she would calm down a little bit, but she continued to freak out. I was determined not to let her blow my high.

"Ryan, that was the scariest, most disgusting thing ever! I didn't realize the blood actually came out of you and into the needle and then went back into your body! You're going off the road. You're so messed up, you can't even drive; you're going to get us both killed!" Her screeching was only a mild annoyance, because I was guarded by the glowing warmth of my high.

We made it to the apartment safely, despite Ashley's concerned scolding, and I led her upstairs to the bedroom. After hours of lovemaking with no sign of climax, I pushed an ice cube in and out of her, swirling it around with my tongue in between her legs. I knew she was still angry with me, but somehow she still found me irresistible, just as I found her. It was hard to explain, but we had a special kind of bond that even drugs couldn't break.

Ashley agreed to let me use Suboxone to assist with my detox, as long as I took less and less of it every day and it was taken orally. Making her watch me shoot up did the opposite of making her feel more comfortable. To me, it was no big deal, because I had become so used to it. Even horrible things slowly become normal if you're around them a lot; eventually, you will be accepting and even defending things that once appalled you.

When I was using Suboxone I couldn't get high on opiates anyway, and if I did use opiates of any sort, Ashley would immediately know, because of the drug tests. Staying with her was more important than getting high, so remaining clean was a little easier than it had been before I was getting tested daily. Although it was easier, it was in no way easy at all. I still silently struggled every day and was just barely able to pull through. Ashley's smile, her encouraging words, and my deep-rooted attraction to her physically, spiritually, and emotionally were the only things that kept me going. The insomnia, restless leg syndrome, and intense desire to use were still very present and real.

When Ashley graduated from Arelington College in December after finishing her extra semester, I was both ecstatic and panicked. It was an awful combination, similar to when I was coming down from a high. I was happy she graduated, because it meant I would get to spend a lot more time with her in the immediate future, but I was petrified that she might get a full time job and I would have to be without her for longer periods of time than ever before.

She had planned on moving to Colorado, Oregon, or somewhere out west with killer snowboarding after graduation, and I begged her to stay. There was no way I was going to let her leave me. I couldn't do a long distance relationship, because drugs would reclaim me for sure. After my dreadful time in Virginia, I was not ready to move away from Vermont again. Part of me really wanted to go with her. I missed snowboarding and could have probably been happy out west, but I was way too nervous to leave. Even when I was not using, my addiction still controlled me. Being so far away from known connects was too scary.

One of the things I loved and hated about Ashley was her passion for snowboarding. Ever since the accident, I had only ridden once, with Ashley, when she begged me to. It hadn't been the same stress-relieving bliss I used to experience. My once cherished love of the sport was now a painful scar in my memory.

We finally came to an agreement that she would stay, but if she hadn't found a full time career in Vermont within a year, she was going to leave. It wasn't ideal, but it would do.

The summer after Ashley's graduation was pure bliss. It was just like our first summer. We drank, rolled, partied at her house, at friends' houses, had beach bonfires, and spent the evenings dancing the night away at the bars and days on the beach. We filmed a lot of our shenanigans and uploaded them onto Ashley's computer to preserve the memories and I sold weed to keep busy and make some extra money. As summer came to an end, Ashley picked up more shifts at the bar and focused on refining her resume and applying to job after job. The six months I'd been granted in our written contract had passed, so she begged and encouraged me to do the same, but I needed more time.

I told her I didn't want to get a full time job until I was

ready to begin my career, and I wasn't ready. This frustrated her and she frequently brought it up, calling me out in front of friends and making me feel like a failure for not having a career. Her friend Good Vibes stuck up for me often, but I feared Becca and her other friends were encouraging her to leave me.

"At least I'm off opiates and not using needles," I would tell her, to calm her down slightly. As time rolled by, she complained more and more that she didn't want to drink, she was sick of partying, and she wanted to start a career. This frightened me inexplicably. Drinking, selling weed, partying, and constant fun were my distractions. They kept me from gravitating back to heroin and other opiates. I needed to party. It didn't help that I had recently gotten robbed at gunpoint while selling weed. One of my old oxy custys had hit me up to buy a 20 bag of weed, pulled a gun on me, and taken an entire ounce. I almost didn't tell Ashley, but she kept a watchful eye on my funds, and would have noticed the missing cash and thought I was spending it on something I shouldn't have.

# CHAPTER SEVENTEEN:
# Destruction

"God, Ryan, don't you care about me or the future at all?" I spat in frustration, staring at my boyfriend, who gazed back at me with pathetic pleading puppy dog eyes.

He had convinced me to take a break from my tireless job search to daydrink with him, just as I got an e-mail about a job interview for my dream job, doing public relations for Shredders Snowboards, a local snowboarding company.

"You just said you would drink with me today," he pouted with a frown.

"Seriously? You should be happy for me. This is a really important interview I have tomorrow; my future depends on it, and you're going to make me feel bad because I won't spend all day drinking? You promised me that you would look for real jobs in six months—roughly a year ago! I agreed to let you sell weed, and you got robbed by a dirtbag junkie! You have sketchy people showing up at my house! It has basically been a year, you haven't applied to one legit job, and you're still selling weed! You broke our agreement; just because you want to throw your life away doesn't mean I do!" I shook with rage.

In the couple years Ryan and I had dated, I had only yelled at him a few times. We rarely argued and almost always enjoyed spending time together, but after I had graduated college and started looking for a career, things had gotten a little tense. The more I applied for jobs, the more Ryan wanted to drink and slack off. He made me feel guilty, like I wasn't fun anymore, whenever I didn't agree to join him, but he was still passing his drug tests. As long as he wasn't shooting up or doing any form of opiates, I couldn't bring myself to leave him.

I loved him way too much. We had a special connection—a spirit love that I hadn't been able to find with anyone else. Ryan had the ability to convince me to do almost anything, but I had worked hard all my life to get a good job. I wanted to have children someday, and to be able to offer them the support my mother had given me. I also didn't want them to have a dead or junkie father. Ryan said he wanted the same things in life, but his actions were making me think differently. I would have been even more upset he wasn't happier for me if I hadn't been so nervous for the interview. My thoughts were interrupted by Ryan again, voicing his irritation.

"I'm going to get alcohol and call some friends to drink," he said, storming out of my apartment like I had wronged him.

"Fine. I won't be here when you get back. I'm going to prep for this interview at a friend's house, because I can't be distracted by a bunch of drunks," I shouted at his retreating back. Some nerve he had. I paid for rent and he lived for free (occasionally chipping in for utilities), and he acted like he owned the place.

Stuffing my computer, notebook, and a few pencils in my

backpack, I jumped in the car and headed to my friend Becca's to study. I had only made it a few minutes down the road when my heart lurched into my stomach.

There was Ryan's car on the side of the road. It was not parked near anyone's house we knew. My gut told me he was shooting up, but I just had to be wrong. If he was shooting up opiates, he would fail his daily drug test, and I would leave him. It had to be something else.

Slamming on the gas, I sped up and quickly swerved over, off to the right, to park behind him. If he was doing something wrong, I needed to catch him in the act. Ryan could talk his way out of anything unless he was caught red handed. I quickly exited my car with sweaty palms, my heart pounding loudly in my chest. What was I going to find? I had no time to hesitate or speculate; I just had to run. Quickly sprinting up to the door, I looked in the window. There was Ryan, with a needle in his arm.

I pounded on the window and he looked up at me, pure terror etched across his thin face.

"What the fuck, Ryan? The drug test! You're seriously shooting up? How could you, when you knew I would find out tomorrow when you failed?"

He expertly extracted the needle from his arm and opened the door with trembling hands.

"You wouldn't have known. I'm not shooting up opiates. I would have passed the test," he said, with a shaky voice.

"Well, what are you shooting up, then?" I screeched, not even knowing if I wanted to know.

I had no choice now; I had to leave him. He had been using

needles for God knows how long, and would ruin my career for sure if I stayed with him. My heart continued loudly thudding, and adrenaline nearly burst through my veins. I hated Ryan. I hated that I was in love with Ryan.

"It's only Adderall. I was shooting up Adderall. I'm really fucked up. I don't know what's wrong with me. I just missed needles, but I hate needles. I guess I missed the rush, the instant gratification," he stammered.

"You have some serious issues. I hope you're happy. Good luck finding a place to live. I'm glad drugs mean more to you than I do," I said, turning and sprinting back to my car. There was no way I could concentrate on my interview after what had happened, but I had to try.

I arrived at Becca's house, surprisingly not crying. I think I was still in so much shock that I was unable to have a physical reaction. My phone was blowing up with texts from Ryan, asking where I was, apologizing, and begging me to forgive him.

I changed my status on Facebook to single, to show him, my friends, and myself that the breakup was permanent. I ignored his pleas, only responding to let him know he had a week to get all of his things out of my house. Gone were the good times. The daydreams of marriage and a family with my soulmate crumbled before me. Deep down, I had known this was coming, but it didn't make it any easier.

After a long studying session, three interviews, and a lot of nervous waiting, I was thrilled to be offered the job. Moving out west was still on my mind, but that could be done later, after I was more established in the working world.

It was weird to live with Ryan, but not be dating him. I had given him a week to get his stuff out and find a new place to live, but the week turned into three months of him treating my house like a hotel, before I just boxed everything up. Not wanting to bother his family, I drove it to his junkie friend Seth's house. I couldn't be his free storage anymore; as much as it hurt me, he needed to be removed from my life.

The door was cracked open when I arrived, and I could hear Seth's girlfriend screaming into her cell phone before I even got to the front steps.

"I don't care if you don't think I'm fit to raise a child. It's bullshit that my baby was taken away from me as soon as he was born! No, I am not a junkie, I use opiates because I have back problems!" she screeched.

I had sent Ryan a text to let him know that his things were going to be dropped at Seth's, but I desperately did not want to be any part of the scene that was going on when I arrived. Luckily, the sun was shining with no sign of rain, so I placed the box of Ryan's clothes, CDs, posters, and various other items outside Seth's front door, and snuck away before anyone even noticed I was there. Breathing a sigh of relief, I tiptoed back to my car.

"Thank goodness someone took away that girl's child," I thought. I could only imagine the poor, helpless baby, born addicted to opiates, screaming out in agony, experiencing horrific withdrawals. I hated opiates with a passion, and despised anyone who would put an innocent child or unborn child through the torture of withdrawal. I had seen what it did to Ryan, and I could only imagine how it would affect a baby.

"They should require all pregnant mothers to get drug tested, and force them into rehab if they fail," I thought to myself, driving home. There were too many unpleasant images in my head; I couldn't bear thinking about innocent babies and children, neglected by addicted parents and born with drugs in their systems.

Ryan showed me the ugly world my father and brother had lived in before they passed; a world that was present side by side with the one most people live in, blissfully unaware. It seemed like almost every day, I found out another friend, relative, or schoolmate, who I never would have pegged for an addict, was addicted to opiates. Robberies and deaths in the Arelington news increased, and the repeated mentions of overdoses and funerals flooded my news feeds in social media.

Even though I was now very acutely aware of the drug epidemic our society was experiencing, I was still able to focus on my career and move forward in my world. It was difficult, because it meant I had to leave loved ones behind. Even the addicted people who were still alive were basically dead. Their personalities and looks changed so drastically, it was like they were human zombies. Although I could easily spot an addict in the crowd, they seemed to blend in to people who had never had direct experience with their world. Droopy, faded eyes would get mistaken for tired eyes; track marks were covered up by clothing, Band-Aids, or choosing a discrete vein to inject; the changes in weight and personality were so subtle that no one seemed to notice until it was too late.

I threw myself into work at Shredders Snowboards, traveling all around the United States, and got to know some really great people. My first year with the company, I worked a lot of overtime and was still bartending on the side. I saved a good amount of money for a down payment on a house—only I didn't buy a house, because, without Ryan, I had no motivation to start a family. I tried online dating for a while, and went out to fancy restaurants with some nice, generous, and even good-looking guys, but my soul still felt empty without Ryan. I longed for our hiking and kayaking days, and wished he would have been able to overcome his addiction and get back into snowboarding again.

One weekend evening, I was having a few friends over at my apartment to play cards and beer pong. Ryan showed up. He came with one of our mutual friends, Good Vibes, and some guy named Mark. Good Vibes was originally my friend, but he had become close to Ryan, and Ryan's annoying friend Mark (whom he'd met in CRASH years ago). I had heard about Mark prior, through friends of friends, and had only been told bad things. I should've told Ryan to leave, to not show up at my house unannounced with a dirtbag junkie in tow, but as soon as I saw him, I knew there was no way I could make him leave. Even though his face was slightly puffy, with blotches all over it from opiate use, and he was even skinnier than before, he was still beautiful to me. I loved him so much that I'd made some stupid choices—enabling his behavior in our relationship by allowing him to drink and do other drugs, believing that he was actually going to look for a career after signing my contract—the list goes on, but even though he was no good for me, he still had my heart.

"Hey, Ash," he said, shyly giving me a half smile and scooting closer to me with a beer in his hand.

"Hi," I replied, feeling like a can of butterflies had just been set free inside my gut. Just looking at him made me tingle all over, and I began nervously ripping the label off my Corona.

"I see you have some sexual tension," he joked, pointing out the tattered remains of the bottle wrapper.

The rest of the room fell away, and all I saw was him. Normally I would have felt rude ignoring all of my guests, but I couldn't focus on anyone else. I had finished a few drinks before he had shown up, and we were engrossed in tipsy conversation. My love for him made me so blind, I didn't stop to think about what he might have been doing while we were not hanging out.

His droopy eyes, pinned out pupils, torn clothes, blotchy face, and puffy scarred hands should have given away that he was still obviously losing his battle with addiction, and wouldn't be a good fit for my successful lifestyle.

When you're in love and tipsy, you don't think rationally. Moments later, I found myself locking lips with Ryan in my apartment bathroom, with no concern that our drunk friends would soon have to pee and be knocking on the door.

I felt his body press up against mine as he shoved me into the wall, grabbing my curves and passionately kissing my mouth and neck. Moments later, we were removing each other's clothes, and he hoisted me up onto the sink. The tingling sensation I had felt just by looking at him earlier quickly multiplied, exploding through my body, and I moaned out in pleasure as he pushed himself deep inside me. I lost all sense of time, my body filled with exquisite pleasure, until there was a knock on the door.

"You two bangin' in there? Let me join!" Good Vibes laughed jokingly from the other side of the door. Loud and comical, he could always brighten up the room, so even though his real name was Rich, we all referred to him as Good Vibes.

I snapped out of the haze of intense pleasure and stared at Ryan. Still a little shocked at what was going on, I starting to freak out a bit, but then Ryan looked at me, laughing.

"Kid, I told you not to be that loud. You got us busted by Vibes, now the whole party knows what's up."

I couldn't help but smile. I'm not sure why I loved it so much when Ryan called me "kid," but there was just something about the way he said it that was so endearing. We put our pants back on and shamefully exited the bathroom.

"Thanks, Vibes, you cock blocker," Ryan said to Rich, laughing, and we all went back to drinking and playing beer pong like nothing had happened.

For a minute, I felt like it was just a sweet summer evening when Ryan and I were dating, like I had gone back in time. Everything was the same. I wished we could rewind time for real and change the future. Even if I could have gone back in time, I doubted anything I could have done differently would have saved Ryan. I'd done everything I could to get him out of drugs; I just had to enjoy this little flashback as much as I could, and not let myself ruin my own life, falling for someone who was addicted.

———•◆•———

"Push over, kid, my head is dripping down the crack," Ryan laughed, sticking his head in between my bed and the wall and shoving me playfully toward the other end.

I had a pounding headache, an unwelcome hangover, and no memory of the end of the previous night, but here I was with Ryan, in my bed, laughing uncontrollably.

We spent the morning watching old videos of us that we had recorded when we were dating and cracking up with laughter over old memories. I hadn't felt so happy and complete since the day before we had broken up. It was nice, but I knew it was false comfort. Ryan would take me back in a second, but I couldn't let myself go back to him. He even went as far as begging for me back, but he was unable stay away from the drugs. He said he would, but I knew better.

The conversion turned quickly from light and playful to dark when I questioned him about sexual partners, and he mentioned hooking up with a junkie from his job.

"You told me she has hepatitis C," I said fearfully, hoping he didn't contract it.

"Yea, I think she might, her ex-boyfriend did, but you can't get that from having sex. I didn't share needles with her," he said. Suddenly, I felt dirty and repulsive for letting him into my house and back into my heart.

"Let's go. Right now," I said, and he looked at me quizzically. "I'm taking you to Planned Parenthood to get tested. It's rare, but I'm pretty sure you can get hepatitis C from sex, and I want to make sure you don't have it."

He shrugged and slid off the bed, following me to the door.

The results of the test didn't come in for a few dreadful weeks. I kept replaying what I could remember of the night over and over in my head. Ryan had disappeared again with Mark, who, I found out from Rich, had gotten a big check from the military and was singlehandedly funding Ryan's opiate addiction, in exchange for friendship.

There was something about Ryan that made everyone want to spend time with him, and made almost everyone want to do things for him. Throughout our relationship, he made me give in to countless things that I knew I shouldn't. He got Brandon to keep his shooting up a secret from Tim in Virginia, got Terrorist to let him back into Causeway Block, and convinced Good Vibes to give him free beer frequently and call into work sick, just so they could hang out whenever I had been busy.

I was just getting out of a work meeting when Ryan's name showed up on my phone's caller ID. Even seeing his name still made my stomach drop, after everything we'd been through.

"I'm clean, kid. I told you!" I heard Ryan's happy voice from the other end of the phone. It really sounded like he was telling the truth, but I knew there was no way he was off opiates. I paused, unsure of what to say.

"Told you that you could only get hep C through needles."

"Oh, that kind of clean, as in no STDs; well, that's a good thing," I thought to myself.

"You mean you're lucky, and so am I. According to Google, you actually can get hep C from sex, it's just not commonly transmitted that way. I don't know why you ever slept with that nasty girl anyway," I corrected him.

"Me either. I was really fucked up, and yea, I know that's not a good excuse," he said.

I paused, not wanting to hang up, because just the sound of his voice made me happy, but I had a lunch meeting.

"I have to go, but I'm having a barbeque this weekend, if you want to come over?" I asked hesitantly.

We'd gone such a long time not speaking, and then hooked up the first time we hung out again. I didn't know if it was such a good idea to invite him over, but I couldn't help it—I desperately wanted to.

"Hell yea, text me, I'll see if Mark can buy me some beer and give me a ride over."

I wanted to tell him to leave Mark at home, but I didn't want to be the one supplying his beer and picking him up from whichever house he was crashing at, so I kept my mouth shut.

"Okay, see you this weekend, bye," I said quickly, hanging up the phone. After removing it from my ear, I muttered, "I love you."

"I don't know why I'm doing this to myself," I thought, as I drove to pick up my client from the airport for our lunch meeting. Seeing Ryan was painful pleasure. It was torture, getting a taste of the wonderful past, while being painfully aware that he didn't fit into my future and wasn't going to change.

The weekend rolled around, and I was in the middle of smothering barbeque sauce on the cheddar bacon burgers I had on the grill when I saw Mark pull up. Good Vibes, Ryan, and a girl jumped out and headed toward my backyard. I recognized the girl, Rose, from mutual friends. She was decent, not a junkie, and had hooked up with Good Vibes in the past, so I welcomed her as she approached. I gave Ryan and Vibes hugs, barely acknowledged Mark, and went back to cooking.

"Did you text her back?" I heard Rose ask Ryan. I strained to listen to their conversation, pretending to be focused on grilling.

"Naw, she's obsessed with me. I told her I'm not hooking up with her again, but she still wants it," Ryan said, laughing.

Rose looked relieved; when he said he hadn't responded to the text, I assumed it was from the dirtbag hep C junkie. The relief on her face transformed to slight jealousy as he walked away from her and toward me. Vibes engaged Rose in conversation, but I could tell she was still watching Ryan out of the corner of her eye as he came up and put his arm around me and nuzzled my cheek with his nose.

"Smells good, babe," he said, giving me a little squeeze that sent chills of excitement up my spine. "I always did love your cooking, you're so good at it," he continued, taking a deep breath in.

Ryan knew how to compliment me. He knew just what to do and say to make me happy. I wished so badly he would give up the drugs, get a decent job, and live a normal life. We chatted briefly about how the week had been, then I said exactly what I was thinking, which was never hard to do with Ryan. I could talk to him about anything at any time, and I never felt uncomfortable or judged.

"You're going to date Rose, aren't you?" I asked.

"What! No! She's not my type," he said, glancing over at Rose, who was clearly drooling over him. "I don't even think she likes me, and she hooked up with Good Vibes. What makes you think she does?"

"I can just tell. Just like I knew you would hook up with that girl from your work, but not date her, I know Rose is going to be your next girlfriend, and it makes me sad. I wish that I could be your girlfriend, but I know you won't stop opiates. Rose seems like such a pushover, she probably won't even ask you to stop. I'm jealous that you'll be sending cute pictures and weird texts to someone who isn't me, but I just can't bring myself to be with you when you're using," I continued.

"I want you to be my next girlfriend, and my last, and my only, but you won't," he pouted.

"Ryan, you know how much I want to date you, but unless you're clearly off drugs and have your life together, I can't, and you know that. You've lied to me and given me false hope too many times. I need proof before we date again," I said sternly, as Vibes strolled over.

"Kid. I told you, I'm not on drugs," Ryan lied.

"What are you lovebirds talking about? You're burning the burgers," he said, good-naturedly helping himself to the biggest burger on the grill. He pulled it off and onto a toasted bun using his dirty hands, making everyone around crack up in the process.

"No! Cheese! Don't leave me!" he said, trying to catch a melting stream of cheese in his mouth by crouching down under the burger and holding it above his head. The scene was even more comical because he was sporting a graphic tee that said "Milk, I am your father." My phone buzzed.

"Of course, an email from work on my day off, what else is new," I thought to myself, pulling my inbox up and squinting to read the e-mail.

"Shit. You've got to be fucking kidding me," I said out loud, catching the attention of many of my guests.

"What is it?" Ryan asked, concerned.

"I have to go to Oregon for a Shredders Snowboards sponsored event the week of the festival I was planning to go to."

"Electric Zoo! No! I forgot to tell you that I got one of my friends to trade me his tickets in exchange for some, uh, stuff, so I was going to go too!" Ryan exclaimed.

My heart sank. The email said that my boss acknowledged that I had taken time off, but this event was really important and could get me promoted. All expenses were paid, and I would be getting paid time and a half for attending.

"I guess I have to sell my Zoo tickets," I muttered under my breath.

"I'll buy them; I've always wanted to go," Rose piped up.

I nearly vomited. Here was my prediction, unfolding right before my eyes. I couldn't turn down this opportunity to further my career, and there was always next year for Electric Zoo. I was kind of dreading partying for more than a day anyway, because recently just a night of drinking tired me out. I didn't know if I was up for hours of rolling and no sleep, but I did know that if Ryan and Rose hadn't already hooked up, they would for sure if I sold her my tickets.

"Ryan isn't going to change. You can't hold on to hope that he will forever; you have to let him go," I told myself, holding back tears.

"Sure, Rose. I'll give them to you for a hundred dollars. Let me go get them," I said, walking toward the house.

"Ash, come on! Please come to Zoo! It won't be the same without you!"

Ryan had followed me into the house and was begging me to ditch out on my work trip, a perfect example of why I couldn't date him if I wanted to succeed in life. Suddenly, he stopped talking and grabbed me by the arms, studying my face.

"Are you crying?" he asked, confused.

"I just know if I sell her these tickets, you're going to date her. I really want to go, but I can't. I have a career, and I want a house and a family someday. I really want it to be with you, but I can't live recklessly and irresponsibly. It's just not who I am," I whimpered.

"Chill, babe, I am not going to date her. I don't even want her to go; I want you to go." He wrapped his arms around me and began kissing me all over, which only made me cry harder, because I had a feeling this would be one of the last times we'd ever have a moment like this.

Finally, I was able to wipe the tears off my face long enough to find my Zoo tickets. Ryan cracked me open another Corona, and we headed back outside.

"Here," I said reluctantly, handing them to Rose. She happened to have cash on hand. She made decent money and wasn't into drugs.

"Thanks!" she said, enthusiastically, and I resisted the urge to vomit.

I really wanted to go to the festival, even before I knew Ryan was going, but now I wanted to go even more, and this innocent little peppy girl was going to take my place.

"You're welcome. I'm really jealous. I wish I could go. Now you're going with Ryan, and I can tell you like him," I said, trying to hide my distain.

"Yea, we're friends," she said, blushing.

"Well, I love him very much, but he's a serious drug addict. He shoots up heroin and lies about it all the time. He's also very manipulative and persuasive, so he will probably try to get you to buy him things. Just so you know," I said, walking away toward Ryan and Vibes.

I can only imagine how awkward she must have felt afterward, but she didn't leave. She also didn't speak to me for the rest of the day. She just kept making googly eyes at Ryan.

# CHAPTER EIGHTEEN:
# Letting Go

"Wow, I can't believe Rose is doing opiates now. I mean, I guess I can, Ryan can be pretty convincing, but I dated him for two years and never would have even thought of doing that. I even warned her about how he's going to ruin his life and anyone else's who chooses to go down that path, and that she should stay away. How could she be so stupid?" I rambled on and on, as Vibes and I sat at my kitchen table gossiping.

Vibes was one of my best guy friends, and he had become very close with Ryan as well, so we always had plenty of things to talk about. Just as I had foreseen, Rose and Ryan had started hooking up either at or after the festival. He admitted to hooking up with her, but still said she wasn't his type, and that he wouldn't date her because he was in love with me. We'd been talking less frequently, because I knew he was bad for me and I was only torturing us both by prolonging the relationship.

"Yea, she's a follower. She will do anything to make people like her. Ryan is basically using her right now. She pays for all of his drugs and anything he wants, so he keeps her around, but he's really in love with you. I wish you guys would get back together. It was so much more fun when we all had beach fires, went for bike rides, and Ryan wasn't a junkie. Now, I feel like he's barely my friend anymore, and you're always busy working," he laughed, knowing my thoughts on the subject.

"Vibes, you know I can't," I protested, wishing that there was a way that I could.

"Yea, I know. You have a good career and don't want to be dragged down by drugs, but I miss the old days. I miss the summers when we would all go out and party every night and chill at the beach all day, and Ryan wasn't using opiates."

"Yea, me too," I said, wistfully gazing down into my Corona, wondering if there was anything I could have done differently to save him.

"This is a great taco," Vibes said, laughing. He had the most comical laugh.

I couldn't help but smile, even though my mind was on Ryan and how he was destroying not only his life, but the lives of those around him. His mother, brother, and stepfather had all stopped talking to him, and I knew I should do the same.

"Not as good as they were on the original taco morning, when Ryan was with us, but any tacos with my homie are good tacos," I said, giving Vibes a high five and taking a bite of my taco.

I knew I shouldn't ask for details, but I couldn't help myself, so I pressed Vibes for a little more information. He launched into a series of stories about how Ryan first got Rose to try heroin. She'd vomited for hours the first time she snorted it, but that didn't stop her. She had tried again and again, quickly transferring from snorting to injecting, building her tolerance. This lead her to do a hit and run on a vehicle, overdose, land herself in the hospital, and get fired from her high paying job for missing shifts and stealing, all in a matter of months.

"Wow. Most people don't go downhill that fast," I said in shock.

"Yea, well, I'm not surprised. She's probably gotten so bad so quickly because she basically went right to using needles. I used to hook up with Rose, and that girl will do anything to please someone she likes," he said, with an almost evil laugh.

"I don't want to know about that!" I said, giggling.

When I first met Vibes, I thought that he was gay, because of his pink shirt, and nose and nipple piercings, but he loved to make it very clear he was straight by hooking up with numerous girls and laughing about it.

"I just need to forget him. Don't let me talk about him anymore. Let's talk about something else," I said to Vibes, shoving another piece of taco in my mouth.

Just then, my phone rang. It was work. What could they possibly want? I rushed to chew the huge bite of taco quickly enough to answer, with Vibes pointing at me and laughing. It was almost an impossible task, and I nearly missed the call.

"Hello," I said, trying not to laugh as I drooled taco sauce onto the floor.

"Ashley, I have some exciting news, and it couldn't wait until Monday!" my manager's voice boomed through the phone. By his tone, I could tell this was something big.

I think Vibes knew, based on my facial expression, it was not time to joke around, because he stopped doing his taco dance and sat silently on his barstool in my kitchen.

"Don't leave me in suspense, what is it?" I asked, intrigued.

"We're opening a new Shredders location in Portland, Oregon, and I've recommended you as the new marketing director," he said.

"So, I would have to move to Oregon?" I asked, open-mouthed, even though I knew the answer was yes.

My manager continued to go on and on with details, and then ended with, "You have until Monday to decide, we need to get moving on this; I really hope you take this opportunity, Ashley."

"Thank you very much! I will let you know for sure on Monday!" I bubbled.

"Move to Oregon! What did he say?" Vibes was standing in shock.

"Shredders Snowboards is opening a branch in Oregon, and they want me to be the director of marketing!" It didn't even sound real as I said it. I was still in shock as I felt Vibes wrap me up into a big bear hug.

"No! Don't go, homie! You can't leave! I'll miss you too much! Congrats, though, that's awesome!"

I laughed; he was just like Ryan, begging me not to excel in my career, but he was joking, and meant it in a good-natured way. Ryan really didn't care about my future, as long as he had me. Vibes was just a good friend who wanted me to stay, but would be more than happy for me if I left, which was what I had to do.

———•———

Less than a month later, I sat looking out the window of my new office in beautiful Portland, Oregon. It was a gorgeous city and I was happy with my choice to move, but my thoughts were still entirely consumed with Ryan.

As time went on, I found out he was homeless, jobless, and dating Rose, who also had no job or home. I would periodically check his Facebook for updates, just to see if he was still alive. Every night, I prayed for him to get better, but we rarely talked. When we did get in contact, he would beg me via text or Facebook message to come back home, promising he was clean and vowing to leave Rose if I did.

Not a day went by that I didn't dream of the past or fantasize of a day in the future where Ryan would kick his awful habit and we would get married and live happily ever after, but I knew it would never happen. The only way I could function and focus on my job and my new life was to pretend he was already dead.

It wasn't dreadfully hard, because the Ryan I loved already was dead. His personality and looks were entirely transformed. I could tell, from his Facebook posts and pictures, his random and pathetic attempts to contact me and win me back, as well as my frequent phone conversations with Vibes, occasional texts from Tim, and from how my mother said Ryan's mom was doing. Sifting through images of him in dirty, unmatched clothes, with puffy and scarred hands, feet, and face, I barely recognized him as a ghost of the person I loved. There were shots of him clinging to Rose, who had lost an incredible amount of weight in a short amount of time, and looked just as bad as Ryan. He was always smiling; even though he had lost almost everything, he still had drugs and Rose. The nights were the hardest. Sitting alone in my bedroom, I often added entries to a diary of poems written mostly with Ryan in mind. My favorite is titled Loving a Living Ghost.

*Loving a living ghost really takes a toll on the soul;*

*You see them in your memory exactly how they used to be;*

*Your heart yearns for their beauty;*

*Then you see them on the street, and you're forced to accept reality;*

*Life never is what you think it should be.*

## Chapter Nineteen:
# Fate

Clutching my worn jacket, I scooted closer to Rose on the park bench, where we sat waiting for the bus. We had no destination, but I couldn't stand another second in the frigid Vermont winter. My whole body ached, and I was in so much pain my vision was blurry.

"Did you update your Facebook status again to see if anyone has a couch we could crash on for the night?" I asked Rose for the third time.

"I already told you. I updated my status and texted everyone I know. No one wants to let us crash. They all know one night turns into as long as we can stay until they kick us out. Maybe if you didn't leave your needles all over my friends' houses, I would be able to find a place for us to crash," she snapped.

Too weak to respond, I let out a sigh and checked my phone for the thousandth time. I wouldn't even care if we had a warm place to stay, if only my dealer would respond. I had one hope left. All the others I had ripped off so many times they no longer trusted me, or they had gotten busted and were in jail for God knows how long. The Arelington police were working with the

DEA to set up controlled buys and bust dealers. They offered junkies shorter prison sentences if they would wear a wire and help bust dealers.

The bus pulled up, and it took all the strength I could muster to get off the bench and teeter on frozen, aching legs to the opening doors. The warmth was my only motivation. I longed for the warm summer days. Rose and I hadn't had a place to crash all summer. We'd gotten kicked out of her apartment and countless friends' houses, but during the warm summer months, we spent nights on the beach, camping, faded out of our minds, not bothered by our homelessness. I hadn't ripped too many people off then, and I was hooking many of my friends up with stuff to support my habit and Rose's. Hustling heroin, coke, weed, Adderall, and basically anything I could find, just to keep from being dope sick, was a full time job. I missed the summers with Ashley more than anything, but the hope for ever having another one of those was so lost, it almost seemed surreal.

"Ryan, what you got for me?"

I looked up, seeing the bus driver's greedy, longing stare. For a while, Rose and I had hooked him with dope in exchange for free rides, but we were out and my dealer wasn't responding.

"Not shit, man, as soon as I do, you know I got you," I said, starting to walk by. He put his arm up and stopped me in my tracks.

"Can't pay. No ride," he said to me, continuing to block my entrance.

"Wow, this is bullshit. I've helped you out so many times," I said to him.

"What's the trouble, do you need money, dear?" I heard a sweet old lady behind me offer.

Turning to look, I could see she was already pulling cash out of her purse. What a kind old lady; she reminded me of my grandmother. I was grateful we were going to be able to get on the bus and have a few hours of warmth.

"Yes, we do! Thank you so much! We've been having a really hard time, and haven't even had money to eat in a while," I heard Rose exclaim. Before I could protest, she was snatching the money from the old lady for the bus fee, and a little extra for food.

"Thanks," I mumbled, and the bus driver reluctantly moved his arm to allow us on.

The bus was nearly empty, but I could feel stares from a few people as we sat with the dirty duffle bags that containing everything we owned, which was not much more than a few soiled outfits. My wardrobe used to be expansive. I would put as much effort into coordinating my clothes, hats, shoes, and sunglasses as I would into design projects. Ashley had always made fun of me, but I hadn't cared. Studying my shaking hands, I longed for those days. I couldn't remember the last time I showered, brushed my teeth, had sex, or even had something to eat. Rose had stopped getting her period as a result of extended opiate use, which was a blessing because we couldn't afford tampons, but it made me a little nervous. She wasn't on birth control, and there was no monthly visitor to let us know she wasn't pregnant.

My mother had reached out to me many times, begging me to come home, get clean, go to rehab, and leave Rose, but

I couldn't. Don had made it clear I wasn't allowed in the house unless I was sober. Sobriety was even more frightening than the never ending spiral of blissful high and painful withdrawal. I desperately wanted to get clean, but was afraid of failing. Every time I'd tried to get clean, I had always relapsed. Whenever anything wasn't going perfectly, or even if I was just bored, or let my mind drift to how badly I had screwed up the great life I could have had, I turned back to opiates. It was just too heartbreaking to get my mother's hopes up and fail again. People who have never had an opiate addiction don't understand. It's not that addicts want to return to drugs; they have to. I briefly recalled attempting to explain it to Ashley, long ago.

"Imagine your worst hangover ever. You're in so much physical pain that you truly want to die, and the cure is out there. You have to do whatever it takes to find it and use it."

"But you know using it will completely destroy your life," she had argued.

She was right, but it didn't matter.

Letting out a sigh, I slumped down further on the uncomfortable bus seat. This wasn't fair. Why was I here? I was so depressed I wanted to die; after all, I'd never asked to be born in the first place.

"Ryan, what the fuck are we going to do? I'm dying!" Rose pouted in the seat next to me, clinging onto my arm. I shrugged her off. I couldn't bear to be touched when I was withdrawing, and I didn't know any more than she did about how we were going to get our next fix.

I contemplated going to visit Mark, but the last time we

spoke, he had used up his military money and was withdrawing badly. He had begged me to help him out, but I was flat out of funds as usual, and took to ignoring his calls. I never would have been friends with Mark if he hadn't funded my habit. His jokes were repulsive, his laugh was annoying, and he used the weirdest phrases, like 'pantie lover,' 'fart box,' and 'moist magnet,' in excess. Who even knew what he meant by any of those? I was always too fucked up to care.

There was also the matter of him living with his parents, who were also both in the military and thought I was a bad influence. Every time I went over there, I got the feeling that if I made one wrong move, a grenade might go off and kill me, so I did my best to avoid his place.

The last text I had gotten from him read, "You were never even my real friend. You used me for money, you piece of shit! If I ever see you again, imma blow your head off." Most likely an idle threat, but I didn't want to chance it. Mark's PTSD made him a little crazy sometimes, and unless he had money again, there was no way I was going to meet up with him. His folks would never allow me to crash, especially if Rose was with me. It was difficult enough begging friends to let me stay, but when you have to convince someone to let two bums stay on their couch, it gets twice as tough.

"Let's just show up at Seth's place. Maybe he will have passed out with the door unlocked, and we can just let ourselves in," Rose suggested.

I knew he would be pissed. Seth had banned Rose and me from his place when he caught her stealing a ticket from his stash, and he refused to front me anything because I no longer had items to post for collateral. He had to be slightly smarter about his opiate use, because he was burning through his trust fund money at a rapid rate.

Mary was even worse. Before we'd been banned from Seth's place, she'd gone into a rapid downward spiral, burning through Seth's money and overdosing twice, after their child was placed in foster care. If Seth hadn't been there to revive her with the Narcan he'd copped from the exchange after Will's overdose, she wouldn't have made it. I must have zoned out thinking about Seth and Mary, because I was suddenly acutely aware of Rose's whiny voice.

"Ryan, I know they told us never to return, but Seth is our only hope; he's always so junked out anyway, he might not even notice us there. We have no choice."

I nodded. "Okay, we can try going to Seth's, but I highly doubt he's going to let us in."

By some lucky chance, we were on a bus route that passed Seth's spot, so we didn't have to find some way to get on another bus with no money. We were running the risk of getting off, getting denied by Seth, and then not being able to get back onto a warm bus, but the busses stopped running at midnight anyway, and it was nearing that hour, so it was worth a try.

Drug-sick, tired, and freezing, Rose and I trudged along in silence down the sketchy streets that led to Seth's rundown apartment. Chills went up my spine when I saw Mark's car parked out front.

"What the... I didn't even know they were friends," I

thought out loud, and wondered for a brief second if we should just wait around the corner until he left.

Rose must have sensed my hesitation, because she said, "Don't be ridiculous, Ryan, he's not going to shoot you for using him for drug money. Since he's at Seth's place, maybe he got some more money from the military. You can pretend to be his friend again, so he will hook you up. It was really weird how much he liked you; actually, it was kind of creepy."

I had no energy to respond. We plodded through Seth's un-shoveled driveway, up to the door. It hung open. That would have been normal for summertime, but during the winter, Seth always kept his doors and windows shut tightly and made people enter and exit quickly to avoid letting out precious heat.

"The door is open already! Let's just go in and sleep on the couch," Rose suggested, taking another step toward the entrance.

"I have a really bad feeling about this, Rose, maybe we should try to catch another bus," I said, hanging back.

"To where? We have nowhere to go, Ryan, this is it. Are you with me or not?" she demanded. The sliver of a moon cast shadows over her desperate eyes, and I gave in to her plea.

My feet were soaked from the snow. There was no point trying to pack down a walkway or follow where Rose had stepped to get to the door, because my shoes were already filled with freezing water on the inside and caked with ice on the outside. Seth had to see how desperate we were and let us stay just the night, at least.

Rose put her index finger to her mouth, in a gesture to stay silent, as she entered the front door. I didn't want to spend the night without asking Seth first, but I also didn't want to wake him up.

I was about to step through the door when I heard Rose let out a piercing scream.

"Shh! What is it? You're going to wake Seth for sure!" I exclaimed. "That is, if he isn't already up!" I added, remembering Mark's car was parked on the street next to his driveway.

I pushed past Rose, who was quickly trying to back out of Seth's door, a look of pure terror etched across her face, dimly lit under the moonlight. There were no lights on in the living room, but a ray of light coming from the bathroom shined brightly enough for me to make out the bodies.

I almost stumbled over Mark's lifeless corpse, which was just inside the door. There was a needle still stuck in his arm, and his gun lay on the floor close by.

Seth's body was hunched over on the couch. I could tell he was dead from the amount of blood oozing from multiple bullet wounds, and the lack of color in his complexion. Deep red steaks of frozen blood showed the spots where it had sprayed across the torn couch and up onto the wall.

Mary's body lay in a pool of chilled blood just outside of the bathroom door.

"What. The. Fuck." I whispered more to myself than to Rose, who had re-entered the apartment. I expected the lives of my three former friends to come to an end sooner rather than later, because of how prevalent drug-related death was becoming in our community, but not in this violent of a manner.

"Let's get the fuck out of here," I uttered, turning toward the door.

Rose blocked me. "Not yet, don't you think we should at

least see if he has any dope, or money?"

"Seriously, Rose! My friends are dead, and if we don't get out of here quickly, it might look like we had something to do with it," I said. Even as I spoke the words, the ropes in my stomach and pain oozing from all corners of my feeble body told me I was going to give in to her suggestion.

"They're dead anyway, so what does it matter? They would probably rather we get their money and drugs than the cops anyway," I thought, trying to reassure myself as I gingerly stepped over Mark to search the place.

"Score! I found some dope and one last needle that hasn't been used! Thank God, because I didn't bring one, and I would hate to use one Seth, Mark, or Mary had already used." Rose rejoiced, quickly prepping the heroin for injection.

"You're going to go first?" I pouted, not wanting to wait another second to be relieved from my agony.

"I found the stuff, so, yea. I'm going first." She selfishly sucked the concoction into the rig and pressed it into a waiting vein.

The very second it entered her body, I grabbed for the needle. Rose appeared to be pretty knocked out; in my haste, I didn't even stop to think she might have overdosed. The only thing that mattered was getting the precious poison into my bloodstream, so I could feel well again and get out of Seth's before the cops showed up.

———•———

"This one's still alive!" I heard an unfamiliar voice that seemed very far away. What was going on? I felt so dazed, I wondered if I was dreaming.

"Pass me the Narcan!" the same voice screamed, and the opiate antidote was launched into my nostril.

I screamed out in agony, pissed off, as the Narcan took effect and stripped my opiate receptors clean, tearing me from my blissful high and bringing on a shattering wave of dope sickness. Through my blurred vision, I could see bright lights and people everywhere. Cops. It all came flooding back; the gruesome scene Rose and I had stumbled upon at Seth's apartment, listening to her suggestion, and taking his drugs.

"Shit. Rose and I are going to be in so much trouble. We're fucked. I'm going to have to detox in jail," I thought, wondering how I could have possibly overdosed on such a small amount. Even though I had overdosed before, I hadn't in a long while, and my tolerance was high. It suddenly dawned on me that Rose must have overdosed too.

"Shit, I took the needle right out of her arm to use for myself before making sure she was okay," I thought to myself, trying to piece the memory back together, crafting it in my mind so I didn't look guilty.

"There you are. How are you feeling? Can you tell us what happened here?" My thoughts were interrupted by an Arelington police officer in my face, asking a bunch of questions.

"I'm feeling like shit, you asshole. I went from feeling great to full blown agony! I have the right to remain silent, and until I can figure out what the hell went on, I'm going to use it. I'm just as confused as you," I yelled at the officer.

"Fair enough. Let's get you to a hospital for now, but you're going to have a lot of explaining to do in court, mister. Being found with four dead people isn't something you can easily talk yourself out of," he said.

"What? Four dead people? What do you mean? Rose is still alive, right?" I begged, not knowing if I wanted to know the answer. A sinking feeling in the pit of my stomach told me she wasn't.

"I'm afraid none of your friends made it; if we had been a few minutes earlier, the Narcan might have saved Rose, like it did you, but we were too late. This batch of heroin is laced with a good amount of fentanyl, and is highly lethal. You're lucky to have made it," he said.

Lucky was the last word in the entire world I would have used to describe my situation. My girlfriend was dead. I would probably go to jail for a long time for being involved. They would know from blood tests that she had used the needle right before me, and I hadn't done anything to try to save her. I was the only reason she'd started using opiates to begin with.

Overwhelmed with guilt, I tried distracting my mind, hypothesizing what went down at Seth's prior to our arrival. Mark must have been detoxing hard and tried to rob Seth. Maybe he went nuts and killed him on purpose, or maybe there was some sort of squabble that resulted in an accidental death. I'm fairly sure he killed Mary on purpose, because she had witnessed whatever happened.

"I bet he was going to get down and then make off with the drugs and money, and hope he wasn't pinned for their murder, but then he overdosed, and we came in and found them all," I thought to myself.

As I was being hauled into a waiting ambulance, I noticed it was still dark out and wondered who had alerted the cops.

"Thanks for saving me. How did you guys find us anyway?" I questioned the officer by my side. I'm not sure if he was supposed to tell me or not, but he must have thought I was too dazed for it to matter, so he answered.

"We got a call from a well-respected military family, worried about their son. This was not exactly what we were expecting to find when we tracked his phone's GPS. Fortunately for you, we had Narcan on hand. If you start to fade out again, the hospital may administer more Narcan via injection."

I nodded, shaking from withdrawal pain and wishing the Narcan would wear off. "Of course Mark's overprotective parents were the reason the cops showed up," I thought to myself. I wondered if I would have survived the overdose without Narcan, since I had done some of the same drugs that had killed Sean and put Will in a coma with no problems. I figured I would have made it, since I was able to faintly hear before they shoved Narcan up my nostril.

I would never know for sure, but I did know how extremely disappointed my mother was going to be when she found out about everything. I thought I had hit the lowest of low and shattered any hope I had for a future when I was living out on the streets, but this took it to a whole new level.

# CHAPTER TWENTY:
# Wasted Potential

Staring down at my weathered hands, I turn the page of the dictionary my mother sent to me. My youthful skin is camouflaged with an array of scars, reminding me of the countless times I shot up in my hands, when the veins in my arms retracted, tired of being punctured. Despite my dismal surroundings, I am desperately trying to better myself in jail.

Depression and anxiety are still a daily struggle, but nothing compared to the withdrawal that is inevitable if I do any of the opiates I could get my hands on. Drugs are plentiful in jail, but only if you have something to trade, and I have nothing. My gaze falls upon the D section of the dictionary, and a word catches my eye: "Dissipation: a wasting by misuse." That pretty much sums up the past ten years of my life. I feel tears begin to well up in my eyes, and quickly banish them from my face. No matter how you are feeling, you have to act tough in jail if you want to make it out alive and not sexually violated.

I can't shake the word 'dissipation' from my thoughts. It reminds me of how much potential I had growing up. There are so many children, teens, and young adults who struggle or suffer financially, physically, or emotionally who are doing far better than I am now. I didn't have any disabilities, and I came from a fairly affluent family. My college tuition was paid in full. I had an immediate and extended family who loved me. I had a talent and a passion for photography and web design. I could have been great. Now I have nothing, because drugs had me.

Addiction knows no boundaries. When you're an addict, there is no right, there is no wrong. Your once strong-held morals quickly dissipate; the only thing that matters is the high. Addicts are stealthy. They can go days, weeks, months, and even years blending into society, but eventually the money runs out or they get sloppy. Once their addiction is so bad that people who aren't addicts start to notice, it's usually too late. Many people, including myself, can hold a conversation, drive a car, and attend class or work strung out. Unless you're specifically looking for signs, my unchanging pinned out pupils, droopy eyelids, and lazy disposition don't raise any red flags. I wish someone had stopped me before I started shooting.

I saw friends, loved ones, and strangers from Arelington and far beyond die before me. Family, friends, and acquaintances stopped talking to me, because hanging out with an addict is no fun. I was selfish and blind. I lost money, apartments, jobs, cars, and worst of all, I lost respect from others and respect for myself. I stumbled down a dark path, where I narrowly escaped death time and time again.

This is where it ends. I refuse to succumb to the force of drugs again. Once I am out of here, I vow to stay clean and lead a prosperous life. I know it will be a thousand times harder for me now than it would have been, if I hadn't gotten caught up with drugs, but better late than never. Once I realized there was a life after mistakes, and dwelling on them only made things worse, I've developed a new found self-confidence.

There are many lessons I have learned, but in order to have a successful recovery, I need to never forget that I am an addict. I will always be an addict. My battle with drugs has forever changed me. I cannot have just one drink, one line of coke, or one opiate. In order for me to stay clean, I must be clean from everything. They told me this in rehab, and it scared the shit out of me. I had convinced myself I was fine, and slipped back into using because I was still in denial about my addiction. Now I fully admit it, and remind myself of it constantly.

I still live every day in fear. The anxiety and depression are overwhelming, but not as great as the pain, suffering, and destruction that is inevitable if I invite drugs back into my life. The light at the end of the tunnel seems dim; the love of my life hasn't spoken to me in what seems like a lifetime, and I am partially responsible for the death of the girl who was by my side during the last leg of my struggle. My mother and Tim are the only people who have been to visit me in jail. Once I get out, I know gaining employment and meeting people who will be accepting of my situation will be difficult, but I have to try. I'm very thankful I never contracted HIV or hep C from sharing needles with Rose. We promised to only share needles with each other, but with junkies, you can never be sure.

After being released from the hospital and instantly thrown in jail, only to come out for countless court dates, I was blessed with a mandatory detox and rehab during a two-year prison sentence, to be followed up by strict parole. I say blessed, because Mark and Rose's parents were out to get me. They hired fancy lawyers and tried to pin me for the deaths of their children. Time of death and a testimony from the bus driver (who, luckily, decided to be an honest, stand-up guy) proved that Rose and I weren't present at the apartment until after Mark, Seth, and Mary were deceased. It was more difficult to prove that I wasn't at fault for Rose's death. Luckily, the judge ruled that Rose was a grown adult who made her own decision to shoot up, and even if I had realized she had overdosed before taking the needle and pleasuring myself, I wouldn't have been able to save her in time with no Narcan on hand. I was charged with breaking and entering and involuntary manslaughter, because my reckless and grossly negligent behavior resulted in Rose's death. I could have been given a longer sentence, but the judge was informed, from countless similar court cases, about how drugs steal your humanity. The Arelington community is in the midst of an opiate epidemic, and rather than throw a large chunk of the population in jail, the government is helping fund a variety of mandated rehab programs for people like me. Good people, who have had their humanity robbed by drugs and were in desperate need of help, rebuilding their lives on the solid foundation of rock bottom. The person who grabbed the needle out of Rose's arm was not really me; it was an addict, a junkie, someone who I never want to be again.

"Landry, mail," barks a guard, sliding me an off-white envelope.

In shock, I avert my gaze from the dictionary to the single piece of mail on the table in front of me.

"Who can this be from?" I wonder. I never receive mail. Scanning the return address on the envelope, my heart drops into my stomach. I gasp for breath. Never in my life have I felt this many butterflies fluttering hopefully in my gut.

It reads "Portland, Oregon," with no name. Clutching it in shaking hands, I gingerly peel open the seal, praying it is from Ashley.

# HELP RAISE ADDICTION AWARENESS

Dear Friend,

1. Thank you for reading *Moral Dissipation*. I encourage you to help me spread addiction awareness. You can help by…

2. Taking a picture of yourself holding your copy of *Moral Dissipation* and posting it to Facebook, Instagram, and other social media.

3. Including the caption I Hate Heroin Because: (Insert your personal reason).

4. Use as many hashtags as you can to help spread the word

5. Please tag the following pages:

   www.facebook.com/SMJarvis

   @writing_for_social_change

   @AuthorSMJarvis

Your efforts to help in the fight against addiction can make all the difference.

*Sarah*

# NOTES FROM THE AUTHOR:

Ten percent of the profits from Moral Dissipation will be donated to organizations focused on preventing drug abuse and helping recovering addicts. I hope to help stop people from going down the wrong path, and maybe even save a few already headed that way. There are thousands of real people going through these experiences every day, and I hope reading this book will help prevent you from being one of them.